SHARKS
IN LAKE ERIE

A NOVEL BY **H. JOHN HILDEBRANDT**

Casa Flamingo Literary Arts
NASHVILLE, TENNESSEE, USA

Also by H. John Hildebrandt

NON-FICTION

Lake Erie's Shores and Islands
(co-author Marie Hildebrandt)

Always Cedar Point, a Memoir of the Midway

*This book is dedicated to the
Guardians of Lake Erie.*

PREFACE

Although it is the southernmost Great Lake, Erie was the last to be discovered by European explorers. Most historians credit a Frenchman, Louis Jolliet, as being the first to see the lake in 1669, although it had long been home to several Native American tribes. At the time, the Wyandots occupied the southwest corner. The southeast corner had been until very recently the home of the Erie, sometimes referred to as the Cat Nation. However, the Erie were casualties of the Beaver Wars of the mid-16th century. The powerful Iroquois were successful in destroying the Erie. A few scattered groups joined other tribes, but the Cat Nation was no more. The name of one of the greatest lakes of the world is their epitaph: Lake Erie.

Erie's profile is fascinating. It is the shallowest of the Great Lakes by far. It is only 210 feet at its deepest point in the eastern basin. The largest river to drain into Lake Erie is the Maumee. It is the largest river to drain into any of the Great Lakes.

It has the distinction of being the southernmost, shallowest, warmest, most nutrient enriched and most biologically productive of all the Great Lakes. Lake Erie is home to more than half of all the fish in the Great Lakes including approximately 150 million walleye. No other Great Lake comes close. The Lake Erie watershed is also home to approximately 12 million people.

From Buffalo at the eastern end of the lake it is 244 nautical miles to Monroe, Michigan at its western end. It has a foot in both doors, the Midwest, and the Northeast, culturally and historically.

It is big water, true wilderness. There are many places where there is no land in sight. It is the shipwreck capital of the Great

Lakes with more than 1,700 documented wrecks. It is the quickest to anger and the roughest to sail. Its wave action is ferocious.

In winter, in the depths of a cold January, the ice can cover nearly all the surface area of the lake. Wind and current can create huge hedgerows of ice. The view from shore is a vision of the high Arctic. One expects to see polar bears or the Northern Lights.

In the height of summer, the Bass Island Archipelago in the western basin could be a stand-in for the Florida Keys.

We share Lake Erie with our Canadian brothers and sisters, whose love for the lake is no less than ours.

The Great Lake we love so much is under constant assault by a variety of forces, including invasive species like the sea lamprey, zebra mussel, Asian carp, and round goby; algal blooms, especially in the western basin, which can contain harmful toxins like Microcystin LR; agricultural run-off carrying heavy loads of phosphorus from fertilizer and animal waste.

My maternal grandmother loved the lake, although she did not swim or boat or fish. It was enough that it was there. She loved to just look at it. In a long life spent almost entirely on the west side of Cleveland in the grit of the city, she was always close to Lake Erie and said she would never leave it.

Lake Erie is mystical for some, science for others.

But we all need to be guardians of the lake.

John Hildebrandt
SUMMER, 2021

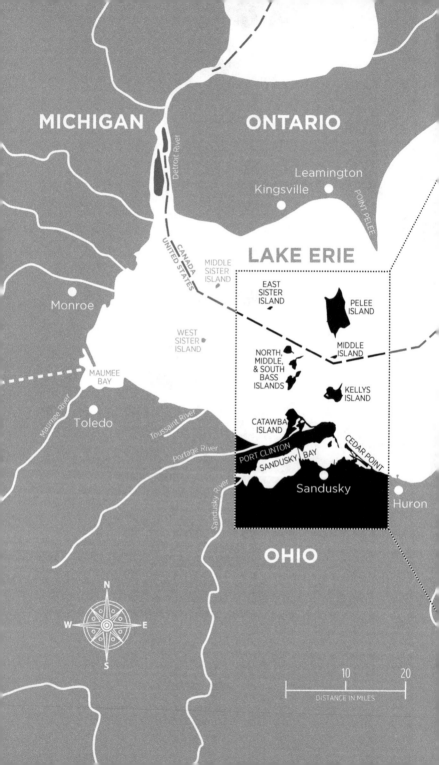

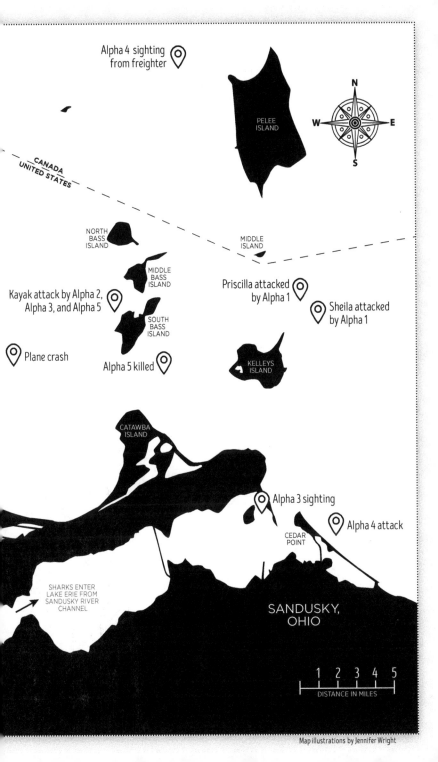

Alpha 4 sighting from freighter

N
W E
S

PELEE ISLAND

CANADA
UNITED STATES

NORTH BASS ISLAND

MIDDLE ISLAND

MIDDLE BASS ISLAND

Kayak attack by Alpha 2, Alpha 3, and Alpha 5

Priscilla attacked by Alpha 1

Sheila attacked by Alpha 1

SOUTH BASS ISLAND

Plane crash

Alpha 5 killed

KELLEYS ISLAND

CATAWBA ISLAND

Alpha 3 sighting

Alpha 4 attack

CEDAR POINT

SHARKS ENTER LAKE ERIE FROM SANDUSKY RIVER CHANNEL

SANDUSKY, OHIO

1 2 3 4 5
DISTANCE IN MILES

Map illustrations by Jennifer Wright

CHAPTER 1

The fin cut the water erratically, not smoothly, as it would were it attached to a machine and not to a fish. The great fish was moving west slowly, searching for food, somehow sensing there were more opportunities to the west.

It was mid-June, a Friday, approaching high summer in western Lake Erie.

Frankie Visidi had spent most of the afternoon fishing at Kelleys Island Shoal, an area about a mile north and east of Kelleys Island, the largest island on the United States side of Lake Erie. The bottom was rocky, and in spots, only a foot or two below the Lake Erie surface. The reef was conical in shape and thin. It was not a large area, but over the decades it had always been a favorite fishing spot for walleye, the prize fish of Lake Erie's western basin.

Frankie liked to stand behind the wheel of his 25-foot center console and look toward Cleveland, more than 50 miles east. Cedar Point, with its giant coasters creating a unique skyline, was much closer, just eight miles south and east.

A slight shift of view to the left and it was all water, all steel-colored water, an ocean view, a stare into the horizon any deep-water sailor would know. If you sailed northeast, it was more than 200 miles to landfall; it was wilderness, the open water of the central and eastern basins of Lake Erie. Frankie often felt the eastern emptiness when he was fishing alone and

anchored on the shoal. It was scary in the way it is when you are in a small boat and cross the blue highway of the Gulf Stream and know that the next landfall is Portugal. The western basin is the beauty queen of the lake, a world apart biologically and geologically, from the deeper and darker central and eastern basins. It is one of the most productive freshwater fishing areas in the world; it produces more fish, and more variety of fish, than all the other Great Lakes combined. There are two dozen islands in the western basin, all limestone and dolomite, gifts from the last great glacier, the father and mother of the greatest lake, Erie.

Half the lake flies the Maple Leaf, and it includes the largest island, Pelee, at 10,000 acres. Pelee Island has greatest collection of plant diversity in the world's second largest country.

This afternoon the chop was very light. The wind was a gentle push from the southwest. The surface water temperature was 68 degrees. It was a weekday and there were few boats out, the closest about a half mile away.

Frankie was 31 years old, unmarried, by trade a computer programmer for a medium-sized auto parts manufacturer. It was not glamorous work, but it paid well by the standards of small-town Ohio. Frankie was just over six feet in height with small gray eyes and thick brown hair. By the standard of age 31, he was reasonably thin, which meant he could lose 10 pounds. His face was open and friendly. Most women his age would rate him a solid B, and maybe in good light and in the right clothes a B+ or even an A-. However, he did not dress well. Clothes were not important to him.

He was born in Sandusky and was a proud graduate of Sandusky High School. He was also a proud graduate of The Ohio State University. He was not much interested in ancestry issues, but he was proud of the fact that he had been told his Greek ancestors had been fishermen.

He had been around dogs since childhood, and in general he felt they were superior beings. His current dog was a black lab. Her name was Priscilla, but mostly he called her Pris. She was young, only two years old, and Frankie knew she needed a companion. Labs were social dogs, and she was in danger of going a little crazy if she were left alone too much.

"I've had to turn down a lot of overtime for her sake," he would often say, but in truth he felt no resentment. He loved the time he spent with her.

He had nothing against cats, except that they were cats and therefore sly, sinister, and secretive.

Frankie had several fishing buddies, but he also liked to fish alone. He didn't do it at night, and he didn't do it in the fall and spring when the water temperature was in the killing zone; but he savored the occasional day alone on the water, just he and Pris. His boat was a center console, so it was essentially an open boat from stem to stern with the wheel in the center. He had a blue canvas Bimini top he put up for sun protection, but captain and passengers, including dogs, were in the elements, something Frankie deeply approved of; he did not like boats with cabins.

His boat was fast, very fast, powered by a big Yamaha 350.

He looked at his watch. It was nearly five p.m., and the sky was still bright, a combination of being located at the western end of the eastern time zone and the time of year, mid-June to mid-July, when the days are at their longest. These mid-summer weeks you could still see a slash of red in the western sky at 10 p.m. He had one line out with a bobber and a hook with a tangle of night crawlers just to catch whatever came along. He had the other line in his hands, specifically an Orvis rod set to a Pflueger Supreme XT spinning reel with 10-pound test line. He was using an Earie Dearie ribboned with nightcrawler. His plan was to flick it out there by the edge of the shoal and attract a walleye to come after it.

He flung the line out as hard as he could. It sailed through the air, then landed softly with a sweet pop and began to sink. Frankie started retrieving. In his experience, walleye hit sooner, not later. There were lots of them out there. For the past, several years the walleye hatch had been very strong, according to the Ohio Department of Natural Resources (ODNR). They estimated there were 130 million walleye in Lake Erie. Most were in the western basin. The average size walleye in the western basin weighed 2-3 pounds and was 22 inches long. The biggest were 8-10 pounds. The state record was a monster caught in Lake Erie in 1999: 16.19 pounds and 33 inches long. Walleye were not fighting fish like trout, but they fought honorably well, and Frankie believed they were significantly better eating than any trout that had ever lived.

But nothing, a dry cast. He tried several more in quick succession. Same results. He pulled the worm remnants off the hook and tossed them into the lake and then stowed the rod. He did the same with the second line.

It was Pris' time now. Frankie had made a few modifications to a portable swim platform so Pris, with some assistance from Frankie, could get in and out of the boat without too much trouble. Sometimes he would get in the water to help her back in. It was shallow at the boat, less than four feet to the gravel below.

Pris knew what was coming when Frankie took out the toy bone. She started getting excited, shaking, and yelping; she knew she was going into the water. Frankie pulled off his shirt and kicked off his sandals. He waved the toy bone in the air and Pris got even more excited; barking and crying in anticipation of the fun to come.

"You go, Girl!" he yelled and tossed the bone in the air and toward the edge of the shoal. It landed with a barely audible splash. Frankie had a good arm. He had been a pitcher in high school and once hit 87 mph on the radar gun.

About 30-40 yards away and swimming slowly toward the boat, was a female bull shark, a large specimen nearly 11 feet long and weighing almost 700 pounds.

At the same time, Pris jumped up to the gunnel and then into the water, her eyes on the prize.

Frankie's eyes were on the toy and the dog. He did not see the fin nor the fish.

The fish closed in on the dog from behind. Its favorite technique with prey was a preliminary bite and a push or bump. It would then continue swimming as it made its decision whether to return or not. It was not a good thing to be bumped by a bull shark. There was usually a second act.

Frankie jumped into the water to get in position to help Pris get back in the boat. He hit the water just as the fish hit Pris.

The dog made a terrible sound, part bark, part whimper; its head dipped below the surface as the fish bit into its back. Frankie was only 15 yards away. He felt something enormous pass in front of him and he screamed Pris' name. He saw the fin now, saw it move and almost flap as it started to turn to come back.

Was it for him? He saw Pris' face, her eyes, and they locked together for an instant.

The fish was coming back for the dog. The dog had passed the taste test; it qualified as prey, though it knew it wasn't a fish. The blood was an easy tracker. The fish went straight for the dog, ignoring Frankie, and bit it in half, consuming much of it in two fast bites.

A huge shark had killed and eaten his dog. He had just watched it happen. It was real. Frankie was only about 10 yards from the swim platform, and he swam to it with a manic fierceness. He was in the boat in a few seconds. When he stood up, he could see the blood in the water, and he could see what he knew were bits and pieces of Pris. He saw the shadow of the fish moving away, into deeper water.

Frankie shook like a martini canister in the hands of an expert bartender. Then he vomited big chunks of the ham and cheese sandwich he had eaten as a snack an hour earlier. Then he calmly and purposefully took his fishing net and gathered what he could of Priscilla, stopping frequently to scan the water around him.

Frankie knew some people believed dogs lived forever. He had read a book about it a few years ago. He considered himself a believer. Pris would have the last word.

CHAPTER 2

Tina pulled him closer. She was 17 and it was a warm June night, and she was out behind the horse barn at the Erie County Fairgrounds and this guy was a keeper. Bobby Schmidt, German farm boy to the core, but also slim and beautiful and strong with deep blue eyes that drove her arms around his back and lifted her mouth to his.

They kissed on and off for several minutes. He gently pressed her back against the wall of the barn. He suggested they go to his truck, a Ford Ranger. She knew it. It was small.

"Kind of small in there," she half giggled. It felt strange.

"There's a trailer over behind the horse barn," she said softly into his ear. "It's the 4-H office. "We can go there." She kissed him again, just to make sure he didn't lose interest.

"Do you have a key?" he asked.

"I got a key," she replied. It was true. She was considered a responsible young woman by the 4-H staff and most others who knew her. She smiled to herself because she certainly did not feel like a responsible young woman when she was kissing Bobby Schmidt. There was a couch in the trailer. They could sit on the coach in the dark and kiss. It was a plan. A lot better than the Ford Ranger. She looked at her watch, saw the hands a luminous green. I was just before midnight. The fairgrounds were quiet. There was a horse competition the next day, but the Erie County Fair itself was a month or more away.

19

Tina took his hand and led him into the first horse barn. There were still lights on in some of the stalls. The smells were heavy and sweet, welcoming. Tina had been around horses all her life. The day before she had ridden her horse, Top Thrill (named for a Cedar Point roller coaster), in the preliminary dressage competition and had finished second.

They had passed perhaps seven or eight stalls when she noticed the gate was open on one of them. Not all stalls were used, some participants took their horses home to rest in familiar surroundings. She stopped and looked in.

She saw the feet first. Big feet. Big boots. Farmer boots. Sticking straight up. Brown boots, the soles caked with mud and straw. Her eyes lifted. There was a man lying on the straw, a big man. She knew instinctively he was dead. Knew it. His hands were crossed on his chest and he was holding a bunch of flowers. There were flowers and green plants scattered around him. His eyes were open and bulging like they had been punched forward by something inside his head.

He looked familiar to her, despite the all the colors of his face.

That was as far as she got. Bobby Schmidt had never heard such a scream.

———————∧———————

Mary Susan Massimino got the call at 6 a.m. She was in a good dream.

"This is Bill." Bill Cleary was the police chief of Perkins Township. He was also Susan's first cousin, the son of her late mom's brother. They were good friends, but not regular 6 a.m. friends.

"What's up?" she mumbled. But she was ready for his response.

"Sorry to wake you. But we had a homicide at the fairgrounds last night. I need to talk to you about it."

"Who died?" she asked clearly. She stood by the side of the bed lightly scratching her butt. It was a good butt, not too big and not too small. She liked it. In fact, she was proud of it, unlike most other parts of her body. She was average in height and weight, but she seemed taller, helped by long legs and a narrow face. Eyes and hair were brown. She thought her breasts were too small and that her ears stuck out her head at an angle. She used to joke with her sons that she was part elf. Her skin was smooth and clear. All her life men had described her as cute, but she felt she was cute leaning to average as opposed to cute leaning to good looking or hot.

She heard him suck in air, "William Robert Krupp."

"No shit," she replied. She knew Krupp slightly. Mid-60s. Successful farmer and landowner. Local politician. President of the Fair Board. Past Erie County Commissioner. Susan considered him pompous and most likely dishonest, but he was a power in the county, the leader of the agricultural community. This would be news, even in Cleveland and Toledo.

"What happened?"

"No freaking idea. But I think we can rule out natural causes. Don't know. Coroner has him now. But something weird."

"What?" she asked quickly.

"Flowers."

"What?" she said again.

"We found him holding a bunch of flowers in his hands. Two kids found him—a Tina Davis and one of the Schmidt boys. Perkins High School kids, seniors. Probably looking for a nice place to get frisky—but she claims they were walking through the barn as a short cut to his truck."

"They found Krupp lying in a goddamned horse stall at the Erie County Fairgrounds, laid out like he was ready to go under.

Surrounded by flowers. Lots of different colors. They were scattered all around him.

"Whole thing freaked out our Romeo and Juliet. They found the night security guard. The guard was useless as an observer, but at least he knew how to give us a call."

"You got all the flowers?" Susan asked. One of her hobbies was gardening and she belonged to the local Master Gardener group.

"Yep. Well, a lot of them. Some are on their way to Toledo. But we got pictures of everything."

"So, you think it's a homicide?" she said.

"Absolutely. Breckenridge still thinks it might be a suicide—a weird kind of suicide—but I don't see it." Tom Breckenridge was one of Lewis' officers and the first on the scene. "Too much work. Somebody stuck the flowers in his hands and scattered them around. It's a sign, a symbol. Any idiot could see it. Besides, Krupp was a nasty man."

"No sign of foul play?"

"Nothing obvious," he said. "No one shot him or stabbed him or whacked him with a barn shovel."

They were friends and could talk about death this way. It was part of his professional language.

"The whole scene screams foul play. I know the flowers mean something, "he said, "but I have no goddamned idea what."

"What kind of flowers?" She had to pee. She had to pee bad. She crossed her legs. She thought about going into the bathroom, but she knew there was no such thing as a silent pee and she and her cousin were not at the level of friendship where bathroom noises didn't matter.

"That's why I'm calling you. I don't know a pansy from a freaking daylily. I need you to come down here and identify the flowers. There's a lot of them here."

———————∧———————

Susan got to township hall by 7 a.m. She left a note for Tim, her youngest son, home from college and working as a deckhand on one of the Jet Express boats that took visitors and residents out to the Lake Erie islands. He got home late, and he slept late whenever he could, true to his time of life. He would leave for Ohio University in the fall, and she'd be alone. Her oldest, Jeremy, was spending the summer taking some academically questionable courses offered by a university in England, and at every opportunity taking off with his girlfriend to visit Dublin or Paris or Rome. Europe was still jittery over the coronavirus pandemic, and just now returning to normal. Jeremy would be a senior. He thought he wanted to be a lawyer. Susan was ambivalent about lawyers, especially the divorce kind.

Their biological father was long gone, at least long gone to Chicago, where he lived with his second wife and their two young children. Mary Susan—some of her friends shortened it to MM but most just called her Susan—and Brian had been married their senior year in college; a terrible mistake she counseled others not to make. Good lovers don't always make good mates. They were done before they were 30. Susan was fatalistic about it. He had remarried within three years of the divorce and the selfish prick moved to Cleveland and then to Chicago. He saw his sons only occasionally. She was torn up about that. His second wife, a tall good-looking legal assistant from Cleveland (where they met) was focused entirely on getting Brian to spend time with their children. Susan couldn't imagine trying to be loyal to the interests of two sets of kids. Brian sold esoteric financial services to mid-size and larger companies. He was good at it, good enough to get promoted and moved to the Chicago office. He contributed to their support, including the college bills, she had to give him that.

Susan was from Huron, the small city, population about 8,000, just east of Sandusky. She had gone to Ohio University and had majored in history. After college, Brian got a job in Cleveland and she followed him there. For several years, she worked for the Western Reserve (Cleveland) Historical Society.

Susan had stayed true to her love: history. She had almost become a librarian, but ultimately it was not for her. Sandusky had several smaller museums and one large one, the Museum of Lake Erie. The area visitor bureau often referred to Sandusky as the City of Museums in marketing materials. In addition to the Museum of Lake Erie, there was the Follett House Museum, general local history; the Merry-Go-Round Museum, the history of carousels; and the Maritime Museum of Sandusky, the history of the maritime industry in the area.

The Museum of Lake Erie existed due to the generosity of one man, Erik Vankirk, who had given the money to build what he had named the Museum of Lake Erie. In 11 years, it had become one of the finest regional museums in the country. As Susan saw it, his continuing support really meant his continuing control. The way Vankirk had set it up, he retained the final say on everything—should he choose to exercise it—as long as he was the largest contributor the museum. He was now a sporadic visitor to Sandusky, and to the museum, but Susan was always impressed by how much he knew about local events. He had hired her almost 10 years ago, when the first director, a much older person, had died unexpectedly. He and Susan clicked in the interview. They were a good team.

The Museum of Lake Erie was only 11 years old. It was located on the west side of Sandusky on the edge of downtown.

Many of her museum and historical society colleagues were envious. Her situation was almost a don't-pinch-me-I-might-not-want-to-get-up category for someone who loved old stuff even if it was not famous old stuff.

Tall, blond, with clean features, Vankirk made women look twice, but he did not smile much and was not naturally outgoing. Vankirk looked like an athlete but he hadn't played sports much as a child or as a high school student. He had bright blue eyes, something women always commented on. He did not have a rich person's ego, at least outwardly, and she suspected he might have a good heart. He was always well dressed and well groomed.

He was an only child. He was often called by his last name.

His wealth came from financial services. There was a lot of wealth, some thought it possible that he was close to being a billionaire. He was certainly the richest man or woman in Erie County. After college, he and two partners started a firm which provided a new kind of stock portfolio analysis which, it turned out, everyone just had to have.

Vankirk was the only really rich person Susan had known so far in her life. He seemed to be normal in most ways. She wondered what it was that made the difference for him.

She knew he had at least four homes: a small castle (she had seen the pictures and it was a far cry from what most Americans would call a castle but it was still a castle) in Bavaria in southern Germany just outside Munich; a large apartment in New York on the Upper East Side, which was really his primary residence; a place in Key West near the Truman Annex; and a large house on the Cedar Point Chausse, the thin seven-mile-long barrier island that separates Lake Erie from Sandusky Bay.

Vankirk avoided grandstanding at public events and tended to arrive late and leave early. But he was not a recluse. He had grown up in Sandusky. His mother had taught biology in the local high school for many years and his father had been a quality engineer at the local GM plant. Both parents had gone to college in Ohio but had grown up in Upstate New York. Eric had left Sandusky to go to college, Princeton, where he had majored in finance with a minor in German. He returned 15 years later a multi-millionaire. He had been married to an attractive French-Canadian woman named Madelaine, but had divorced, amicably, several years ago. They had no children.

Handsome, rich, and under 50 is a powerful combination.

The German thing, as people referred to it, was Eric Vankirk's defining aura. The joke in Sandusky was that Vankirk liked everything German, but Nazi's, which he hated. His great grandparents on both sides were German, one set from Bavaria and one from West Prussia on the Baltic.

Vankirk took German in high school, and he managed to learn the basics well. His German was flawless in terms of commanding the language, but he had, to native speakers, a strong and distinct English or American accent. He had done everything he could to lose the American accent, but it was a losing battle, and he was resigned to the fact he would take it to the grave.

Sandusky benefited from the huge wave of German immigration to the U.S. in the 19th century. Sandusky was founded in 1818. Most early settlers were from the northeast, specifically Connecticut, residents who headed west after the Revolution to settle on land provided as compensation for the loss of their homes to the British. The Germans came in the 1840s and 1850s, along with some Irish, but the Sandusky community, like many other Great Lakes towns, had a distinct German subculture for decades.

————————∧————————

It was hot, swampy, summertime heat, even at 8 a.m., and Susan loved the slap of cool air when she walked into Township Hall. She walked down the steps and turned to the right and headed to the Perkins Police Station. She was wearing khaki shorts and a white cotton polo with an iris embroidered over the left breast pocket. She carried a small purse and a backpack.

The dispatcher, Sandi Saint-Claire, greeted her warmly. Her son and Tim had played on the same Little League team. Sandi was chubby and bubbly with big breasts and big hair. She cursed at every opportunity. Her son was a catcher and hit monstrous home runs in high school.

"Chief in?" Susan asked.

"Yep, he's in there" she replied with a smile, gesturing with her thumb. Sandi was a good dispatcher with a voice that cut air like it was a lightning bolt. Susan loved the cop/dispatcher lingo. She didn't know what they were talking about half the time, but it sure sounded cool.

Sandi buzzed her in.

"This is the deal," the chief said, directing her to sit in front of a computer. He sat next to her and began moving the mouse. It always looked ridiculous and unnatural when people in uniform wearing guns worked at computers. Bill Cleary was a large man, tall with big shoulders and big hands. He was over six feet and beefy, almost the caricature of the small-town police chief. However, he wore his hair long. It was a strange look. The mouse was completely covered by his hand.

"Susan, I hope you are ready for this," he said, but not looking at her. "This is not pretty, not pretty. The funeral home will earn their money making him look acceptable."

In a few quick clicks, Susan was staring at the corpse of William Krupp.

"Pretty freaking weird," she said quickly. It was bizarre. She couldn't help but think of The Beatles' *Sergeant Pepper* album cover. There he was, holding a bunch of flowers, stretched out on a pile of straw, eyes wide open. The flowers were scattered around him in no observable fashion.

"It must have freaked those kids out, finding Krupp like that," she said.

"The boy handled it better."

Krupp's face was multi-colored, a clown's face. It was puffy and discolored but was not cut or broken. The eyes were the worst, bulging out like two Jacks-in-the Box.

Susan started listing the flowers she could identify. She had brought a notebook and pen. The "bouquet" around his body had daylilies, daisies, a few irises, but also a few wildflowers. The arrangement made no sense; it was nothing a florist would ever put together. Altogether, there were at least eight to ten different flowers. Scattered around the body were more flowers. Most she recognized, a few she did not.

"I'm not seeing any pattern, any obvious message," she said. She felt like she had let him down. His face said he believed her.

"Come with me to the fairgrounds," he said. "You might see something there that tells you something. I'm meeting the Bureau of Criminal Investigation—that's BCI—guys there in an hour."

The BCI guys were from Bowling Green, an hour drive or more west. They drove a standard van tricked out with some of the equipment they might need in the field. Susan watched them park their vehicle and then start to walk toward she and the chief. They were three garden-variety nerds, but probably smarter than anyone within 50 miles. They were dressed in civilian clothes. One had two cameras and one held several black plastic bags.

They looked like the people who come to spray for spiders.

The entire horse barn had been sealed off as a crime scene. The horses had been moved to an adjoining barn. There was a Perkins Township Police officer stationed at either end of the building.

Bill Cleary was convinced that Krupp had been carried in. He could find no drag marks anywhere, nor had anyone else. There were lots of boot and shoe marks in and around the barn. Sorting through them would be a wearisome job. In his mind, the crime scene had already been compromised.

Why put the bastard in the horse barn? It was in the middle of the fairgrounds. It would have been far easier to use one of the barns on the periphery of the fairgrounds; and why in the middle of the barn, was there something special about Stall 11?

And the flowers, the goddamn flowers.

Bill nodded to the BCI guys as they approached him. No smiles. He introduced Susan as a local gardening expert, assisting him with the case.

Together, almost like the offense breaking and heading to the line of scrimmage, the group walked inside the horse barn. It was cooler inside now, but by late afternoon it would be steaming. It was an old wooden building, low roof, the stalls old and beat up. Leather, dirt, dung, horses, straw, each contributed to the mix.

"This is it," Bill said, stopping in front of the tape. The door to the stall was open. The number 11 was painted on the door.

The chief's cell phone rang. He snapped it off his belt in a quick, practiced gesture and spit out his name "Cleary." He stepped back a little, then turned slightly. "I'm at the scene. I'm with the BCI guys now. They just got here." He listened for several seconds, many seconds, and Susan and the BCI crew and a Perkins officer all watched him and tried not to be completely obvious about listening to him. Susan assumed it was the coroner's office in Toledo. The local guy, Dr. Groves, didn't waste any time before calling in the cavalry.

"No shit," the chief said. "You've got to be kidding." A few moments later he said, "Amazing."

All eyes were on the police chief. He waited several seconds, getting himself together so he could deliver the news in the best way possible. This was training for the press explosion that was coming in a short time, probably late afternoon at the latest.

"It was bad chemistry," Chief Cleary said, "not bad drugs." He looked right at the BCI guy as he spoke. "Old Krupp was injected with a series of really bad poisons, including the stuff found in bad algae. All stuff that could, and in this case, would be enough to kill 10 men. I didn't understand him on some of the scientific stuff. And he isn't sure if they were administered separately, or if they all got mixed and became one Super Bowl size poison needle. Pesticides. Herbicides.

"Gruesome either way," he said, owning the floor and enjoying it. "It wasn't a good way to go, at least according to Reynolds at BCI. A real witches brew."

"How long?" Susan asked, not quite believing that she had asked it.

"Not sure."

"About?" she asked again.

"Twenty minutes, something like that. His organs just began melting and then burning and then almost disintegrating." Chief Cleary gave a nod and motion of his hand to the group and they fanned out to examine the stall. This was no five-minute affair.

Chief Clearly wondered how long in fact it did take him to die. Was he tied down? This was new territory. In Cleveland, it was mostly bullets and a few knives, once or twice a hammer or some steel pipe. And once a bow and arrow. He remembered the guy who had shot his wife's lover twice with his compound bow.

The chief's phone buzzed again. It was Sandi.

"You are more than popular," she said, loud enough that Susan had no trouble hearing her. "I need help! I feel like Santa Claus on Christmas Eve. Everybody wants what we've got: a nasty murder."

She barked into the phone: "The Cleveland TV stations, the Toledo TV stations, the *Toledo Blade*, the *Plain Dealer*, the *Akron Beacon Journal*, even Columbus media outlets. They are all on their way here." What should I do?

The chief ignored her. He was looking at the spot where the school kids had found Krupp.

"So, how'd he get there?" the chief asked the group. "He was no small potatoes. With that gut, I'd say he was 250 pounds, maybe more. Not a one-man job. No single person could have done it. Unless he's Hulk Hogan. Ever carry somebody who weighs over 200 pounds? Break your goddamn back. "

Susan tried to look at the spot where Krupp's body had been. She could see a few of the flowers were already starting their transformation into Erie County dirt. The BCI guys said little as they worked. It was just like TV, she thought. She finally took out a pen and a notebook from her daypack and started writing down the names of plants she recognized. There were at least three she did not know. She took pictures so she could share them with certain people who should know. And there were her books at home.

The Chief chewed on what he knew and what he didn't know.

It would have taken four strong men to transport Krupp's body from whatever vehicle brought him to the fairgrounds and then drove to the front door of the horse stall. They chose a stall in the rear of the building. Why? There was no easy way to get a vehicle back there. It made everything harder.

He decided to see for himself. He told the BCI guys he'd be right back.

There was a gate in the back, but it wasn't much of a barrier. The floor was dirt and it looked it. Cleary could not detect anything suspicious, no collection of strange footprints, no telltale furrows from dragging a heavy object across the floor in the direction of Stall 11. When he stepped out the back of the barn, he was nearly at the fence line that separated the fairgrounds from Oakland Cemetery, the largest burial ground in the county. The barrier was an eight-foot-high steel chain-link fence. He looked up and down the fence line. Not a goddamn thing. He was tempted to just turn and leave; certain the body dumpers had brought Krupp in the front door. Somehow. But he knew it wasn't the right thing to do. He started walking in the grass behind the building, looking for signs that a vehicle had been there. He followed the fence line carefully and deliberately. The grass was thick and rough-looking, and he saw what might have been disturbances from a vehicle. He had walked about 200 feet when he first noticed, looking ahead, following the fence line, a spot where the top of the fence dipped slightly for several feet before raising up even again.

He started walking faster. Out of the corner of his eye he saw the lead BCI guy walking toward him. They met at the fence.

It was obvious what had been done. Someone had cut a hole in the fence, probably using a standard bolt-cutting tool. Not an easy thing to do. It would require cutting each link. It would take some time, but perhaps they had two cutters working it.

Access to the fairgrounds was controlled. There was no just-drive-in option. When they delivered Krupp's body, they would have had to pass through a staffed security gate or find some way to unlock one of the unmanned gates or create their own gate. These guys had chosen the third alternative, but it was risky.

The chief stared into the cemetery for a moment. It was leafy and green. He had been there many times. Several family members were buried there, some of his friends, too. He hated cemeteries.

The paths through the cemetery were narrow. There were so many paths, and so many trees, and it was all so poorly marked that it would be easy to become lost or confused, especially at night.

"I would guess your garden variety bolt cutter, something that once upon a time you could special order from Sears." It was the BCI guy.

"Not anymore," the chief replied. "Now it's Lowe's."

They took turns examining the fence but not touching certain areas.

"We'll dust it all, Chief, but I'm sure they were wearing gloves of some kind."

The chief nodded.

They both looked down at the grass and dirt on the other side of the fence. It was a mixture. They could see tire marks. The right set of eyes, and the right tire recognition software, might tell them a lot, including the manufacturer, or maybe more.

They stood in silence a while longer, then Chief Cleary said, "So they drove into Oakland Cemetery sometime after dark. They somehow avoid the cameras."

"We don't know that yet, Chief. You haven't talked to the cemetery folks yet. They might have it."

"I don't even know if they even have much of a camera system. They only need it for the occasional ghost sighting," he laughed. "But for now, let's assume they had a way in and out that avoided detection. They had to drive with their lights on. Couldn't do it in the dark. You'd be slamming into trees and knocking over headstones."

"But maybe they did do it without lights," the BCI guy interrupted. "Full moon last night. It could be done if you went slowly and carefully. And if you knew the lay of the headstones.

And maybe they did hit something. And if they did and we found what they hit we could determine the color of the car. And lots more things."

"Not worth the effort. That car is long gone, probably in the next state," the chief replied.

The chief was getting hungry. Police work did that.

"Well, we know the car was here." He paused, then said:

"I knew this guy." He looked back at the horse barn. "You definitely didn't see him at his best, but you could see he was a big guy. I figure 250, maybe 275. Not a one-man job, not a two-man job, not a three-man job. I figure it took four guys to haul him out of the vehicle, get him through the fence, carry him 200 feet to the barn, then take him to Stall 11. And they had to bring the flowers too and arrange everything and then get the hell out."

"I suspect they didn't think he'd be found until morning."

The chief felt the morning heat on the back of his neck. He thought about Krupp.

The BCI guy shook his head and said "There's a lot of candidates out there to be the guy who did it. I understand he wasn't too popular in Columbus."

Cleary jumped on his remark. "What do you mean?"

"I have a few friends in the Ohio EPA. They used to tell stories about this guy. He was always trying to screw the government. But it was probably drugs. It's almost always about drugs. You'd be amazed how much drug work we do."

The chief made a note to call the Ohio EPA to see if Krupp had ever been in trouble on environmental issues. The BCI Guy had made a logical jump. This murder might be payback, punishment for something gone wrong. Or perhaps a warning. Or both.

CHAPTER 3

It was not a short trip back for Frankie Visidi, even with the engine wide open and a declining lake chop. He thought about stopping at Kelleys Island on the way back, but decided he needed the time to figure this thing out. What he had just seen was impossible. Everyone would think he was crazy. He had seen many movies and he knew how the game was played. His cell phone stayed in his day pack. It would take too much time to try and convince some dispatcher he wasn't crazy.

So, he continued course past the Marblehead Light, the sandbar east and north of Johnson's Island, then into Sandusky Bay. His dock was at the Cedar Point Marina.

His legs felt like rubber as he zipped the canvas cover over the console. His throat was crackly, and his stomach hurt. His mind was worse. It had been almost an hour since the killing. Did it really happen? Was it a nightmare? The sky was a creamy blue and blobs of white clouds scuttled by above. The sounds of the Blue Streak roller coaster were distinct and real and barley a hundred yards from the slip where his boat was docked. He knew he was in the right universe.

Frankie took the net and shook its contents into a white plastic garbage bag. He thought about his Uncle Shane, his mother's brother, who one night after drinking many beers, had told him and his brother the story of how he was once

detailed to pick up body parts and put them in body bags after a North Vietnamese mortar attack.

Frankie looked in the bag. There were bits of flesh. Blood. Hair. Fur. Other stuff. Everything was wet. There had to be shark DNA somewhere in there. Had to be.

He wasn't alone on Pier 5. He would have to pass a few boats where the owners were busy trying to get their boats shipshape before nightfall. They were all friends, a few were fishermen. Frankie carried the white garbage bag in his left hand along with his day pack. He had a small cooler with four walleyes, all about 17 or 18 inches in length, in his right hand. His rain jacket was tossed over his shoulder. He was determined to get to the Ohio Department of Natural Resources (ODNR) office in Sandusky before it closed at 7 p.m.

"Where's Priscilla?" It was Bill Gilliard, shouting as he jumped from his boat to the floating pier.

The question startled Frankie. He should have seen this coming and figured out a defense to handle it. Instead, he told a lie, "I brought her in early," he said. "I think she sensed something wasn't right. She looked sick. I called my cousin, and he came over and met us at the dock." It was mostly plausible, but why would he not just call it a day and care for his sick dog, which is what he in fact would have done?

However, Gilliard seemed to accept it.

"Taking her to the vet?" Pete Hafner asked. He docked his 25-foot Sea Ray on the other side of Gilliard.

Frankie was feeling a little lightheaded; he had not lied like this since childhood.

The other guys loved Pris, too. How the hell was he ever going to be right in the head again.

There were alternative lies.

Pris was a great dog but she had graduated from this life early. But now Frankie liked to imagine her as free. Her DNA was on the move. Maybe now she would know about her ancient father, who had been mostly wolf and who was known as Buffalo Killer to a band of Cro-Magnon's residing in the Rhine valley 15,000 years ago.

Frankie made eye contact with a few others as he walked off the dock and exchanged greetings. He walked quickly to his car. He was thirsty as hell and he had to piss. He could still taste a little of the left-behind vomit in his mouth and throat.

The ODNR Sandusky office had extended hours from Memorial Day to Labor Day, which meant staying open an extra two hours on Mondays, Wednesdays, and Fridays. The office was in downtown Sandusky on the waterfront, only a 10-minute drive from the marina parking lot. When he crossed the causeway bridge, he quickly shot a look west toward the main bay. The shark could be there, he thought; "the shark could be there," he said aloud. Then a voice said it could not be there, not yet. Sharks don't swim that fast. The shark was still near the shoal, hunting for dogs.

The ODNR guy was starting to close shop when Frankie got there. The office was shared by Division of Watercraft ("water cops" as they were known) and the Division of Wildlife (which had many Ph.D.'s). They took turns covering the late shift in the summer.

Frankie was feeling better when he opened the door to the office. He drew a water cop.

Frankie looked at the face of the officer. He looked to be in his mid-30s, well-tanned by a life spent outdoors, especially in the summer months.

"My name is Frank Visidi." Frankie broke eye contact and looked at his watch—it was 7:15 p.m.—and then went back to the officer's face and said, "My dog, a black lab named Priscilla, was killed and pretty much eaten by a shark about an hour and a half ago at Kelleys Island Shoal. I loved my dog."

The officer flinched. He found himself lightly touching his service weapon. But he said nothing, his tanned face frozen. He had already written Frankie Visidi off as a wacko.

"Mr. Visidi tell me what happened. Go slowly."

When he was finished, Frankie said it again, "I loved my dog."

"Mr. Visidi, you realize there is no credible account in the roughly four-thousand-year life of Lake Erie of a shark attack. There are no sharks in Lake Erie. They live in salt water."

"This was a shark. It was huge and it was gray-colored, and it had shark teeth." Then he added: "Goddamn shark teeth. I never saw its underside. It had a big dorsal fin."

"This water turns to ice in winter. Sharks don't like cold water," Officer Mylett interrupted. What kind of wacko, Mylett wondered? He didn't doubt the guy had seen something and, unfortunately, he didn't doubt the dog was dead. He figured he had the dog out swimming, and they got too far from the boat and one or the other or both panicked and only one made it back to the boat. The dog might be doing the float in a day or two and spotted by a fisherman. Or it might be something more bizarre. When he was in the training academy, he remembered studying a case where a guy from Port Clinton claimed his wife and dog were washed overboard by a huge wave. The guy never accounted for the float, and two days later the bodies surfaced and were spotted by a fisherman. The husband had killed them both with a boat anchor and dumped their bodies in the lake. It was something joked about now, 30 years past the incident, but the scene inside the boat must have been horrific. Turns out, the wife had been screwing the guy's best friend. Human behavior at its best. The dog had been a gift from the best friend.

People see strange things on the lake, especially at night. But daytime, too. There are always surprises. He liked it that way.

The guy looked rattled, trying his best to look calm but failing. Byrne did not think he was drunk or high, but there were some who could really fool you.

"I'm going to ask you to write all this down, Mr. Visidi, and we will put out the word that your dog is missing, last seen in the water on Kelleys Island Shoal." Officer Mylett started toward a gray desk to get the form.

"I have the shark's DNA, and Pris' DNA, in this bag," Frankie said loudly, holding up the white garbage bag. "I have some blood, I think, but I know I have bits and pieces of my dog, some fur, part of a leg. The shark's DNA must be in this mess somewhere."

Frankie stepped forward to hand the bag to Officer Mylett. Mylett hesitated at first, but then took it.

"I will refrigerate it and give it to the Wildlife people in the morning. They can take it from there. I know it will go to a lab either over at Gibraltar or in Columbus. Don't expect a quick turn-around."

Frankie shook his head. He was starving and he needed a shower badly.

"There's big shark out there, "he said, pointing north, toward the lake, with his deeply tanned arm.

CHAPTER 4

When Susan got home there was an email from Jeremy. She resisted her first impulse—to immediately click the mouse and open it—and instead, went to the refrigerator and got out a Diet Pepsi, popped it, and enjoyed the sound, kicking off her shoes as she walked across the family room carpet and dropping down into the soft chair in the corner by the computer to read it with pleasure and at leisure.

Europe had finally recovered from the pandemic.

They were in Paris. Paris. Her flesh and blood, Jeremy, was in Paris with a beautiful young thing wandering the Louvre and sipping cheap but good wine in cafes. Soft sunsets. Hazy warm skies. Then lights on street corners and the smell of bread and cheese. There was a part of her that resented him a little. She had never been out of the U.S. (Canada, Mexico and the Caribbean didn't count)—Europe only existed in her imagination—but mostly she was glad for him. She just wanted him to know in his heart that this was a lark and the girl, Alexis, would likely be gone by Christmas, and he had to get his ass into law school.

There they were. The magic words, coming to life across a deep and dark ocean, or perhaps shot to her computer seemingly at the speed of light from a grab bag of metal from the stars above.

Hi Mom. We're in Paris. Mostly raining. Kind of cold. Staying at a hostel not too far from Montmartre. View of the city at night is amazing. Met two kids from Penn State. They are going to go with us to Rome. I saw a Cedar Point cap on the Metro. He was young, maybe a kid that worked at the park a few years ago. I wanted to talk to him, but I couldn't catch him before the train left. We went to Notre Dame yesterday. Not many people praying, everybody looking around. It's certainly impressive. I can better appreciate now why it's taking forever to repair after the fire. No diarrhea yet!

Susan printed the email, then stuffed it into a file with emails going back a year or more. What a great goddamn thing email was. If Jeremy had to take out pen and paper and sit at a desk and scratch out a letter and then trot off to the post office and all of that, well, she'd be in the dark. She thought about how much to tell him about Krupp. She knew he probably hadn't bothered to check the *Sandusky Register's* website. She went fast, she always did. She told him everything. Then she hit send.

Flowers. Herbicides and insecticides. A murdered farmer. If she were a cop, she'd be combing the internet looking for similar cases. The world was a big place. The world of nurseries and flower shops not nearly as big. Start there.

She and her boys lived in a small housing development not far from the mall and close enough to Ohio Route 2 and US 250 that traffic noise at certain times was on the edge of being bothersome. She had good neighbors on either side. That was one of the blessings of Midwest life: the odds were stacked in your favor that you'd have two good neighbors.

It was Saturday. She belonged at the museum. It was normally the biggest day of the week, especially if the weather was bad. There was more than one business in the area that not only survived but thrived in bad weather. In summer, she worked six days a week; her day off was unscheduled and she took it when she could. The museum had a large staff by regional museum standards. In addition to Susan's position of executive director, there was an archivist /curator and an operations manager, as well as several part-timers. The ops guy wore a lot of hats: exhibits, retail, IT support, building and grounds maintenance. The executive director handled marketing and finance, and served as spokesperson, as needed.

She drifted off thinking about Jeremy looking at the Eiffel Tower.

About 1 p.m. the chief called and requested her presence at the press briefing. When they left the fairgrounds in the morning, he had told her he might want her there, so she wasn't really surprised. This was a big deal for Perkins Township and Erie County. He told her he might have to mention her by name, just to confirm his office was following up on the flowers.

"Just don't speculate, Susan, and don't rattle on, either. This is what you say, 'Yes, there were flowers. We are in process of identifying all of them. End of goddamned story, only don't say goddamned story."

CHAPTER 5

The press briefing was not a disaster, but it could have gone better. Her cousin didn't like reporters to begin with but had never really learned how not to show it. Some people were good at it from the jump, others had to learn it, and, of course, some, like her cousin, never learned how to do it. Reporters were not some alien species; they responded much as others do when they sense they are disliked, which means they choose some level of flight or fight, especially if the stakes are high. The ones who chose flight flew off to do Christmas cookie recipes for the Home page; the ones who chose fight readied another question and planned to show no mercy.

Susan watched from the front of the room, but off to the side. It was a good spot; she could see everything: all the summer colors; the crazy t-shirts; ball caps worn both ways; short sleeved white shirts with theme ties (a few); lots of golf shirts; the impact of a mid-afternoon summer day in a room with weak AC and too many people. A part of her wanted to be napping at home with the doors locked and the AC at full roar, but she felt the desperation in her cousin's voice.

She sat next to an overweight young man who worked for the *Lorain Journal*, the largest daily newspaper between Sandusky and Cleveland; Lorain was about 30 miles east. He had been to the museum several times. They remembered meeting but reintroduced themselves. He was new to the beat,

freshly minted from the Journalism School at Ohio University. There were big irregular sweat stains on his shirt. His editor was probably calling every three minutes to find out what was going on and why he hadn't asked a question yet.

Susan had forgotten what a big deal Krupp was in Erie County. Well, not anymore.

"We have a report from a good source that Krupp's body was half-buried in straw and horse manure—and covered with flowers? Is that true, Chief?"

It was Dee Williams, the woman who worked for worked for one of the Cleveland TV stations, one of their stars. She had been helped quite a bit in her career by her striking good looks, and they were on full display this Saturday afternoon in Erie County. You could not help but look at her. She was tall and thin with creamy skin. Susan did not hold her good looks against her.

Her cousin was used to the local media, which meant the local newspaper, the *Sandusky Register*, and one local radio station, WLEC-AM, but not the big show—Cleveland and Toledo—where murders were more routine than not, a newsroom staple.

Too many people already knew about the flowers. He saw no benefit to hiding it.

"Yes, there were a lot of flowers at the scene," the chief replied. "We assume there is some significance, but we don't know what it is."

"What kind of flowers?" Williams asked, a fraction of a second before anyone else could reply. It was a learned skill.

"I am not a horticulturist," he said seriously. "However, we have a local expert who is assisting us and who is helping us determine what kind of flowers were left at the scene."

There were perhaps 100 people in the room. Way too many. Another reporter, one she did not recognize, asked about the expert.

Chief Cleary, her first cousin, ratted her out. "Her name is Mary Susan Massimino," the chief said, looking right at Susan, who was only 15 or 20 feet away. Every eye in the room swiveled in her direction.

Dee Williams got to her first, as she was closest to her.

"What kind of flowers were left at the scene?"

Susan had the list in her pocket, but she didn't try to look for it.

"Mostly standard summer flowers," she said, looking straight into the camera.

"What do you think they mean? The reporter quickly responded. "Can you be more specific in terms of the flowers you found with Mr. Krupp? What are the names of the flowers? Are they all local flowers?

The Chief came to her rescue and cut in:

"We just don't know at this juncture. We are still processing the scene. For now, that's all we have to say about the flowers. They are part of the investigation." He closed by asking the public to call the Perkins PD if they had any information about what happened, all the standard stuff, including some good words about the deceased.

CHAPTER 6

Perkins Township had a camera system. It had been extremely easy to hack it. Now Z could watch all the proceedings in real time from his laptop. He zoomed in closer so he could see Susan's face clearly. He thought she was extremely attractive. Certainly not young, probably 40, but she had a presence he felt across the more than 4,000 miles that separated them. He wanted to meet her.

It was 7 p.m. in Munich, Germany.

Watching on his laptop was Paul Gutten, a German national, 44 years old. He was single, wealthy, childless, and nice to look at (according to most women). His good looks belonged on the fashion model or TV anchorman side of the sheet vs. the star quarterback or CEO side.

Z was a nickname from boarding school days. It had no special significance.

He led two lives. In one, he was a Swiss-German businessman with homes in Bavaria, Lake Geneva, and Los Angeles. In the other, he was a senior leader, the number one, two, or three man, depending on a variety of measurements, for a secret organization that had its roots in the European eco-terrorism movement of the 1970s and 1980s. Z's business was executions. World-wide.

William Krupp had come to them as a referral from an associate in North America. The area where Krupp lived,

several miles southeast of the City of Sandusky in Erie County, Ohio, was 60 miles equidistant from Toledo and Cleveland. All three cities were located on the southern shore of Lake Erie. The lake still had a damaged reputation nationally and internationally because of environmental tragedies like the burning of the Cuyahoga River in downtown Cleveland in the early 1970s. The water plant in Toledo shut down for several days in August in 2016 because of problems caused by toxins from the algal blooms, which were a huge problem in western Lake Erie due to the phosphorus from agriculture. Much of the city had to use bottled water for a few days for drinking and bathing.

Z usually did not question the reason behind a particular execution. He did try to honor special requests, but there were no guarantees. Once his organization had accepted an assignment, the execution was done Z's way.

Z had always had an interest in the biological sciences. He studied biology and chemistry in college. He thought of himself as an amateur scientist. On a business trip to Central America several years previously he learned about the existence of a freshwater shark that lived in Lake Nicaragua. The shark had a well-earned reputation as man-eater. Scientists had recently confirmed that the shark is not a separate species but in fact is a bull shark. Why not introduce bull sharks to the Great Lakes? What a wonderful uproar it could create! It would focus more attention on climate change, showing the world that this is the future of the Great Lakes as its water warms. The sharks would probably not last through a Great Lakes winter, but they would have their best chance in Lake Erie.

For the first time, he would have two projects, quite unrelated, going on at the same time and in the same place. Others would be concerned, but Z was anxious for the challenge.

Z considered himself a very successful man. His grandfather would have been proud of him. His grandfather had managed to live through World War II, an accomplishment itself, especially for someone who had been a front-line commander. His grandfather had disappeared in 1972 while on a visit to the local library. He simply vanished. Z had his theories about the disappearance, including one that he was killed by a Russian, Jewish, or Ukrainian, death squad as payback for his World War II actions in Russia. He disappeared four years before Z was born.

When Z was 25 years old, he received a phone call from a Swiss lawyer named Franz Nedelhof, who said he was the son of another lawyer who had been an associate of his late grandfather. His grandfather had arranged with their firm to safeguard a letter he had written to an as yet unborn grandson or granddaughter. The lawyer's job was to hand deliver it that person when he or she had turned 25 years old.

"No one knows about this except you and me," said the lawyer. He was a tall and austere-looking man, as Z pictured him. By his voice, Z pegged him to be in his mid-30s. "I really don't know what's in the letter. I have not read it and you have my word that no one else in my firm has either. Your family does not know of its existence unless your grandfather shared it with them. We have not."

They met a week later in a small town in southwest Bavaria. Nedelhof had family in the town and planned to call on a cousin after their meeting. They had lunch in a small beer garden. It was a beautiful September afternoon, but it was a weekday and so they had a corner of the garden to themselves.

Z had arrived 30 minutes early, which was his life-long pattern.

After a few pleasantries, Nedelhof handed him a brown 8 x 10 envelope. It looked old but it also looked clean, as though it had not been moved much in its lifetime. The letter was 18 single-spaced pages, all apparently typed using a manual typewriter. There were many typos. At the end of the letter, his grandfather had signed it *Your Opa* (Papa). There was a name printed under it: General Otto Schmeltzer. However, no signature.

"I will be in town at my cousin's home for an hour or two," the lawyer said. If there is anything you want or need me to do as follow up to this letter, give me a call and we can talk in person before we leave. If there is no need to contact me, you still have my card for future reference," he said, handing him a business card. Z watched him walk toward the door. He decided he had largely told the truth.

Z ordered another pilsner and sat down to read. His heart was beating noticeably, and his hands felt klutzy; he was perspiring heavily. He had not felt that combination of physical feelings in a very long time, if ever.

Z savored each word, each page, words written for him nearly 40 years earlier. It was a dead man writing.

It is a difficult thing to write to someone who you do not even know exists.

My given first name is Otto. I was named for my mother's brother, Otto Stenzel. Your mother's maiden name was Freika. I was born in Leipzig. I had two brothers and a sister. My parents operated a small shop, and my father was also a schoolteacher. I had a great uncle who immigrated to America to a small town in Ohio. My two brothers died in Russia. Erwin froze to death outside Moscow in 1941. My older brother Max died near Leningrad in 1943. My sister, Gisella, died of typhus in the spring of 1945, as the war was ending. I could not save her. Her husband was a pilot but not a very good one. He was shot down by the Russians in 1944 near Minsk.

My parents died in the fire-bombing of Dresden. They were there to visit family.

The letter spent several pages reviewing the wartime fates of everyone his grandfather knew growing up in Leipzig. The names meant nothing to Z.

As an officer and commander in the Wehrmacht, I had the opportunity to acquire many things. I was a thief and a good one and over the course of the war in the Osfront I had many opportunities to steal. To the eternal question: Why? My answer would be another eternal question: Why Not?

I served in the Wehrmacht for four years. I was a practicing attorney when the war began, but they needed soldiers, so I was sent to officer training and then panzer school and eventually assigned to the Third Panzer Army, just in time for the German invasion on June 22, 1941. I spent three years in Russia, all on the southern front.

In the late winter of 1943-44, Otto began to organize a group of army officers who were smart enough to know Hitler couldn't possibly win, and when they lost the war, the Allies would want retribution, especially the Russians. The name of the group was *Die Ruckkehr* (The Return).

I operated under great risk of being hung with piano wire in some Gestapo prison if caught, but I was good and I was lucky. I did not get caught. I even stole gold, a lot of it, from the stupid SS.

I had no interest in escaping to South America. I knew many who did. I think it worked for some, others not. But I knew it was not for me, which meant that I had to change identities. I worked hard to find the best people to help me do this. My investment was considerable, but it was crucial. I felt my life depended on it. My wife's as well.

I suspect the Russians are going to find me soon. There are some mysterious things happening. Or, it may be one of the Jewish groups.

A few weeks before the end of the war, General Otto Schmeltzer disappeared into the "Missing" category in the Wehrmacht's long list of casualties, never to be heard from again.

At the end of this letter are precise directions to a cave in the hills above Kreut Alm. In that cave are many bars of gold and silver and other valuable items. This treasure is all yours now. You are the only person who knows of its existence. I never shared this information with your father for many reasons. I provided for him, but he never really knew where the money came from. I did not think he had the strength to bear the burden (and in many ways, it is a burden). He would have been looking over his shoulder every day of his life waiting for the Israelis or the Russians to want their money back. With interest.

If my lawyer cannot locate you within five years, you will be presumed dead, or never born. If this occurs, the letter will be passed on to the next oldest of your siblings (if they ever exist). Otherwise, the treasure will remain in the cave until some lucky person stumbles upon it. That might not be for 200 years.

The letter recounted in some detail how Schmeltzer was able to create *Die Ruckkehr*. Several pages told the story of the day he and other members of the group deposited the gold in the cave and the bloodbath that occurred immediately afterward.

--------Λ--------

Z was not superstitious, or religious, but he felt some anxiety as he walked through the woods. He had not been to the cave in almost a year. There was always the possibility he would find nothing but a thank-you note from the lucky person who stumbled upon it.

He parked his Mercedes Benz in the pull off area and began the long walk to the cave entrance. There was no trail, so he had to navigate by memory, and it was tough going because of the undergrowth. He used a hiking staff, but he still tripped several times. The forest was mixed, both deciduous and evergreens, with the latter holding the edge. There were many wildflowers. He occasionally checked behind him, even stopping several times and waiting for more than five minutes to make sure he was not being followed. The forest was still, just a little insect buzz and some occasional birdsong. It was a warm day and soon he was sweating even though all he carried was a small backpack with water, a compass, an apple, a granola bar, and two small but powerful flashlights. On his belt was a Glock. It was a beautiful place. Many similar places existed now in western Europe. Wildlife had returned to some areas, even predators like lynx, wolves, and bears were making a comeback.

In 30 minutes, he came to the entrance to the cave. He marveled every time he saw it. The side of the mountain was rocky in spots. Near one huge jumble of rock, on a south-facing slope, was the entrance to the cave. The opening was tight and given the size of the rocks and boulders and the weak light, it was very easily missed. Z approached the cave cautiously. It was as he remembered it. Z slithered in between the rocks like a snake, parted some branches just at the entrance, and he was in.

The cool air was welcome—at first. It was a steady 57 degrees. He pulled out one flashlight and pointed it at the wall where he expected the treasure to be. There they were, all neatly arranged by those young Wehrmacht soldiers so many years ago. The value of each of the gold bars, as of that morning, was approximately $675,000. Z walked over and touched one the bars, each of which weighed about 26 pounds. He planned to take two bars back with him.

There were some additional items, including silver bars, and several containers that included a wide variety of jewelry, most of which General Schmeltzer had acquired in his time spent in the Ukraine. Years ago, Z had done a detailed inventory of everything in the cave. He estimated the treasure to be worth over $500 million dollars.

The cave was about 40 feet wide near the entrance. Z turned and aimed his flashlight at the opposite wall. The cave art was still there, colored images showing various Ice Age animals and representations of hunters. Z resisted the impulse to deface them in some way or to enter his own graffiti.

The cave ceiling was about 12 feet high. It tapered slightly as you moved back into the cave. Z walked back to where his grandfather and his allies had dumped the bodies of the soldiers and where Schmeltzer and General Ansbach had in turn dragged the four generals. The cave floor was flat, packed dirt, so it was relatively easy to drag the bodies to the pit. You could look down on the ground and see drag marks where they had dragged the bodies. There was soot on the ceiling. Schmeltzer approached the pit opening slowly, nervously. There was no need, he knew, for him to be nervous, and no need for him to look down into the pit. If the treasure was intact, that was all that mattered. But he looked. He could not help himself. The pile of bodies was still there, maybe 15 feet down, a gray mishmash of bone, uniforms, and metal objects like buttons. The skulls stood out, grinning up at him. It was ghastly.

The shell casings that littered the floor of the cave crackled when he stepped on them.

Satisfied that his treasure was safe, Z went to the pile of gold bars and picked one out and slipped it into his backpack. It would be a long walk back to the car.

———————∧———————

Otto Schmeltzer knew who he was. He was a killer. And he was a thief. And he was good at being both.

In the summer of 1944, he helped organize a small, secret group of Wehrmacht officers, all fellow thieves, to protect their assets when the inevitable arrived, which they all believed was a matter of months, not years. The general had a contact in Switzerland, a family friend for many years, a fan of the Nazi way of doing things, who could be trusted (or incentivized) to convert, when needed, their assets from physical gold and create a kind of shadow bank, a private group without any official existence, at least initially. The collateral for the shadow bank would be gold, silver, jewelry, and other assets hidden in a location in southern Germany. The location would only be known to a handful of men, essentially the members of Die Ruckkehr. The benefits of membership in Die Ruckkehr were threefold: protection of their assets in the immediate aftermath of the war; seed money for starting a new existence, most likely in Brazil or Argentina; and the benefit of a network which could provide contacts and protection for each of the members. Finally, a way to pass on their assets to family members when they were gone.

Schmeltzer was under no illusions. He had to be on several lists in the Soviet plan for de-Nazifying Germany. His name was known. He had burned villages, participated in the killing of Jews and Ukrainians, and killed thousands of prisoners. He had fought brutally, as he was ordered to do, and felt no remorse.

Schmeltzer had no plans to go to South America. He would change his identity, and his wife's, and remain in Germany. He did not think he was on any American lists, and he thought he could outsmart the Russians if it came to that. Switzerland was always an option. It was a beautiful place and they spoke German. The creation of a new identity required the ruthless elimination of the old one.

The biggest issue for Schmeltzer was the fact that the members of Die Ruckkehr did not really trust each other. The second issue was that to do this correctly too many people would know about it. It would be impossible to control, to keep the story quiet. More people would want to be cut in.

Schmeltzer was relatively young and had no trouble with establishing a new identity. He had no plans to run to Argentina or Chile or some backward hell hole. He had been working on his plan for almost a year, soon after the Battle of Kursk in the summer of 1943, when he realized what he had known in his head and his heart for an even longer period: The Allies were going to win; Germany was going to lose. He did not like to think about what that meant for people like himself.

———————∧———————

The gold and jewelry arrived at a small military airport about 30 miles west of Berlin. The gold traveled hidden in wooden boxes marked with a swastika. They looked like standard boxes.

All the available conspirators had arrived by 9 a.m. They met in a small room in a hanger on the edge of the airfield. It was chilly and damp. Most of them were chain smokers and the air was a cloud of gray. There were several ME 109 Messerschmitts in the hangar. All were badly shot up and would never fly again. They were being scavenged for parts.

There wasn't much shop talk. All the news was bad, worse, or worse than worse. The Russians were only 30 miles from Berlin, the Americans had crossed the Rhine and were rolling across Germany. The Wehrmacht was disintegrating. The Allies were victorious everywhere. The only remaining area where the Nazis still had control was a corner of Bavaria and contiguous parts of Austria.

Nearly all the conspirators were young, all under 50.

Among the conspirators there was an agreed-upon story line if any of the participants were caught or if the entire group were compromised: the gold was being saved for the Fourth Reich, for Die Ruckkehr, the Germany that would rise, someday, from the destruction all around them. But for most it was just about the money, the assets that would allow them to build a new life somewhere besides Germany. None of the men in the hangar were Nazi ideologues. They were smart, practical men, men whose first loyalty was always to themselves.

There are many wooded areas in the mountains south and east of Munich. Schmeltzer knew the area well. He had accidentally discovered a cave in a remote area on a hiking trip when he was in his early 20s. He had kept it secret, never sharing its existence or its location with anyone.

The plane took off at 9 a.m. The city below was a charnel house. Most of the passengers could not resist looking down. It was spring, but everything was the color of mud. The pilot kept the plane low. This was a very dangerous flight. If spotted by a P-51 Mustang, they would be shot down easily. They had no fighter escort. Schmeltzer felt their best chance for survival was to fly as low as possible and remain solo. In a short time, they were flying over a late winter landscape, mostly bare trees, and naked buildings. By air, it was 315 miles to Munich. They were headed to a small airport on the east side of the city, a training base for Luftwaffe fighter pilots. Schmeltzer had arranged for a small group of soldiers, men from his division, to meet them at the airport with two trucks. The soldiers, and the sergeant who led them, had been told they were going to assist in the creation of the Fourth Reich by the preservation of part of the Third.

The soldiers were very nervous about being ordered to wear blindfolds after they had filled the trucks with the cargo from the plane.

The meeting at the airport occurred on schedule. Schmeltzer led the group into the mountains and through thick woods, eventually onto dirt roads. They traveled for over an hour. This was southern Germany, not the Rocky Mountains, and wilderness did not exist in the way it did in America, but this place seemed as dark and empty as any place any of them had ever been, even in Russia. The ground was rocky and wet from melting snow and hard spring rains. The cave was perhaps a 1,000 feet off the road below a ledge and impossible to see until you were right in front of it. It took more than two hours to unload the truck and drag everything into the cave.

The cave had been used by sporadically by both animals and men for at least 50,000 years. The walls were black in spots from untold fires. There were drawings on many of the walls. The treasure was piled several hundred feet into the cave. In the far back, Schmeltzer knew, was a hole that dropped down into another cave.

The second to last box held the weapons. Schmeltzer lifted out two Stg 44 storm rifles, handing one of them to General Ansbach and keeping one himself. Several of the Die Ruckkehr had sidearms. At the signal, a nod of the head all opened fire. The generals opened fire on the soldiers, and Ansbach and Schmeltzer opened up on the generals. The noise was fearsome, a combination of small arms fire, bullets ricocheting from wall to wall to ceiling to ground and mixed in with the screams of the men being shot. Outside, almost nothing was heard, certainly nothing distinguishable or identifiable. It was all over quickly. A dozen men, actually at least half were boys of 16 or 17, were dead. Schmeltzer had to finish a few off with his pistol.

The cave smelled of blood and feces and cordite. Ansbach and Schmeltzer did a quick head count. No one had escaped. It was not easy work, but they succeeded in dragging each body back to hole at the back of the cave and dumping it into the pit. They could hear—and feel—each body when it landed below.

They did not talk while they worked.

Then it was time to go.

Each man drove one of the trucks. They did what they could to cover up the tracks in the dirt near the cave, but they both knew they couldn't get everything and were counting on time to wash away the unnatural for the natural.

General Ansbach and General Schmeltzer did not trust one another. The marriage was strictly of convenience, as they had to be a two-man team to pull this off. Schmeltzer was the better planner. He had arranged for General Ansbach's plane to be shot down by one of the few German fighter planes still flying. They were a plane full of officers deserting the Reich, as Schmeltzer had patiently explained to the officer in charge of what was left of the German air command in Munich.

————————∧————————

In the closing days of the war Schmeltzer left his headquarters and drove himself to the rendezvous point to meet his wife, Katrina. He took off his uniform and began his new life as Lars Gutten. The name he chose had no special significance. In the small town he settled in there were no Guttens, but there may be in other places in Germany. He used his cache of gold periodically. When he needed money, he paid a visit to the cave. He transferred appropriate amounts to his banker in Switzerland, who made certain there was enough legitimate cover for these transactions.

The family fortune, and indeed it was a fortune, lived in a cave in Bavaria, accessible only by Lars, formerly a German general. He and his wife, Katrina, had one child, a son, Franz, who was born in 1946. Franz married a woman from Munich in 1972. They had one child, a son they named Paul, born in 1976.

Z believed in science—what rational man or woman could not? And he believed in what he told himself was the common sense of science. He had been involved with various environmental groups and organizations since adolescence, thanks mostly to his mother, who was a convert in her 20s. He did not consider himself a zealot, however, he knew others did.

Z's parents were in their 70s now and less interested in life with each birthday. They did not know his secret life. They did not want to know. They were like the German people who had lived downwind of Dachau.

Z belonged to all the appropriate green organizations and was active in many. He thought globally, that was his perspective. No country was green enough, but he was particularly disappointed with the United States and China.

People understand fear, a universal of the human experience. His immediate calling, in part, was to instill enough fear in the farmers of north central and northwest Ohio that they would change their behavior and stop dumping phosphorus into their fields. Not an easy thing to do—changing a longtime behavior.

The team leader, a man known as Shooter or The Shooter, had reported a clean operation. They were now all safely scattered across three continents. To use an English expression: the deed had been done.

In time, the local police or whomever would end up the power in the investigation, would figure out what had happened to this farmer. He was killed because he was a polluter. He was guilty of the worst kind of crime: killing the unborn, those who might have come after you. To Z, nothing was more heinous.

He was CEO of an organization whose mission it was to punish people who harmed the environment in a significant way. It was a simple concept.

He smiled to himself as he thought about what he had just done. He was in a café in Basel, Switzerland alongside the Rhine River. The river had dropped even more the past few weeks. He preferred a low river level. Another murder. Just one. No, they were executions. He had not committed any murders.

However, the fish were his greatest accomplishment. He felt like a father to them.

The first shark captured was named Alpha 1 and would always be his favorite. She was not the largest—that was Alpha 6—but she fought the hardest when captured—and seemed to be the most aggressive. Alpha 1, Alpha 2, Alpha 3, Alpha 4, Alpha 5 and Alpha 6 (these magnificent fish were all alphas to him), moved steadily around Lake Erie's western basin where there was food, high water temperature, and relatively shallow water. They did not understand they were under a death sentence. Although bull sharks thrived in fresh water, they were warm water sharks. They were seldom seen north of Long Island, unlike their Great White friends, and not likely to survive a winter in Lake Erie, especially if there was much ice. According to Dr. Evans, one of the shark specialists at the Zeiger Institute, the most reasonable scenario for a bull shark to survive the Lake Erie winter was to hang out near the warm water discharge at the Davis Bessie Nuclear Power Plant near Port Clinton, eat lots of carp, and hope for a mild winter.

Small bull sharks have been seen in the Mississippi as far north as Illinois.

CHAPTER 7

Tomorrow, it would be Saturday; it was summer, and the weather was good. It was time to be on the lake. Frankie had gone home from the ODNR office, showered, ate two Stouffer's Lean Cuisines, and then sat in his TV chair and drank three beers and thought about Priscilla. He teared and shuddered at the same time. He wanted to talk to Sheila and tell her what happened, what he had seen, why she would never see Pris again. But it could wait, it had to wait. He texted her from his chair while watching the late innings of the Cleveland game, a nice win over the Yankees. It was a concise message: *Erie will NOT be dreary tomorrow. Meet at dock at 9. KI? PIB?*

Sheila Piersall was the third woman Frankie had been in love with. He had had loved April Lockhart in high school and Christina Bretz his senior year in college. Then there was a long dry spell. He had had several girlfriends in his 20s—but no one to send him on a trip around the moon. He and Sheila clicked because neither felt all that strongly about getting married. They were both single and never married. They had been dating for more than a year but even the subject of moving in together was rarely discussed. It made sense economically, maybe even spiritually, but they still wanted separate lives, at least that is what they told each other.

He told her he loved her, and not just before or after lovemaking, and he felt like he did when he was gaga over Christina Bretz so many years ago.

Sheila's spirit was much freer than his. She was a nurse who liked to have fun, a great combination. She was better with people than he was. Talking came easier to her. Frankie didn't consider himself anti-social—a term his late father had used a few times when referring to him—and could list many friends; but he also liked being alone. She was better looking than he was, but not dramatically so. Shelia was on the high side of average in height. She was also just on the high side of average in weight. But she looked like an athlete—strong, sleek muscles trailing down from her shoulders to her hands and her hips to her ankles—but she had soft spots, too. Her hair was light brown, near to dirty blonde, and she wore it short. Her eyes were a rich brown, and she sometimes referred to herself as the "Brown-Eyed Girl" from the Jimmy Buffett cover of the famous Van Morrison song. Always with a smile.

Sheila was a nurse survivor, and one of the heroines of the pandemic. She was trained as an OB nurse, and she felt that was her calling, but she stepped up to be a back-up for the virus floor at Firelands Hospital in Sandusky. She felt she had gone from assisting in life to assisting in death on the same day too many times.

Sheila was not a fisherman. Too much sitting around and waiting for something to happen, and when it did happen it was over fast. She was not particularly fond of eating walleye, which was an affront to nearly every resident of Erie County, including her boyfriend. She took a lot of good-natured grief over it. She would tirelessly explain to servers that it was the dipping sauce that made the difference. She preferred perch.

Sheila grew up in Fremont, 20 miles southwest of Sandusky.

She liked dogs but was not passionate about them. She came from a large family, four kids and mom and dad. They had several dogs while she grew up, all mixed breeds. She had been friends with each dog, some more than others. She didn't have strong feelings about cats. If pressed, she would vote the canine ticket, but she had also petted her share of cats.

Sheila liked Priscilla and felt no jealousy toward her even though she knew Priscilla was the woman of the house, not her. Pris was big and energetic and happy and devoted to Frankie.

Frankie thought about calling one of his boating friends, Ed McNamara, or Eddie-Mac, as he was generally known, and tell him about Pris and the shark. But it was not going to be an easy conversation, so he put it off.

At 9 a.m. Sheila was at the dock, holding a beach bag and wearing a Cleveland baseball cap. As he walked toward her, he noticed the tufts of blonde hair poking out the sides of her cap; she did not have enough hair to stick it through the back clasp, a look he always liked. She was wearing white cotton shorts and a starting-to-fade yellow golf shirt. The shorts were a half-size too small, and the shirt was a half-size too big. It made for an interesting look. Underneath the shorts and shirt was a bathing suit, a rather small bikini. Frankie approved. He was wearing a wrinkled white fishing shirt, long sleeved, the kind with a collar and tags that said it was rated 55 SPF. He wore a floppy fishing hat with good sun protection but no style. In his backpack, he had an Ohio State cap he planned to wear when they got to Put-in-Bay.

He always felt a surge of excitement, anticipation, a little jolt of happiness when he approached the boat and could look at it up closely. He was very proud of the way it looked. It looked better than it did when launched for the first time. Frankie did not begrudge the time he spent keeping his boat in showroom condition. Cleaning it was fun.

But today was different.

Neither of them smiled much as they got the boat ready for action. It went quicker because this was not a fishing day. Sheila knew the routine, the way he wanted the lines coiled, the right place to put her bag, where to stick the extra fender. They were an efficient team. They cleared the dock in less than 10 minutes. Some days they hung out on the dock and talked to their boating neighbors, but she sensed he did not want to talk to anyone.

"What's different?" he asked, as they motored slowly toward the entrance to the marina. Sheila looked along the edge of the break wall. She saw a big water snake moving quickly only a few inches away from the rocks. Looking for gobies, she thought.

"No Priscilla," she quickly replied, and then added, "so what's the deal?" Sheila was glad the dog wasn't along.

"I am going to talk about it a little later."

There were several boats out already. Frankie had to pay attention to where he was going, or they could easily end up surfing the pier or ramming into another boat. It was the usual craziness. Six months from today there might be several inches of ice on this part of the lake. You had to grab your time on the water when you could. The whole boating fraternity understood that.

They cleared the Cedar Point light and started on a course for Kelleys Island Shoal off the rocky northeast corner of Kelleys Island. There was little breeze, and the lake was like a pile of dry leaves, harmless and soft.

Frankie opened it up a bit more and with minimal strain the boat climbed up to 30 mph, plenty of top end for weather and wave conditions.

"We are headed to a spot on the shoal. I need to show it to you," Frankie yelled over the sound of the big Yamaha.

In 30 minutes, they were there. Not alone, of course. In western Lake Erie, you were never the first to the fishing spot. There was always at least one boat whose captain got up earlier than you did.

The sun was hot now, as Frankie pulled back on the throttle and, while scanning the horizon to the east, into a sun that was now climbing high into the sky, he said, not looking back, "I just want to drop a line for a few minutes."

Frankie brought the boat in tight to the reef. The water depth was about six feet. He checked the depth gauge.

"Go for it," she said without hesitation.

Sheila felt the mid-summer sun, too.

There were several boats in the area, but widely separated, all of them intent on catching a good walleye drift.

They were getting very close to the spot where Pris had been killed. Frankie had plugged in the GPS coordinates before leaving the spot yesterday. He carefully guided the boat close but not too close to the reef. He wanted to get as close to Pris' spot as he could. He scanned the depth finder and saw they were at six feet. He suddenly felt Sheila's arm around his waist.

"So, what's the surprise?" she said.

He needed cheering up, she decided. She could tell he was preoccupied. Frankie stepped in front of the console to get out the anchor. Now was her chance. His back would be to her for a short while. Sheila reached back and grabbed her collar and jerked off her shirt. Then she reached back again and unhooked the back of her bikini top and slid the straps off her shoulder. The shorts came next. Then the bikini bottoms. In 21 seconds, she was as God made her, including a smile.

"Hey, Babe," she said, in her best Lou Reed imitation, "want to take a swim on the wild side?"

Frankie had both hands on the anchor line but immediately turned around in response to her call.

God, she was beautiful, he thought, even with her hair on the short side. Then Sheila lifted her leg over the gunnel and then half jumped into the water. There was a modest splash. A moment later her face was above the water and she started waving him in. They had gone skinny-dipping together more than once, and it was always fun, but not now. Not now.

Frankie was thinking about what he should say to her to get her back into the boat when he saw the water move behind her, like an invisible rake had just been dragged over it, or a school of baitfish had been spooked. It was full late morning sun, the sparkly kind, and he could see nothing below the surface.

The fish was coming from the opposite direction today. It was picking up food noise, a combination of Sheila's arms and legs dancing in the water and a big school of walleye nearby, whose movements were more subtle, but still very recognizable to the great fish. She was drawn to Sheila. She slowly lifted toward the surface, as though she were a submarine about to breach, then leveled herself for the attack.

Frankie finally saw the fin. He was paralyzed for a moment, then began screaming "Get out! Get out!" He jabbed his finger in the air. Frankie could see by the look on her face that she did not understand.

Finally, he screamed "Shark! Shark! There's a shark behind you!

Sheila could read the terror on his face. Whatever it was, it was real. Instinctively, she kicked her leg and swiveled in the water, so she was looking backward. She saw the fin dancing above the water. It was not far away; it seemed like the Empire State Building was riding high above her. Her eyes were at surface level and she could see its head and the mouth and the teeth.

She did not scream. Nurses do not scream. Her legs may have to be sacrificed, she thought, but her head and torso must get in the boat. Sheila kicked furiously. She aimed for the big Yamaha. She knew the prop wasn't turning. She would have to climb into the boat by the outboard well. She couldn't hesitate. The swim platform wasn't in place yet.

Frankie knew what he had to do. He had to brace his left leg in the well and reach down and lift Sheila into the boat. She would have to pull, too, and it would not be easy. She was only several yards away and kicking furiously. The fin was close behind her and closing fast. When she got to the motor, she thrust her right arm out of the water and Frankie grabbed it and pulled hard, really hard, putting his whole life force into it. He felt her body coming up with it. Sheila's right foot found the propeller. It was not engaged, thank god, but It was sharp—the pain was like an electric shock through her foot—but she pushed back, she had no choice—and thank god Frankie was strong enough to lift her. But the shark's jaw arrived at her left foot just as Frankie gained the leverage to get her in the boat. Her foot felt like it was being dragged across razor blades. In a tug of war, they would lose. For an instant, the fish released its grip to get more purchase perhaps, and it was enough that Frankie was able to get her foot free and into the boat. The fish bit the propeller hard enough that It shook the boat like a rag doll. The boat absorbed the hit, but jerked forward and upward, the bow shooting up as the weight of the fish pressed the stern into the water. She seemed to linger, the huge body shaking in the water. But there was no growl, no roar, then it slid back down under the water.

Both feet were a bloody mess. Red water was smeared all over the bottom of the boat. Frankie put his arms around her waist and pulled her back to the seat. Sheila used her heels to help him. But then the nurse took over.

"Get me a towel, Frankie, and get me the first aid kit," she said. Her voice was steady, calming.

She bent forward and looked down.

The bad news was that her big toe on her right foot was hanging by a thread, or, more appropriately, a tendon; the good news was that there was no artery nearby. She had never seen a wound like this. There was no way she could apply direct pressure. The cut went deep. They could see the flash of white that was her toe bone. Sheila could feel the pain arriving like a F-15.

Frankie did a good job with the kit. It was open. There was a roll of surgical tape. She decided her strategy would be to wrap the tape around her first two toes as tightly as she could to keep the big toe in place. She tried to block out everything else, including the fact that she was naked.

"Hold my heel, Frankie," she said calmly. "I'm going to go to work now." She quickly but calmly cut a piece of tape and reached down and put the two toes together and started to wrap. It was going to work, she thought, at least for a while. She dabbed some antiseptic all around the wound. Full out, they could reach Battery Park Marina in Sandusky and a waiting ambulance in 30 minutes.

Her left foot was cut along the bottom. One of the shark's teeth had just barely reached her, just enough to dig a trench down her foot from her heel to just below the back of her middle two toes. Thankfully, it was not a deep cut. If the tooth had gone in deep, most of her might be in the shark's belly by now. She wrapped the remaining tape around her left foot and fastened it.

"Frankie, you've seen enough of my privates for one day," she laughed. They both laughed. "This isn't 'Naked and Afraid.' Get my pants on. I can't stand up."

Frankie got her shorts, knelt in front of her and slowly and carefully lifted each foot through the legs and slipped it up her legs. It was not easy getting the bottoms up over her hip, even though she helped by lifting her butt up at the end. She didn't worry about the bikini top. She pulled on her shirt. She was good to go.

"Frankie, what just happened?

"A shark just tried to eat you."

"There are no sharks in Lake Erie, Frankie."

"Well, we know there is at least one," he half-smiled.

"Thank you for saving my life, Frankie."

"I couldn't save Pris," he said. It was true. Pris was part of the shark now.

Frankie moved forward and began pulling up the anchor. Sheila looked down at her feet. She was afraid she would go into shock. She looked out over the water toward the north tip of the island. The land was a beautiful deep green. She scanned the water for the shark. The closest boat was perhaps a quarter mile away, but there were dozens within her line of sight. Frankie went to the stern to get a bucket so he could dump water in the bilge. As he reached for the bucket, he did a quick visual inspection of the outboard. Something white and shiny caught his eye. He looked closer. He reached down and pried a shark's tooth from the metal jacket surrounding the exhaust portal on the engine.

"Well, maybe they won't think we're crazy," he said, holding up the tooth. There was even a bit of what he thought must be shark tissue on the bottom of the dagger-like tooth.

"Babe, I was so freaking scared," Frankie said and gave her a long hug. He stepped around her to the console and turned the key in the ignition. The big engine got even bigger, humming almost instantly. "We're going full bore. Hang on." The boat started to move. Frankie picked up his phone and began the communications process that would have a squad waiting at Battery Park Marina in Sandusky when they arrived in less than 30 minutes.

CHAPTER 8

The drive out to the Krupp place seemed slow in the afternoon heat. Susan sat in the back seat, occasionally staring at the back of Bill's head and the young detective's head. The back of Bill's head was damp with sweat and he needed to take a razor to it. The skin was dark, tanned, from his days out on Lake Erie hunting walleye. Detective Bobby Quick's neck was thinner, the skin lighter and tighter, less sweat, and an even, careful line between skin and hair. No question, he had a better neck.

Susan had never been by Krupp's place. He lived in the southwestern corner of the county, out in the flatland. However, there were occasional small ridges, remnants of the ancient Lake Erie shoreline, but the feeling was Kansas. The east-west roads followed these ridges, running straight and true. The soil on the ridges was sandy and rich. It was a sea of corn and soybeans in every direction, broken by the occasional patch of woods, and clusters of buildings and trees that marked the farms. Most of the farm buildings were old, classic white Victorians with cupolas and front porches. Many needed paint. There were windbreaks on either side, lines of white pines or sometimes Austrians. Some places had huge oaks in front with big sweeping branches that cooled the yard. Barns flanked the houses, a mixture of big, massive wooden things, beautiful in their simplicity and history, and smaller metal

things, clean and neat and not very pretty. Farm ponds were common, on one side or the other, in between house and barn, created to water the livestock. A few silos, none looking very well cared for. Junk everywhere, of course, and she enjoyed cataloging it: junked cars, tires, collapsed outbuildings, bikes, bricks, concrete block, barbed wire, chicken wire, rusty poles, signs, benches, aluminum chairs, lawn clippings, and farm equipment she couldn't begin to identify.

The farms were prosperous, however. The land was exceedingly rich, some of the best farmland in Ohio, along the edge of what had been the Great Black Swamp, dark, moist soil. Mostly corn and soybeans, but also tomatoes, beans, pumpkins, some fruit, and winter wheat.

Sprinkled among the farms were stretches of three and five-acre lots filled with newer homes, most built since 1960. When a farmer needed cash, he sold off a little frontage to someone who wanted to live in the country. Susan wasn't one of them; she had no interest in living in the country. They passed the home of Joanne Fehrbach, a fellow Master Gardener. It was a classic brick ranch, probably built in the mid-70s, huge and sprawling, perhaps 3,500 square feet. The lawn was monstrous. Susan hated cutting grass. Even with a rider, it would take hours to cut it all. She thought Joanne was crazy to be responsible for a lawn like that.

Krupp lived back off the old state route that led to Columbus. It was a two-lane highway flanked by dangerous, canyon-sized ditches. Susan hated the ditches. At night, or in winter, she feared losing control of her car and careening down into one. It wouldn't be pretty. It happened all the time.

The police radio scratched and cackled. She didn't understand most of it. Bill and the detective talked baseball. They were both Cleveland fans, so there was a lot to talk about. She sensed the younger guy was nervous with her around. They had met before, but this was different, a homicide investigation. She was a civilian, no matter what her relationship with the chief and her knowledge of some stupid flowers.

"I'm not sure what to expect from the widow," Bill said loudly, addressing Susan as well as Detective Quick. "There will be some family there. He's got several grown children, but one lives in Florida and the other in Pennsylvania. He's got a son in Columbus. He's probably there by now. There's lots of other extended family, too. I talked to the widow and one son last night, briefly, told them about Krupp, said I'd be out in the morning.

"Old Krupp is still on a slab in Bowling Green."

"When does he get to go home?" Susan asked.

"Not sure. Probably tonight, maybe tomorrow."

They rode in silence for another minute. They were getting close.

"He hadn't been home since late afternoon. That's what she told me last night. He did some work on one of his tractors, then he drove to the fairgrounds—at least that's what he told his wife. He called her once, she said, from his cell phone she guessed, about seven o'clock, and said he wouldn't be home for dinner."

"We can get all those records," Detective Quick said. "I'll call the company. It's standard."

"Yeah, but where was he calling from," the chief said. "We don't know that." The chief cleared his throat. "But you're right. It will help. If his phone was Verizon, call John Mosby. He'll cut through the crap for you."

Quick nodded in agreement.

"So, you've got to piece it all together," Susan said, her hands on her kneecaps. "Where he was, what he was doing."

"Yeah, we've got to check through everything. Hopefully, some people will come forward, tell us they had pancakes with him at Bob Evans at seven p.m. and he looked the freaking picture of health."

"Car?" Mary Beth asked.

"Truck," the chief corrected. "Krupp was not the kind of guy who drove a car."

"Do we know that for sure?" Quick asked.

"Find out."

"It's missing?" Susan asked.

"Cars always turn up," the chief shot back. "Usually in an altered state. I remember the time, back in Cleveland, we found this yuppie's BMW. Joyriders. Nothing wrong with it except a pile of kids had a pizza party inside. They had stuffed the leftovers between the seats, and under the seats, and smeared tomato sauce everywhere. At first, we thought someone had bled to death inside. Smelled terrible. I couldn't eat pizza for at least three days."

"This is it," Quick said suddenly.

The first thing they saw was a large, painted sign that read: *KRUPP'S CORNFIELD MAZE, $5, SAT-SUN ONLY.* It was a leftover from the prior year.

Just inside the driveway was a small gravel lot and along the back was a wooden structure, roofed but mostly open, something primarily used to sell fruit and vegetables. Susan saw a sign that read: *ENTER HERE.* The cornfield stretched behind as far as she could see. The corn was about three feet high, ready to explode into mid-summer growth. There were no cars in the lot.

"Krupp the entrepreneur," Chief Cleary said, laughing. "Imagine getting people to pay you to walk around in your cornfield."

"They're starting up all over," Quick said. "Easy money. Some farmers do very intricate designs. People have always enjoyed mazes."

The chief shook his head. "What a freaking world."

The chief turned the cruiser onto the gravel driveway that went back nearly a quarter mile. A massive cornfield stretched as far as Susan could see along the south and west sides of the property. She could see the house sitting on a small rise, the obligatory trees and outbuildings scattered around. Most farms were located much closer to the road. She wondered why the Krupp place had been set back so far. But that decision had been made generations ago.

"How much was his?" Susan asked.

"A hell of a lot," the chief replied, slowing the vehicle. "I heard he owned more than five thousand acres, rented lots of it out."

It looked like a working farm. There were two big barns at the end of driveway, an old wooden one, massive and white, with the year "1849" in big block letters over the door. Susan doubted the barn dated back that far, but she didn't doubt the family had been here that long. There were two big pieces of farm equipment parked outside the smaller, metal barn. They were green, which could mean only one thing, that they were manufactured by John Deere, but she didn't really know what they were or what they did. She did see a tractor next to the smaller barn. She knew what a tractor was. There was a lot of loose junk everywhere, some of it rusty. On one side of the barn was what looked like an ancient steam tractor.

"Lots of junk," Susan said.

"I heard he was big into farm auctions," the chief said. "Loved to buy stuff if he could get it cheap enough."

The house itself was Victorian, certainly late nineteenth century, big, a bit in need of repair. The windows looked old, the shutters misaligned, and the paint was peeling in spots. It had a big, sweeping front porch, the columns featuring some gingerbread scrolling. It had the look of a place loosely cared for. No flowers anywhere. Susan decided Krupp was the type of person who took pride in his bank account but little else. He had been a utilitarian man.

Bill parked the cruiser between the house and the white barn, perhaps two hundred feet from the front porch. There were two pick-up trucks parked in front of the barn and one Chevrolet Blazer. As they got out, Susan thought of the scene in *Saving Private Ryan* where the military men, accompanied by clergy, arrive at the Iowa farm to tell Ryan's mother three of her children are dead. In the movie, the mother is seen from the rear, and she knows what the message is as she sees the car wind up the long dusty driveway to the house. Her knees buckle when she answers the door. This was different. Janet Krupp knew her husband was dead. She even knew he had been murdered. Susan and Detective Quick let the Chief take the lead as they walked toward the porch. Susan's bowels were unpleasantly tight. Janet Krupp would be wondering who the hell she was and what she was doing here.

She could see what she knew must be Janet Krupp standing behind the screen door, a shapeless body in what appeared to be an old house dress. She opened the door and stepped out. The face was ordinary, lined, a woman of sixty, perhaps a few years older, dull brown hair streaked with gray. Her eyes were darting, not dull, and took in the three of them quickly before settling into Bill's. Susan had never met her but knew her a little by reputation. She was very social, a smiler, knew and greeted everyone, active in all the farm organizations. She was popular, much better liked than her husband, but not ambitious or acquisitive as he was.

The screen door slapped shut behind her.

"I'm sorry for your loss, Janet," the chief said, very slowly and sincerely, in a practiced way. His eyes drifted down as he said it. Susan watched her face. There was no reaction. Chief Cleary had, of course, said the words earlier, over the phone, but now it was in real time. Detective Quick said the same words but did not look down.

It was her turn. Before she could say anything, Bill introduced them all. He told Janet Krupp that Susan was assisting him with the case.

"I'm very sorry," Mrs. Krupp," she said, offering her hand at the same time. Susan looked into her eyes. Janet Krupp took her hand. Susan could tell she had been crying for hours. It seemed odd in a woman her age. Older people didn't cry, they were stoics; they were used to death, even the death of people close to them; it was not dignified, especially in German farm folk. But this woman had cried plenty. Susan felt strange; a little shiver ran through her guts, as she thought about this woman crying over her husband. Her heart went out to her.

"Ma?" It was a loud voice, concerned and almost plaintive, male, coming from inside the house.

"The police are here, out on the porch," Janet Krupp answered, not looking back.

Richard Krupp appeared at the door. He was tall, big boned, with a face that had never done well at the high school dance. She guessed him to be 30 years old. More introductions. The son put his arm on his mother's shoulder. It was time for Bill to take charge.

"Janet, we need to sit down and talk about a lot of things. I know this is difficult for you, but we must do it. Can we go inside?"

"So, somebody murdered my Dad?" Richard Krupp said, blocking the doorway, still holding his mother's shoulder.

"I think we can say that now with certainty, Richard," the chief said. "I know this is very hard on all of you, but our job is to get to the truth, and we will, and we're going to need your help."

For several seconds they all stood there, no one talking, only the insect noise and the whistling breeze through the corn. A moment later they were inside, a cool and dark place, fitting the occasion. Bill announced that Detective Quick would be handling the case but that he would, of course be involved as well. Quick asked about Krupp's schedule from the previous day, the time he left the house, the vehicle he drove, how he was dressed, everything he could think to ask.

"Were there any problems you were aware of, Mrs. Krupp?" Susan almost laughed to herself. Everything was unfolding just like it did on TV, but it was also completely different.

The furniture around them was all early American, mostly pine. The carpet was green, 1950s green, and the curtains were white. The house was apparently air-conditioned but set at such a high temperature it barely made a difference. Susan could scarcely believe it. She was sweating already. The chair she was sitting on was scratchy.

Janet shook her head. So did her son. "Oh, I don't know. He had his enemies, but you know, just political enemies, people he didn't get along with in the county or whatever. Nobody that would want to kill him. I just can't imagine that. I just can't. I couldn't begin to think of anyone, think of anything." Her voice trailed off.

"Ma told me he was poisoned," Richard Krupp said. "What kind? How'd they do it?"

Quick hesitated, but Bill Cleary did not: "He was injected with chemicals, probably a mixture of insecticides and herbicides, the BCI office in Bowling Green isn't exactly sure yet. They said he had also most likely shot with a tranquilizer gun." The chief turned slightly so he would look directly at Janet Krupp. "Whoever killed him, put him to sleep first. He didn't suffer, Janet."

"Good God, Man. Somebody shot my father up with insecticides!" Richard yelled. "Shot him up like he was a goddamned cockroach!" He jumped up and began pacing. "This is just crazy, crazy, crazy."

"It's true," Quick said. "I'm sorry. It's what happened. Our job is to find out who did it to him."

In detail, Quick and the chief asked for a review of Krupp's activities the day before. Everything seemed ordinary enough. He was up early, as all farmers are, and spent time in the barn before breakfast. He had a phone in the big barn, and he often made business calls from the barn. She was gone herself part of the day, off to Port Clinton to attend a baby shower for a niece. Janet did most of the talking. Richard had been out of town.

"We don't think the murder occurred at the fairgrounds or in the horse stall." It was the chief. "We think it took place somewhere else, that perhaps your father was lured somewhere. Perhaps it happened there, wherever there is, and then his body was transported to the fairgrounds and brought to the horse barn. The two kids found him around midnight. There were plenty of people around earlier. Whoever brought him there brought him there sometime between eleven and one. It's a two-hour window. Whoever brought him there, didn't come alone. Your father was a big man, probably weighed almost two hundred and fifty pounds, maybe more. It wouldn't be an easy thing to do, especially unobserved."

Richard stood up, put his huge hands into his pockets, walked toward the door, looked outside past the porch toward the corn. Susan sensed he wanted to talk but something was holding him back. Bill and Detective Quick were focused on the widow.

A few minutes later, the chief asked if they could go out and look around the barn and the outbuildings. Janet waved them outside, but first asked if they wanted something cold to drink. They all declined. Richard followed them.

Everything looked like a farm to her. She spotted a few skinny cats, and the air was thick and smelled sweet. Krupp was a grain farmer, no livestock, just some chickens and a few goats. The barn smelled more like a garage. Because it was his barn, and now he was dead, the place felt creepy, and she stepped lightly and looked and listened for things. There was an assortment of equipment in the barn: three junky trucks, old farm equipment, a long workbench, tools everywhere. It was midday and slightly cool and very dark in the barn. It was an old place, a hard-packed dirt floor.

"What are you looking for?" Richard asked.

"Just looking," Bill replied, slightly irritated. "It's our job."

Bill led them out a back door and he stopped to take in the view of the cornfields, which seemed to stretch forever. A farm lane led straight back, separating two fields, and disappeared over a slight rise, perhaps a quarter mile away.

"Good-looking corn," he said. He didn't know what else to say.

There was a second building, a metal pole barn which functioned as a garage. More farm equipment, newer stuff. The floor was concrete. Susan saw a phone on the wall next to another workbench and stacks of paint cans. She could see the frustration on Bill's face. He didn't know what to look for and didn't know why the hell he was here, but he was here and he had to put on a show. Detective Quick stared at everything, as though his eyes were a video camera.

Richard drifted off, back toward the house. They all seemed relieved. Susan certainly was.

"What an accumulation of crap," Bill Cleary said, shaking his head, looking around, back inside the pole barn. "There's no end to it. You couldn't catalog this in a hundred years." There was an immense number of things stuffed into the building: paint cans, oil cans, tools, old furniture, boxes and boxes, clothing, a pile of old rubber boots, the accumulation of decades.

No flowers.

"What's the freaking motive, Detective Quick?" the chief said. He was standing next to the big green tractor. He put his hand on one of the huge tires, stared at it, ran his hand into one of the huge grooves. "We got to solve this shit. And I don't have a freaking clue." Since he had been township chief there had been only one murder in the township and that was a standard domestic: husband shoots unfaithful wife and then shoots himself. Kevin and Patti Gentry, both age 38. He had lost his job at the quarry and she had been scoring with a truck driver she had met at a bowling alley. His family had always considered him a little wacky. In his experience, families were usually right about these things.

In the city it was rare, too, but more frequent. But there was usually no doubt who did it.

The chief did not like this at all.

"It's not domestic," Susan said.

The chief grimaced. "I suspect you're right. But I don't like that kid, Richard. I think he's a wacko. But I don't think he gave his old man an insecticide rush."

"Drugs," said Quick. He shrugged. "It's always drugs. It's the default," he said, glancing toward the cornfields behind the house. Susan couldn't tell if he was serious or not.

"Not likely," the chief said, in a dismissive tone, "but always a possibility."

"Political enemy?" he shot back.

"Christ, this isn't Bosnia. It's goddamned Erie County Ohio. Around here, you screw your enemy by voting him off the bowling team."

"Crazed environmentalists. He's got an underground river that's dumping something awful into our drinking water and now he's been punished," Quick offered. Susan sensed he was half-serious.

"They'd be claiming credit by now," the chief said. Besides, those people don't do things like that. It's not personal with them. Besides, some people will tell you the damn lake is all leaned up now, he said in a deliberate mocking voice, "We saved it. Just ask Mister Walleye the next time you're pulling your Eerie Dearie out of his mouth. He'll tell you. But of course, there is still the little matter of algal blooms."

They couldn't just keep standing in the barn. Susan felt it was weird, almost scary. Through the open door she could see the son, Richard, coming across the yard back toward them.

"We've got to talk to more people," Cleary said, looking at Quick. "I'll help you. I know more of them. We just got to talk to a lot of people."

His cell phone went off. He answered it quickly. He mumbled replies, brief. It was one of the dispatchers. "Get numbers, names, and I'll call them back when I get in." He flipped the cover on his phone and looked at them both. "It's a media circus now, too. Papers all over the state are calling: *Plain Dealer, Blade,* and the TV guys, too. Christ, they were just here three hours ago. We've got to get back."

She saw the son stop in front of the barn. He stood there, watching them, his hands on his hips. She wondered why he didn't come into the barn. He had seemed so excitable in the house.

The chief's eyes swept the barn a last time. "See any flowers, Susan?"

CHAPTER 9

Susan was exhausted. She felt herself nodding off on the drive back to the Perkins PD, but she kept trying to listen to the cop talk in the front of the car. One assignment the chief gave Detective Quick was to individually interview all the leaders of the agricultural community, also people who knew Krupp well politically.

"Talk to family, too," the chief said. "There are Krupps behind every cornstalk around here; they are everywhere. I think you will be hard pressed to find a fan of William Robert in that group. A lot of his land came from wheeling and dealing inside the family. He's the guy who at wakes and funerals finds a way to talk to the widow or other bereaved and give them his card, so if they ever decide to sell the property, they have another family member to help them through it."

"Slime bucket, I take it," said Quick.

The chief was just warming up. "He fell into the category of people who are successful even though no one likes them."

"But he was smart, I guess." Quick said.

"Probably was."

There were two classic responses. Quick chose: "But not quite smart enough."

"I don't think he ever saw it coming," the chief replied. "Well, we need to figure out what he did to make somebody

think he deserved to die, and to die in a very specific way. First things first."

They drove past a small ODOT sign welcoming them to Perkins Township. They were only a few minutes from the station. Traffic was normal for late Saturday afternoon.

"Look, this could be payback stuff. This was done by professionals. We'll check out every angle, but I don't think he had gotten sideways on gambling debts or got caught with kiddie porn. My theory is he did something to someone that involved screwing the environment. And given what appears to be going on around here these days, that means contributing to the algal bloom problem." The chief was a believer; two out of the last four years the late season fishing charter business was way down because of the blooms. The chief was not a politician. He favored a simple and direct approach—just pass a law with major league fines and enforce it a few times and the word would get out to reduce your load of fertilizer and manage it properly. The main ingredient in fertilizer is phosphorus. "

"Speaking of flowers, what do you have in the back seat?"

He had caught her thinking about the flowers. "Let's go through the list again," she announced. Susan pulled out her notebook from her bag and started reading. She walked Chief Cleary and Detective Quick through the list of flowers and included some basic information about each, including what kind of soil it favored, what climate zones it grew in, how much water it needed, whether it favored sun or shade. She knew she was boring them to the power of 10 but really didn't care.

I thought you did a good job at the briefing," Quick said. "You spoke like you knew what you were talking about." Quick half-turned to his left, so he could see Susan's face. "I got a flower question for you. Okay, so the flowers are a message. Is the message 'Flowers,' or is the message daffodils, and petunias, etc., etc. Do they matter, was each chosen for a reason?"

"God, I hope not," the chief said. But you don't know, maybe the flowers mean nothing, and these guys are just screwing with our heads."

"I did see something at the Krupp place that was on the list," Susan said. "There was a bunch of it growing alongside the old barn. Butterfly weed."

Susan's iPhone began to ring. It was Eric Vankirk.

"I've got to take this," she said quickly.

CHAPTER 10

Perhaps the flowers meant nothing. Bill Clearly had considered that possibility early on. It was just the murderer's idea of something funny. Stick a bunch of flowers around the deceased, just like in the funeral parlor. He simply grabbed whatever was at hand. They didn't mean anything. He told himself he should call Susan and ask her if any of the flowers they found around Krupp were flowers her Master Gardeners had planted. Perhaps the killers had just gone out into the fairgrounds and picked them and then brought them back in and spread them around the corpse. But why take a chance like that? It was dark, there weren't many people around, but there were enough. It would be far too risky. It wasn't logical. No, the flowers had come in with the killers. They had meaning.

———————⋀———————

He was home now, sitting in the kitchen, drinking a cold Molson. His shoes and socks were in the corner and he enjoyed curling his bare toes around the chair spindle. The wood felt good, dry, but strangely soft. The air conditioning felt good, too, damn good. Their youngest, Annie, 15, was at band camp over at Kelleys Island. Tom, who had just graduated and was headed to Ohio State in the fall was working at Cedar Point as a ride operator on one of the big coasters. Meg had grilled some brats, which he ate with too much enthusiasm with relish,

mustard, onions, and a pile of slaw. She was on the phone in the den with someone, probably her mother. No one spent more time on the phone than his wife. He spent a lot of time on the phone, too, his cell phone was a constant companion, but the calls were all business and were short, even abrupt, and a call to action. The idea of chit-chatting on the phone for an hour was not a positive thing. He could not imagine it.

He rolled the situation over and over in his mind. He was a logical thinker. He had worked as a detective in Cleveland for eight years. He understood the deductive process.

What did they know? Krupp was seen alive at the Bob Evans Restaurant on US 250 about 8 p.m. He had been at the fairgrounds earlier, probably for three or four hours. He wandered the place, as his custom, talked to a lot of people. Everyone they'd talked to so far said he appeared completely normal. Nothing out of the ordinary. He said it aloud, holding the beer in his hand: "Nothing out of the ordinary." Detective Quick must have talked to 15 people. The stories were all the same: corn, weather, pigs, politics, a dirty joke, fishing conditions, horses, mutual friends.

Krupp had dinner with Sam Munchausen and Gil Radtke, both old cronies. Munchausen was a farmer who also had horses, big Belgians, and he entered them in the horse pull every year. Radtke was the local John Deere dealer. They had sat at the counter at Bob Evans and jostled with the waitresses and acted the standard old coot routine: eat greasy food, drink coffee, laugh, make slightly off-color remarks to the girls serving them, drink more coffee, leave a stingy tip. He knew the drill: he occasionally did it himself. They talked about all the standard stuff: the cost of new tractors, a little sports, the upcoming fair, the weather. According to Munchausen and Radtke, the soon to be deceased was in a fine mood, laughing and joking, not a care in the world. But he had only a few hours to live. Just a few hours before he was retching and exploding inside like an atom bomb. He got in his truck, they said, and drove off into the sunset. They assumed he was going home. But he never got there—or did he? His wife didn't get back from Port Clinton until almost eleven. There was plenty of time to go home—home was maybe 15 minutes from Bob Evans.

No truck. Not seen anywhere. MIA. It would be nice to find the truck. It could be in a barn somewhere, or it could be on US 15 in West Virginia. Detective Quick had called it in early in the morning. In theory, every cop in America was looking for the damn thing.

———————∧———————

Krupp drove somewhere, met his killers, got killed, and then got brought back to the fairgrounds and dumped in a horse stall. So, how did they get into the fairgrounds? There's a fence. Not that it would be difficult to get over, not even wired across the top. You could easily climb over it, but lift a 250-pound body over it? You'd need several people to do it efficiently. There would be lots of places along the back side, which bordered the largest cemetery in the county. Lots of trees. Dark. You'd have to cross an open field to get to the horse barn. Carrying a 250-pound corpse? How likely? He made a note to ask Quick to call Oakland Cemetery tomorrow to see if anyone noticed anything funny in the cemetery Friday night. Of course, they could have driven into the fairgrounds. The gate might have been wide open. The caretaker was supposed to close the gate if he were called away for some reason, but Cleary felt certain he was easily distracted. The caretaker, Joe Bacarella, was supposed to have an assistant who was on patrol except when he had to cover for Bacarella. But maybe Bacarella had spent most of the night having coffee in the kitchen of the fairground office swapping stories with the horse guys who spent the night in their campers on the south side of the fairgrounds. Cleary thought they might have been sharing more than coffee. He claimed he had heard or seen nothing unusual. He could have been auditioning to be Sergeant Schultz. There was the occasional vehicle wandering the grounds, but that was normal two nights before the event opened. He was no help; he was worthless.

So, it could have been done. They could have driven in with the body, parked behind the horse barn, unloaded poor Krupp, carried him into the barn and dumped him in an open stall, scattered the flowers, put the bouquet in his hands, and left. He and Quick had talked about how long it would have taken. Quick guessed 10 minutes.

Not likely he was car jacked. Sorry, truck jacked. They were waiting for him at home, or he had gone somewhere to meet them. He could have been fooled. Most likely, though, he knew who killed him.

He was brought to the fairgrounds because he was the president of the fair board. It was his turf, his workplace, his love. There was an obvious message in it. Someone thought it would be appropriate that he be found at the fairgrounds. It would also guarantee more publicity.

Motive. Who wanted him dead? That was the key to everything. Most of the murders he had been involved in back in his Cleveland days were drug related, the result of gangs fighting over turf or somebody late with a payment. Or, they were crimes of passion: unfaithful boyfriends or girlfriends; disagreements that turned deadly because a weapon was at hand.

Cleary took out his pen and notebook and began making a list: business deal gone bad; bad politics; revenge; wacko serial killer. He put the pen down. Krupp was killed by the lethal injection of herbicides and insecticides. There was obvious message there. It was the key to everything. Any idiot would know that. The manner of death was deliberate. There were easier ways to kill Krupp if that was your objective. The manner of death suggested the motive. That was not always the case but it seemed to him it made sense in this situation. One possibility was that Krupp had committed some terrible environmental crime and was executed because of it. Find out what he had done, or maybe what he was planning to do, and he'd be halfway home. Nothing came to mind, but there was something there, had to be. Krupp was certainly no Mr. Greenpeace, but to Cleary's knowledge he wasn't on any polluter's top ten, either. A few years back, in a particularly bad algal year, the water intake in Toledo had been compromised for a few days. The entire city had to go to bottled water. It was a near disaster. Cleary remembered Krupp had been active in defending the local farmers and their farming practices.

Cleary had to talk to Krupp's friends, his associates. He had to talk to his wife again. He had to go through his papers, his bank accounts, his phone calls. He had to inspect the property, all the property, and he had to do it with someone who knew something about all this. He had to talk to a lot of people. All this was going to be work. And the damn media would be all over him, and the three Perkins Township Trustees—one of whom, Joe Eversharp, was a farmer—would want to know what was going on at every turn. Nothing else would get done until this case was solved. But he also knew that Krupp would be buried by Wednesday, and the fair would go on in August and when it was over the media would lose some interest and he'd get a little breather. But it wouldn't go away.

Susan's flowers. In his mind he was calling Krupp's bouquet Susan's flowers. Perhaps there was something to the flowers, to those flowers, which would tell you something if you were smart enough to figure it out. He opened his notebook and looked at the list: wild blue indigo, butterfly weed, cardinal flower, corn flower, cone flower, delphinium, coreopsis, and day lily.

He wanted another beer. It took only a nanosecond to justify. He went to the refrigerator and opened another Molson. He skipped a glass. Meg always kept three or four beer glasses in the freezer for him because he loved drinking beer out of a frosted glass. He tasted the beer, cold and good, and he decided a glass would be a good thing and reached in and got it.

Meg was still on the phone. He could hear her chattering away. He walked to the sink and looked out onto the backyard. It was almost dark, just a purplish twinge over everything, summer darkness, which was like a lazy, soft hand dropping down over the world and cuddling it. He imagined the big lake right now, the glow on the water, calm and smooth, the sky the deepest blue to the east before going to black, and to the west, between the islands, streaking purples, and reds. In his boat they'd be flying home, the big Mercury singing, the ice chest full of walleye, the wheel solid in his hand; he'd be standing up, his knees and feet feeling the movement of the boat on the water, bending and flexing as though they were physically attached like an arm or a leg. The warm air with just a fingertip of coolness would be blowing in his face and hair, his skin would feel warm from an afternoon of sun. His eyes would be scanning the horizon, picking up the Marblehead light, then the Sandusky light, the lights which marked the big coasters at Cedar Point; and other lights, boat lights, flying at him or around him, close and far, all funneling down to their home port.

The beer tasted good. He wondered if he could talk Meg into having sex later. It had been more than a week. Annie was playing her clarinet over at Band Camp at Kelleys Island. Tom wouldn't be home from Cedar Point until midnight. They had all the prerequisites: time, place, no kids. He would be extra nice to her the rest of the evening and right after the news he'd suggest they go upstairs and take a shower. He was dog-tired, no sleep the night before, lots of tension, lots of problems, but scented soap and his wife's warm, wet body and her giggles would wash it all away.

He was 43. Between Cleveland and Perkins Township, he had 20 years as a cop. In ten years, when he was 53, he'd have his 30 years in, his youngest would be out of college, and he could retire. If Meg wanted to stay a teacher, that was fine. He had no interest in moving away from Erie County. But he would buy a new boat, a 28-foot Grady White with twin Yamahas, and get into the charter business full time. He'd work it hard from April through October, taking people out for walleye, bass, and perch; and from November through March, he'd sit on his ass and drink beer and watch football games. In his mind, it was the ideal life, and he was well suited for it.

Some of the ecology nuts really were nuts, he knew. It had never happened in this part of Ohio, or much in Ohio at all as far as he knew, but the greenies sometimes went crazy and destroyed things. It mostly happened in the West, where there were more glamorous and sexier things at stake: mountains, tall timber, grizzly bears, wolves, Indians. He didn't know much about it, but he figured he should start. Tomorrow, he'd call a friend he knew at the FBI who could educate him a little on eco-terrorist groups. Krupp's death didn't fit the pattern. Then, none of the deaths he had ever investigated really fit the pattern; there was always something quirky or weird about every murder. But it didn't fit the pattern. Eco-terrorists destroyed things—bulldozers, buildings, signs, houses—they didn't destroy people. The terrorists who took down the World Trade Center were after blood. The green people weren't at war with people; they didn't take hostages; they hijack planes and fly them into oil fields. When they did destroy things, they took credit for them.

He had to start somewhere. He had to have a working assumption. In his mind, the manner of death suggested retribution for environmental crime. But there were lots of other options. At the same time, he had to just keep gathering facts and studying the situation. Something would turn up, it always did.

———————∧———————

Chief Cleary punched in the numbers with speed and precision. He took a secret pride in his ability to dial phone numbers quickly and accurately. It was a basic 21st century skill, and a good thing to be good at for a police officer. He had long, thick fingers but they moved effortlessly across the face of the phone. It was Wednesday. Krupp's funeral was now scheduled for Friday. Nothing was happening. He was calling his friend in Washington, Peter Zamboni, who worked for the FBI. He wasn't exactly sure what he did, but he knew he had been in an anti-terrorist division for the past two years. He wasn't a field agent. He worked inside.

The phone rang only twice.

"Zamboni." The voice said, flat and official. A more FBI voice could not be imagined.

"Pete, it's Bill Cleary. Perkins Township. Out here on Lake Erie, the walleye capital of the world!"

They both laughed. "Caught much?" Zamboni asked.

"The sons of bitches are jumping into my boat. They know they cannot escape me. But the truth? Only fair. Water temp is off a bit, and too much high pressure lately. Makes it harder." They had discovered a mutual love of fishing when they had been in class together at one of the special FBI schools. Zamboni was from New Jersey and fished mostly in the ocean. He had never fished the Great Lakes. Cleary had fished the Great Lakes and in Florida but never along the east coast. He was unfamiliar with the fish, the tactics, all of it; it was a different world. Both had almost no interest in pond and stream fishing. They liked the big water, big fish.

They talked fishing for a while longer. Cleary never tired of it. Zamboni was a little younger than he was, very tall and a bit too thin in Cleary's opinion. He did not fit the FBI stereotype: average, average, average. He looked like a first baseman. He had a wife and two kids, the kids still young. He did a lot of surf fishing. He liked to go down to the Outer Banks in the summer. But it was time to get to business.

"Got a strange one here, Pete. Local bigwig farmer murdered last weekend. Two kids found the body in a horse stall at the county fairgrounds, the weekend of a local horse competition. The DOA was lying on a pile of straw covered with flowers."

"What kind of flowers?"

"All kinds. Mostly Local stuff.

"How'd he buy it?"

"This is the fun part. He was poisoned. Nothing ordinary, of course. The lab in Toledo said it was mixture of insecticides and herbicides. A real witches brew, if you will." Cleary was feeling more relaxed. He put his big feet up on the edge of the desk and leaned back in his chair. He wished he had gotten coffee before dialing Zamboni.

"Lethal, I'm sure," Zamboni said. "Point of entry?"

"He was injected with the stuff," Cleary said, "a vein in his left arm."

There was a pause on both ends. Then Cleary said: "So far, no apparent motive, no suspects, nothing. I've got no leads. It's embarrassing." It was. He could be honest with Zamboni or thought he could. Anyway, he was doing it.

"You check out the property?" Zamboni asked.

"One of my current theories is that he did something bad to the environment. Or he was about to. It's the best explanation so far. No girlfriends, no bad debts, no drugs (at least as far as we know). Maybe he got covered in flowers because he either had already destroyed lots of flowers or was going to do so. My three bosses—the goddamned township trustees—are all over my ass on this. They all knew the guy. Didn't like him much, but they all knew him."

"You sure he wasn't screwing the other farmer's wife? I understand a lot of that goes on in the Midwest."

Cleary was irritated, but he ignored the remark. Zamboni had a streak of East Coast snob in him. He thought everyone west of the Blue Ridge or the Alleghenies was a hick. He knew better, of course, but he liked to play the game. "He's had EPA issues, but nothing extreme. "There's nothing obvious."

"Actually, environmental terrorism is on the decline. No longer fashionable. All the action is some variant of Muslim extremism or right- wing militias." There was a pause while Zamboni switched the phone to his opposite ear. Climate change is our religion now, and you know what religions do to heretics and non-believers—they kill them, usually publicly, and usually in a way that generates fear and loathing."

"Have they been out to the farm? The EPA guys?"

"No."

"I'd send them out there. They might find something. Some of these guys are surprisingly good. They find amazing things."

The chief made a note to call the Ohio EPA, adding it to a long list of follow-up phone calls he had to make.

"The property's not industrial, never was. It's farmland. Been that way for 150 years. Before that it was a Indian village or something. You can't do that much damage with fertilizer. Not enough to get killed over."

"It doesn't fit any protocol I'm familiar with," Zamboni said. "The greenies like obvious targets: timber company headquarters, whaling ships, that sort of thing. Or they wreck signs, pour water into the bulldozer's gas tank, something like that. They want publicity. If a group had done this, they'd already be talking to the newspaper. That's what's strange."

"Maybe not," Cleary said. Cleary stared at the picture on his wall across from the desk above the two cheap red chairs. It was a fishing picture, a beautiful illustration (he thought) of a walleye swimming up from the depths about to swallow an Earie Dearie spinner with a big nightcrawler on the end of it. He had a legal pad in front of him and held a cheap liquid gel ink pen in his right hand. It was nearly 90 degrees outside, but here it was cool, almost cold, the way he liked it when he was working indoors. He wanted information.

"They ever kill anybody, Pete?"

"Accidentally," Zamboni replied. "A few times. But what you're describing sounds like a hit. It just doesn't fit the profile. There's a group in the Southwest. They hate golf courses."

"I hate them too," Cleary shot back.

"Freaking waste of time if you ask me." Zamboni paused, and Cleary could tell he was sipping something, probably coffee. It was before 10, still coffee time. "So, these guys like to go out in the middle of the night and take apart the sprinkler systems."

"Sounds like work."

"Exactly. So, last year they decided to blow up the pump system for this big fancy resort course out in Arizona. They put together a bomb. Fairly sophisticated. But not sophisticated enough. It was supposed to go off in the middle of the night—at least we think that was the plan—but instead it goes off at eight in the morning and takes out two landscapers and one poor guy from Indiana who was there attending a conference. There was no claim of victory. I think we all felt they had no plans to hurt anyone and were mortified by what they had done."

"I do know this. The scariest Green people come from Europe. Very unpleasant people. I know they have kidnapped people over there, extorted money, that sort of thing."

"Quit making some chemical or we take away your BMW?"

"Or your wife and daughter." That sort of threat shakes people up. I've been learning more about Europe lately."

"Never been there," Cleary said. He had no interest in going to Europe. None whatsoever. But his wife did.

"I'm not sure what I can do to help you, Bill. But I'll do some checking. Sounds like you've got a good one. The more I think about it, it's pretty darn interesting. Do you mind if I talk to some people outside the bureau? Inside the bureau?"

"Talk to anyone you want," Cleary shot back. "I've got a dead guy full of fertilizer, no leads, and the press calling me every 10 minutes."

They talked a while longer, catching up on family and fishing and more mundane matters. Cleary invited him out to Ohio, something he had done many times in the past, telling him they could go fishing and the wife and kids could spend the day riding rides at Cedar Point.

When they were done, he began dialing more numbers: Ohio EPA, Susan, BCI.

CHAPTER 11

Cleary met the two EPA guys at the farm. It was hot, sticky, steamy, and the insect noise was a cacophony. They both bitched about the Cedar Point traffic. In the summer, in this part of Ohio, it was part of the language. Cleary had no sympathy. Traffic meant money in the community and job security.

Cleary had the property description of the farm with him. It covered almost 1,500 acres, mostly in a lump but with outlying parcels here and there and spreading over both sides of the road. It was a huge job to inspect it all. You would hardly know where to begin.

"I just want you to look for the obvious stuff," Cleary said, after some perfunctory introductions. They were both young, probably around 30, one a scientist or technician of some sort and the other a bureaucrat, not a scientist.

Their truck was in the driveway, halfway between the house and the road, close to the original barn. His vehicle was parked alongside. He had gotten there early, talked to Richard, calmed him down somewhat. Richard had offered to take them around. Cleary told him to stand by.

In his shirt pocket, Cleary had a list of other parcels Krupp had owned, the result of Detective Quick's legwork. They were spread all over the county. None were the size of the family homestead, however. He also owned a large parcel on Kelleys Island, out in the lake. It would take a week to look at everything.

Krupp certainly hadn't looked the part, but he had been a rich man. Like everybody else, Cleary envied rich people. He had no trouble admitting it to himself. However, he didn't envy dead ones.

He outlined the crime theory with them, but he decided not to mention anything about the flowers. The scientist-type seemed interested. He knew something about herbicides, had grown up on a farm near Akron. He was short, thin, the body description classically defined as wiry, an athletic look. Cleary thought he might have been a wrestler in high school. His teeth were a little crooked, unusual in contemporary America, especially in a college graduate, probably someone with an advanced degree. Cleary guessed his family background was blue collar. He was probably 50/50 on the braces, so his parents took the side of the coin that said his teeth might not be that bad when he grew up. They weren't, but they could still use some work. He had plenty of time, Cleary thought. His 50-year-old cousin Patti was wearing braces.

"You know, it could be just some sicko who thought this would be a fun way to kill somebody," the non-scientist said, "not a true environmentalist wacko." Cleary could read in their faces they were uncomfortable being there. They would put up a good front, but this was scaring them.

Cleary gave him a blank, irritated look. "This was no crime of passion," Cleary said. He kicked the ground, something uncharacteristic, and looked out toward the cornfield past the barn. "They shot the guy full of chemicals. To be specific, herbicides and insecticides, that sort of thing. That's what killed him. Not too pleasant, as you might imagine." He reached from under his arm and took out a 9 x 11 envelope, already damp with his sweat, and said, "Here is the report from Toledo. It lists everything they found in him—so far."

They both reached for it, gooey with interest. The non-scientist dropped his hand, let the scientist take it from Cleary.

Cleary could tell by the looks on their faces they wanted to know more, more gory details, all the nasty bad dream stuff. But it wasn't going to happen. They both wore baseball caps. One said Ohio EPA on the crown. The other said Ohio State. It was an interesting combination.

The scientist read the names of the chemicals. They meant nothing to Cleary, but they sounded malevolent. The scientist read the names with some excitement, nervous excitement, "Also, some essence of algal bloom. Lots of chemicals that should never be in a human body," he said finally.

No shit. They all agreed on that.

"How long was he dead when you found him?" the bureaucrat asked.

Cleary shrugged. He wasn't going to answer it. The question had no relevance for the Ohio EPA. "Right now, we've got a dry hole. No suspects. But the prevailing theory—mine anyway— is that he committed an environmental crime. This was all payback. We have no evidence, of course, but it seems logical. If he did something bad to the land, maybe you can find it." Cleary raised his eyebrows a little, let his hand drift up to his cap. He removed it and wiped his brow with the back of his hand.

The scientist-type—his name was Larry Schmitz—looked a little disconcerted. It wasn't quite right, but it was something in the same family. He was wearing an OSU golf shirt in addition to the hat, and no undershirt and it was getting wet on his chest, just under the logo. It was a common mid-summer vision in this part of the world: a male with a polo shirt with wet spots in various places; across the chest (front and back), armpits, stomach. Cleary had gone to Cleveland State University. He generally rooted for the Buckeyes, but his younger brother had played football at Penn State for two years, so he had developed an interest in the Nittany Lions.

"There's not much in his EPA file," the bureaucrat said, "but he was no angel. But then you know that." He shrugged, looking out at the vast expanse of corn, beautiful and green and marching toward the horizon. "But we'll look again. We've got aerial maps we can look at. Maybe something will show up. The sweating Ohio State fan said, "Water's usually the key. The bad stuff always involves water. There are lots of underground rivers around here—well streams, not rivers—that work their way out into the floor of the lake. It's mostly limestone here, very porous stone. The wrong stuff seeping into the wrong piece of ground could get carried out into the lake and you'd never know where it came from. The surface rivers get checked all the time. But we don't know as much about what's going on underneath. It's a different world down there."

They agreed on a plan. Schmitz would drive over to the other side of the road and drive the perimeter of the fields. He would get some soil samples at various locations, water samples in the ditches. There was a creek that ran across the back end of the property through a patch of woods. He would investigate that too, get more samples at various places. Vinci, the bureaucrat, would look around the farm buildings and the immediate vicinity. When he was done, Cleary would drive him down the main farm lane that separated the huge cornfield from the soybean field and he would take soil samples and just look at everything. They would all meet back at the cars in an hour. They exchanged cell phone numbers. What else could they do?

Cleary saw Richard walking up to them. He sent Vinci over to the barns. He waited for Richard to arrive. "The Ohio EPA is headed over to take a look at your barns," he said, gesturing with his head to Vinci. "I know we've been there before, but it's all part of the process." He expected some mild protest from

Richard, but it didn't come. "His partner is over on the other side of the road. He's taking soil samples and water samples."

"He won't find anything bad. Just Ohio water. Just Ohio dirt."

Cleary shrugged. "Then that's what he'll find."

Cleary had an idea, "How about if we take a tour of the property, you and me?"

It worked. Richard got in Cleary's Police SUV and they headed down the farm lane that led into the massive cornfield. Cleary drove very slowly. The vehicle felt its way on the grass and dirt. He could tell Richard felt a little uncomfortable in the police vehicle. People always did. Civilians would check out everything, but always keep their hands on their laps; they never relaxed. Their eyes moved like a bird's, however, checking out the interior: weapons and radios and all that shit. Cleary kept the windows down, despite the growing heat; it just felt like the right thing to do. The insect noise was noticeable. He had no idea what insects were causing it.

"How's your mother doing?" he asked.

"Not too well. None of us are. It's tough on Mom, tough. Your husband calls from the fairgrounds and says he'll be home later and then ending up dead. They were married 38 years.

We didn't know what to do about the viewing. Went back and forth. My Mom doesn't believe in closed caskets, said he would have wanted people to see him to say goodbye. I don't know. Frank Bergman's people did their best, I'm sure, but I thought he looked pretty bad."

Cleary had not gone to either the wake or the funeral, but he remembered what Krupp had looked like lying on the floor of the horse barn on a bed of straw surrounded by lots of pretty flowers. He was green-looking. His eyes bugged out like something had been trying to kick them out from inside his head. He was foamy around the mouth, dried milky foam that stuck to his chin and his lips.

"We're getting a lot of strange calls," Richard said, turning to look at Cleary, more comfortable now in the seat. "You get looks. People say things to you, but it's not like he just died, he was murdered. No one has any idea why. No one. Nothing. Not a goddamned thing. And we're out here wandering around our farm, just chasing our tail. There's nothing here. It's been a week."

"Why are you so sure?" Cleary asked.

"He wasn't that kind of man."

"What kind do you mean?"

"He loved the farm. It's been in our family for more than a century. It was sacred. We were all brought up on that. He'd never do anything to it. Never. I know that as well as I know anything in my life."

They continued to move between the corn. Cleary knew nothing about farming. He was amazed and impressed at the sheer amount of stuff that had grown up out of the earth in this place in the past few months. In the spring, it was just plowed dirt. They were at least a quarter mile from the house, coming up to a rise in the ground. To the left was a small copse of trees, alone in the sea of corn. The farm lane angled off to it, a sidetrack. Now, in high summer, the lane was like a tunnel, a place away from all the world, quiet and alone and mysterious. In winter, it would be naked, cold, and dull.

"What kind of corn is this?" Clearly asked. He figured he might as well know. He knew there were about five thousand varieties.

"This is Schlessman 5-35 High Yield," Richard said quickly.

Cleary was impressed. "Your dad owned a lot of property. I guess he knew his corn."

Cleary was feeling the heat now, and he decided to put up the windows and put the air on. "Richard, what did he like best, the farming and all, or the politics, you know, being a county commissioner, fair board president, all that stuff?"

Richard turned and looked right at Cleary. "He liked doing everything. Not much for animals really. His father had pigs and chickens, but my father always said cows were too much work, too demanding. But he liked farming. He liked owning things. He was good with money, but he never spent any. An old German."

"I'm trying to find someone who would want to kill him," Cleary said.

"I know. You want me to hand over someone who wanted him dead. But I can't help you. There were people he screwed in business deals. Well, you know, not really screwed, just got the better of, you know what I mean. He was a smart guy about business."

Cleary knew what he meant.

"There were people he beat in elections, that sort of thing. But these aren't people who kill people."

Cleary knew he was right. Most people got killed because of family stuff. There was the professional stuff, gang stuff whether old-style or young style. And then accidents: some poor bastard working the wrong convenience store at the wrong time. But here in Erie County nobody got killed over votes.

They drove over to the copse of trees. Under the canopy and mixed in with the underbrush was lots of farm junk. Some of it was very rusty, old. There were piles of it. Cleary parked the SUV and got out, saying nothing to Richard. He looked at it, thinking about whether he wanted to wade in or not. Maybe he should leave this to the EPA guys. There were two or three old cars, pieces of tractors, but he saw no 50-gallon drums.

"What's this?" Cleary asked.

Richard was out of the car, too. "Every farm has a place like this. Hell, most farms have two or three places like this. It's just the Krupp dump. Been here for decades. Might be a little oil from a crankcase leaked into the ground, that's all."

Cleary walked closer.

"You like snakes?" Richard said.

Cleary froze, looked down at the ground. He saw nothing.

"Lots of snakes in there. Lots of them. Great place for them to live. It's dark and it's warm. Fox snakes. Black snakes. Maybe even a copperhead."

Cleary stepped closer but kept surveying the ground. Inspecting this little patch of woods was clearly an EPA job. Cleary had an average human's fear of snakes. He was not at either extreme.

"What do they eat out here? It's just a lot of corn," Cleary said, turning in Richard's direction and smiling a little. He put his hands on his hips. It was hot.

Richard walked up to an old tractor, chocked with weeds, and bent down and flipped over a piece of corrugated metal the size of a small door. There was a huge snake underneath, a big black thing, thick with a big head. It was not happy to be disturbed. It pointed its head toward Richard and hissed.

Cleary instinctively backed up several feet. He was about ten feet away but that was too close. The thing was huge.

Richard had backed up, too, but he was smiling. "I killed my share of these when I was a kid. We had a big black lab liked to kill them, too."

The snake was moving now, twisting in the thick grass, moving back under the tractor, away from them.

It occurred to Cleary he was an armed man, with a pistol on his hip that would fire a bullet that would blast its head off.

His cell phone rang, loud. It was not the EPA.

"There he is, Mr. Blacksnake, and looking very well fed on all the fat rats that are eating our corn." Richard spoke to the snake as though he were its friend.

CHAPTER 12

Peter Newcastle had been working the big boats for almost 15 years. His freighter, the *John Byrne*, was one of the true big boats at 1,010 feet. This season it was running iron ore from Duluth, Minnesota to Cleveland, Ohio. Peter was a wheelsman by training. He never tired of the view from the bridge, 70 feet above the level of the lake; it was almost a god-like view of the world, especially in the early morning or sometimes at the back end of the day, when night starts to softly close in.

It was morning now and his eyes were fresh. He had slept through the big boat's passage down the Detroit River. The freighter now had Ontario to port and Michigan and Ohio to starboard as she edged out into the western basin of Lake Erie. Peter could turn back over his right shoulder and see the stacks of the Monroe, Michigan power plant. This was not deep water. The western basin averaged only about 30 feet in depth and all the freighters had to lock into their course and stay with it or risk grounding. Steering the boat was mostly an academic exercise thanks to all the electronics, but everyone, from the cook to the captain, felt better knowing there was a human being on the bridge who knew what he was doing.

For the larger boats there were two routes through the Lake Erie Islands, officially labeled the Bass Island Archipelago, a northern route, all in Ontario, between Pelee Island and the Ontario shore; and a southern route, called South Passage,

which ran between the Ohio shoreline and South Bass and Kelleys islands. South Passage was one of the highest boat traffic areas in the Great Lakes, nearly all of it recreational. Most of the big boats opted for Pelee Passage.

The distance between Pelee and the mainland was only 20 miles, considered tight quarters for a 1,000-foot ship.

The *John Byrne* moved forward at a steady 15 knots, good speed given a full load and a relatively flat lake. Peter's eyes traveled from gauge to gauge, checking for anything that just didn't look right, then switching forward and scanning the horizon in front of the boat, as he had been trained to do. There were several recreational boats out on the lake. Most were headed to one of the reefs to start the day's fishing. There were also some large groups of gulls, also getting ready for a day's fishing. One group, mostly big herring gulls, was off the bow of the boat about 30 degrees and perhaps three hundred feet away. Peter rested his eyes for an instant on the gulls. Something unusual stopped him from moving on. Trailing behind the gulls he could see a dark gray dorsal fin. It was moving fast in the same direction as the *John Byrne*.

"What the hell?" Peter yelled, slamming the ears of the first officer who was on the ship phone at the back of the bridge, talking with the captain.

"It looks like a goddamn shark!" he yelled again, this time reaching for the binoculars on the starboard side of the wheel. The dorsal fin was moving faster now, closing the distance to the gulls, who seemed oblivious to the shark, and to the *John Byrne*. Peter could see the outline of a huge fish.

"It's a shark!" he kept yelling.

Then the fin disappeared, maybe 25 yards from the gulls. Several seconds later, as Peter trained binoculars on the gulls, Alpha 6 broke the surface and immediately swallowed most of a gull, all but one wing which stuck out above the surface like a crumpled flag. There was a bit of thrash, some white water, then horrible screeching as the rest of the gulls attempted to get airborne as fast as possible. None of them looked back. About 20 seconds had passed. The boat was moving at 15 knots.

The dorsal fin was gone. It was all gone.

"What the hell did we just see?" Peter said, looking down at the lake, then over to the first officer. "That was no walleye or steelhead on steroids. It looked like it was 15 feet long."

"I'm not sure what I saw" the first officer said.

"I am. I just saw a shark."

"There are no sharks in Lake Erie."

They all had seen strange things on the lakes. Although a natural phenomenon, the night he had first seen the northern lights in full power was the strangest. He felt like he was in another galaxy, that a spaceship was going to come hurtling out of that dancing color and carry him away.

Two years ago, in early spring, the water still like ice, three men in the bridge had all seen a ghost ship. They were on Lake Huron, it was early evening just after a spring storm, and they all saw it clearly, a mile or so off the port bow headed north. They were headed the opposite way, south, eventually to Monroe just south of Detroit with a hold full of taconite. They watched it for at least five minutes. The freighter did not register on radar. It simply was not there, but it was there. It was a newer freighter, not a wooden-hulled ghost from the past. Then a cloud rolled in and it disappeared.

The captain, who was off duty at the time, did not believe the crewmen when they told him what they had seen. He dismissed it: "There are no sharks in Lake Erie." Peter knew there were always explanations, but the only explanation for what he had just seen was a shark, a big one.

"You have no photographic evidence," the captain told Peter. The first officer was no help, offering no corroborating story.

"Not sure what I saw, Cap," said the First Officer.

"No photographic evidence? the captain said, looking right at Peter.

"I had my phone, but it happened so fast I couldn't get to it." It was the same way out in Wyoming. He was hiking with friends and he saw a mountain lion and he managed to drop the phone between two rocks in all the excitement.

"You know we keep a camera in the bridge at all times, just in case we get a shark sighting, or we see the Lake Erie Monster." He and the first officer started to laugh. Peter gave them both a silent FY.

"I know what I saw, Cap. That's my story and I'm sticking with it."

Later that day the First Officer told Peter he couldn't rule out a big fish based on what he remembered seeing—it was a blur, but he saw a shape in the water, and he saw the bunch of gulls take off like two dozen rockets—but not to the point of certainty. And when you're in the position of running a thousand-foot boat you must have certainty.

"If we report it, everyone is going to say we saw the Lake Erie Monster."

"Do you put it in the log?" Peter asked.

"No," said the first officer. "But it's the cap's call. He sees it before it's uploaded. But you know he's not going to mention it."

It was mid-day now and the *John Byrne* was moving into the central basin. There was 80 feet between the bottom of her hull and the smooth lake floor.

CHAPTER 13

Vankirk was in town and wanted to meet at the museum Thursday morning. It was courteous of him to let her know so many days in advance, but that's how he was. The next board of trustees meeting wasn't until late August, and they had just had one in June. Susan decided he must have some off the grid idea he wanted to try out on her. But it was also a possibility he just wanted to walk through the museum and talk.

She got there early, her usual behavior. She parked in the rear of the building, but she chose to walk the grounds before heading to her office. One of the names her staff had for her was the "Queen of Clean." Susan had spent two seasons at Cedar Point Amusement Park as a sweep, which meant she had walked the midways with a pan and a broom sweeping up cups and plates and napkins and twenty-dollar bills (twice her second season) and bits of paper and mini juice cans and various clothing items. She had bought into the cleanliness philosophy of the park and it carried over to the Museum of Lake Erie. The first thing she did every morning was patrol the grounds for trash. Gum deposits on the outdoor walkways drove her nuts. The second thing was a quick tour of the interior, especially the restrooms. She expected them to be sparkling.

The museum was only 11 years old, still a babe, still searching for its own unique identity. With Vankirk's wallet, it had been created from scratch, and Susan didn't hold back

from acknowledging Vankirk as founder, benefactor, and creative spirit of the museum. Others in the community had invested in the museum as well, even though Vankirk had held back from what she called roughhouse fund raising, where just about every legal means of persuasion are used to get funding for a project. In contributing so much of the cost himself, he put aside the philosophy of the great Andrew Carnegie, the Bill Gates of his day in the early 1900's, who helped fund 2,509 libraries around the world, including the Sandusky library. Susan liked his way of doing things, which was to require a community to put up half the cost, and once built to be responsible for the library's operation and maintenance. He wanted, he once said, the community to have "some skin in the game."

Susan sometimes fantasized about being wealthy, like the wealth of Vankirk (or more). He seemed, if not one of the boys, at least normal in most respects. She wondered what she would do if she won the lottery? Would she build a museum, like Eric Vankirk? Would she give it all away to what her mother used to call "good causes." There were so many choices.

Susan wondered at times if Vankirk shouldn't have pushed for more local involvement in the project. However, he had also set up a separate endowment fund to cover future operational and maintenance costs. Operations and maintenance were the two costs always hammering directors of local and regional museums. There was never enough money left for exhibits and marketing. Susan appreciated it was a lot more fun pitching sponsorship of a huge new state of the art aquarium for showcasing Lake Erie fish than a new roof.

The three-story museum was located on the west side of downtown and on the water, appropriately. The building was constructed of native limestone, called blue limestone, even though it was battleship gray in color, all of it quarried locally.

Sandusky had more vintage limestone buildings than any city its size in the state of Ohio.

There was no grand architectural plan at work; it was used mostly because there was plenty of it nearby and the price was right. Susan was not a fan. Block limestone buildings, no matter if church, government office, or home, communicated strength, power, order, and a male world view. She liked color, sharp lines, some glitter. A more female expression. But she didn't dwell on it one way or another. Vankirk's architect added enough splash that in the end the exterior worked in the modern day.

Vankirk's vision was that the museum tell the story of Lake Erie in a broad context. Sandusky would be a focus, but not *the* focus. He had instructed his design team to use as a model the Museum of the West in Cody, Wyoming, a world class museum in a town of about 10,000 inhabitants, which was designed as a combination of five different stories or themes held together by a unifying vision of place, which in the Museum of Lake Erie was the lake itself.

The museum had cost $35 million. More than $25 million had come from Eric Vankirk.

The museum invested a lot of space and dollars in telling the story of the natural history of the lake and its shoreline. The museum showpiece was a huge model of Lake Erie. It was an Alexa-type set up where the visitor could ask a lake-related question and a friendly female voice would provide the answer to the question. If relevant, it would be accompanied by a graphic that would appear on the model and instructions for accessing additional information.

Other major exhibits included the wine industry, agriculture, native peoples, shipwrecks, the golden age of Lake Erie passenger steamers, the War of 1812, the growth of cities like Cleveland and Toledo, the tourism industry, European settlement and immigration, the Civil War. One section included rotating exhibits of famous and some not so famous people associated with the lake, from Civil War financier and Sandusky native Jay Cooke to the Wyandot chief, Ogontz, to Lorain Ohio native Admiral Ernst J. King, Chief of Naval Operations in WWII.

The museum also featured a very large aquarium, with displays of Lake Erie fish and other lake animals. The main tank simulated a typical western basin reef.

The most controversial section dealt with the current and future state of the lake, specifically the problems caused by the agricultural runoff which created algal blooms; the growing risk of new invasive species such as Asian carp and snakeheads; the challenges of climate change.

Vankirk was a believer in climate change, Susan was as committed as well. She and Vankirk had talked about the issue from time to time during his visits to the museum. She had seen no direct evidence of climate change in her lifetime, nothing tangible. She could not point to flowers that had appeared in her garden that were never there before. No one in her Master Gardener group had reported Spanish moss on their live oak trees. Susan could not read the scientific papers on the subject without blanking out in about three minutes. So, it did come down to faith. She believed even though she did not see.

Susan was standing at the front of the steps leading to the main entrance when Eric Vankirk arrived in his black BMW sedan.

He did look the part, she had to admit. He was tall and blond and though he was in his mid-40s he looked more late youth than early middle age. Even features. Gray eyes. He wore tan slacks and a fashionably untucked shirt. Expensive sunglasses. No hat. Susan had always been attracted to him, but she did her best to hide it. She didn't think anyone else had any idea how she felt.

The museum did not open until 10 a.m., so they had an hour before the first visitors would arrive.

"This should be a good day for the museum," he laughed, glancing up at the very blue sky. They both understood he was joking, as museum traffic generally peaked on rainy days, when beaches and boats lost to museums and historical sites in the battle for visitor hours.

The morning was still fresh, the summer light still at an angle, and the air was warm but not hot. They exchanged weather observations for a minute or two, then Susan led him to the side of the building and the entrance to the business office of the museum.

"I've got my usual list of things to review with you," she said, opening the door and then holding it open for Vankirk. His typical visit consisted of a meeting with Susan where each would go through a list of issues or information, followed by a walk through the museum. He was rarely there more than 90 minutes.

Vankirk set high standards for the museum. He loved awards and any award the museum had garnered, going back to its opening, was proudly on display on a prominent wall just inside the entrance. There were a lot of awards. At times, Susan thought of him as the owner and operator of a mid-sized travel attraction rather than a museum person. Susan was always a little bit surprised when he asked about guest issues. Vankirk read over every guest comment, good and bad, sometimes addressing an issue personally. Most museum directors would have been uncomfortable with a board chair who wanted to be that involved with the operations of the museum. Susan was comfortable with it.

Most directors of regional museums worked for a committee or a board, as is the case with most non-profits. Susan knew she was spoiled. She had always liked working for one person instead of anywhere from 7 to 17 (or more) members. It was an entirely different political and managerial environment.

"My list is not too long, Eric," she said as they walked down the hall to the administrative office. "Conference Room or my office?"

"Your office will be fine," he quickly replied. "I like the view," referring to the view of Sandusky Bay with Cedar Point, Johnson's Island, and the Marblehead peninsula rimming the horizon from east to west. Susan had set up her meeting table in front of the window.

She offered him coffee, which he accepted. She got herself some bottled water.

"You go first," he said, sipping his coffee.

Susan handed Vankirk a sheet of paper with topics for discussion. Vankirk held the paper and pulled out his reading glasses.

"First thing, Eric, is a possible acquisition. I got a call from a local Civil War collector who has apparently struck gold. A family in Florence Township recently discovered a war journal written by an ancestor. No one in the family knew it existed until a few weeks ago. It was discovered in an old trunk. The soldier's name was John Fritz. I haven't seen it, but the dealer gets downright giddy talking about it. He says it covers three years of service, is well written, almost poetry he says, in some of the descriptions. It includes several combat stories; and includes two reported conversations with General George McClellan and a description of seeing a ghost on the Gettysburg battlefield. The dealer is Norm Mack. I've known him for years. He comes to the museum a lot. Norm's a friend of the family.

"Any connection to Lake Erie?" Vankirk asked.

"Nothing direct—at least so far." Susan reached into her file folder and pulled out some papers. "Here's a few pictures of the journal," she said, handing him the file. Susan wanted the journal. She had a weakness for journals and diaries. If it proved to be half of what Mack described, it belonged with a major auction house in New York. She could see an opening bid of $25,000 or more.

There were four notebooks, all dark leather. The pictures of some of the interior pages showed a fine hand wrote the words.

"I think he must have been an interesting young man," Susan said, as Vankirk continued to look at the images of the journal. "I checked him out as best I could. He joined the 8th Ohio in 1862. He was 20 years old. He died only three weeks after he got home. He was at a church picnic and he and a couple of other young men decided to show off their tree-climbing skills to impress some young ladies. Fritz got up the highest, but on the way down his hand slipped and he fell to the ground. He broke his neck. Died instantly. All this detail courtesy of the *Sandusky Register* archives."

"Who is the competition, Susan—assuming we want it."

Susan took a sip of water before continuing.

"Too far east for the Hayes Museum, but they seem to be interested in anything Civil War these days. Too far west for the Cleveland museums. There are a couple of local collectors. Eventually it will end up in one of the national auctions." She knew he knew that she wanted it for the Museum of Lake Erie. Her voice gave her away, too.

"We're still building our collection of Civil War material. This would put us on the map."

"I will authorize you to go up to $10,000," Vankirk said in a way that marked that the discussion about the journal should wrap up. "It definitely belongs in a museum, not in a collector's basement."

Susan did not push it. She had learned shortly after taking the job that Vankirk did not like back up selling.

A quiet victory—Susan felt $10,000 would be plenty to close the deal—Susan returned to her list: attendance at the museum year to date and compared to the current budget (all good news); the need to get bids for making some roof repairs; approval for Susan to attend a conference of museum directors and managers in Charleston, South Carolina (now that the coronavirus was under control business travel was starting to come back); preliminary discussion on a new exhibit on the golden age of Lake Erie passenger steamers; a general discussion on the year-to-date performance of her full-time staff (all three of them).

It was Vankirk's turn.

"I saw you on TV," he said with a smile. "You seemed a little nervous at first, but, really, you did just fine. Did you know Krupp?"

"Sort of. He would come to the museum. Our terms on the Chamber board overlapped. We were not buds and we were not enemies. I hope they find out he did something really bad to deserve to die like he did."

"You saw the pictures?"

"I saw the pictures."

"Did you identify all the flowers?" Vankirk asked.

"I think we got them all, "she said quickly," but that's all we got. There's nothing beyond the flowers. It's driving my cousin nuts. There is no closure. When there is a murder, there needs to be closure."

"I did not know Krupp well, but, like you, I knew him. I know we talked a few times when he was a county commissioner. I didn't really have an opinion about him, which is odd for me." Vankirk finished his coffee. He always drained his cup, never left a half-filled cup of coffee.

There was a pause, and then Vankirk asked about her sons. It was a routine question, nearly always asked, and it was usually interpreted by Susan as the first step in ending the meeting, at least the portion of the meeting in her office. Regardless of why he asked, she always liked it that he did. He had met her boys several times. He knew their names.

"Tim is working for the Jet Express this summer. He likes being outdoors and he likes being around boats and the water. He just turned 18. He's learning how to clean the head—not his favorite thing to do. No girlfriend right now, but with Jeremy in Europe all summer. He's got the use of big brother's car."

They both laughed.

"And the girls?"

"To heck with the girls," Susan said. Seconds later, she held up both hands, palms out. "I'm sorry. I apologize. That was not professional. It's just that he's barely 18, never had a steady girlfriend, and I don't want to see him with a damn broken heart."

"And your son, Jeremy?"

"Europe."

"Not just Europe." She quickly said, "but Europe with a girlfriend who looks like something out of a *Victoria's Secret* catalog."

"Your son must be a charmer."

"I wish he'd worry more about charming himself into law school," she said. "He claims that is what he wants to do. He got the blue eyes from his father, and the good looks, and he has that quality of making you feel you are the only person in the room, the only one that matters. I've seen it in action. You can't teach it. He's smart, but no genius. He could be a good lawyer in the courtroom: the combination of brains and selling skills. But he's not going to write legal briefs."

They should be going on their museum tour, but it would be impolite to look at her watch. Her staff was on full alert. They knew the drill.

"He's going to apply to a lot of schools, but he has his heart set on Northwestern or the University of Chicago or Notre Dame."

Vankirk shrugged. "They are all good schools."

"They are all good schools that happen to be in the Chicago metro and close to Dad."

"So where in Europe is the charmer?"

"Well, he is supposed to be in London."

"Where else in Europe? I hope he's planning to visit Germany."

"Well, he's supposed to be in school over in London taking a course in modern British poetry and a course in the creation of the British Empire—(essential learning for every young lawyer, she said sarcastically) –but every time I hear from him, he's nowhere near a classroom. But, yes, he will be in Germany, not sure where it is on the itinerary."

"Susan, he—they—must visit me when they are in Germany. I live just outside Munich. I will be back at the castle tomorrow night, staying for at least three weeks. They will stay with me and I will show them around. They can spend the night in a real castle." Vankirk was beaming as they started down the hall into the museum proper. Susan didn't say it, but she doubted they'd be sleeping, more like screwing. She hadn't even seriously snuggled with anyone in two years and here's Jeremy living the dream in a damn castle. She laughed to herself again. It wasn't healthy to envy your children. But she didn't want Jeremy and Alexis to stay with Vankirk, especially without her presence. It just wasn't right for one of your kids, even if he was 21, to spend the night in your boss' house. Jeremy was socially sophisticated for a middle-class kid from middle America, but Alexis may not be up to the task. Susan had met her a few times and was less than impressed. Susan had never been to Europe. Her father's family was from Assisi, Italy, the hometown of St. Francis, and her mother's family was from Warsaw, Poland. She might get to them someday, but for now the ideal vacation was four or five days at the Colonial Williamsburg Inn and dinner at one of the themed restaurants every night. She also wanted to go to the WWII Museum in New Orleans, stay in the French Quarter, and eat at wonderful restaurants.

Vankirk seemed thrilled with the whole idea and kept asking Susan for Jeremy's contact information through the tour of the museum. He would have his assistant arrange everything.

Susan rationalized her acquiescence in not pushing back too much because Vankirk's castle was in fact as much a commercial enterprise as it was a residence. As castles go, Vankirk's was size small. She had seen many pictures over the years. It was a castle in miniature, not like those fortress-style creations from the Middle Ages. It did have moat and a bridge, which led into a courtyard. The exterior walls were painted white. There were turrets and battlements, she remembered. But it was more than a residence. Vankirk's previous wife was a minor celebrity chef, and the castle was the site of an upscale American restaurant. It also housed the European offices of Vankirk's company.

Vankirk stopped in front of the birchbark canoe which hung from the ceiling. It was authentic, not a replica, crafted in the early 1800s by the Wyandots who lived along the south shore of Lake Erie. It was a miracle it had survived.

"I have a favor to ask, almost forgot. I have a European acquaintance who will be traveling in the States this summer. He lives in Switzerland and Germany, not far from Lake Geneva. He has a lot of business to conduct here in the U.S., so it's an open question if he'll make it. If he does it will be a quick visit on his way back from, I think Chicago. He has your contact information. I really want him to see the museum."

CHAPTER 14

Frankie lived in a waterfront condo in Sandusky. It was slightly more than he could afford, but not enough to be a serious over reach. After all, as he told himself while writing the mortgage check every month; he drove a used Jeep Cherokee; he did not take expensive vacations; he did not have to contribute to a college fund; he did not eat in fancy restaurants, except on very special occasions: he did not buy expensive clothing; and the only other debt payment he had was for his boat and motor.

He thought about these things as he made dinner. Sheila was sitting out on the second-floor deck looking at the water. He did not have a prime view, but he had a view. His condo looked slightly east, so he saw more of Cedar Point, two miles across Sandusky Bay, and the Cedar Point Causeway. He knew she was enjoying the view of the water, but he knew she didn't love it as deeply as he did.

Sheila had a big white wrap around her right foot. The ER doctor had known what to do and who to call and there was a good chance the toe could be saved. It seemed to be healing. No guarantee, however, that it would ever be the same again.

If they had told them about the shark, the EMS crew and the ER staff would have wanted them to have breathalyzer tests. Better to control the situation themselves, they decided.

Use the tooth when it made the most sense, when they could use it to their best advantage.

At times on the way back across the lake to Sandusky, Frankie was certain Sheila was falling into shock. Her face became pasty in color. But then the old Sheila would come back and say something very Sheila-like: "That goddamn shark tried to eat me."

He had told the ER staff she cut her toe climbing into the boat, caught it on the edge of the prop, which technically was the truth. The drag line on the sole of her left foot also needed explaining. He told them it was from something in the back of the boat, not sure what it was. The focus in the ER was on trying to save her toe. The ER doc didn't ask a lot of questions as he worked. His job was to keep the toe attached and give it the best chance possible when the surgeon took over.

Small town life had its moments. The ER doc was Sheila's second cousin. She had worked with two of the nurses and one other, who prepped her for the surgery, had been a nursing school classmate. She ended up being admitted. The word spread quickly in the hospital that one of their own was in house after a boating accident. She had lots of visitors and lots of phone calls.

Sheila was drinking lemonade, the tart kind that paints the inside of your mouth with sweet pleasure. She loved lemonade that was made this way. She thought a Miller Lite would be nice, but she decided to put it off until after dinner. In her purse was a bottle of pills clearly marked as an opioid. She called them her little friends, but she had been successful in limiting usage to two pills, one the night of the incident, and one the next night. They sure as hell worked. She remembered the soft dreaminess, the blanket warmth, the almost womb-like peace. It would be nice to go there again. But that could never happen.

They were banned from campus. Besides, they had to deal with the shark.

"Tell me again what you're feeding me," she yelled, though her head kept its focus on the water.

"Pizza-pizza-pizza," he yelled back, but it was not true. He was making shrimp and mushrooms with angel hair pasta in a light cream sauce with a side of asparagus. He had been refining the dish for years. He was completely comfortable making it. His mother had made something very similar.

It was a warm night, humid; there were no warm nights along the Lake Erie shore without some humidity. She had managed a shower on her own while keeping her right foot wrapped in plastic. Her body felt clean, and she hoped it was sweet smelling. She wore her lightest bra and panties under an Orvis fishing shirt that Frankie had given her for her birthday and an old but comfortable pair of shorts. She wasn't one to fuss much with her hair.

Sheila needed her crutch to move from the deck to inside the condo. It was a pain in the ass to have to move like this—it was a new experience for her—but she knew she was getting both stronger and more skilled each day.

"Could the shark be out there in the bay right now," she asked, "maybe somewhere between here and Cedar Point?"

"It could."

"Which means I could see that fin pop up anywhere," she said, picking up the binoculars and starting to scan the horizon.

―――――∧―――――

The day of the attack on Sheila, Frankie had thought about it hard, if not long, and knew he had to go back to ODNR for the second time in two days. He had to show them the tooth. People had to know there was a new risk to being in the water.

129

Twenty-four hours ago, he was headed to Kelleys Island Shoal with Priscilla to catch walleye. Since then he had seen a shark eat his dog; met with an ODNR guy who thought he was crazy; taken his girlfriend out on the lake to the spot where his dog had died, where she decided to go swimming before he could tell her what had happened to his dog; helped save his girlfriend's life when she was attacked by a shark as soon as she started swimming; taken her to the ER after a high speed dash from Kelleys Island Shoal, met with another ODNR officer who thought he was crazy.

Frankie had gone to the ODNR office from the hospital. He had called a buddy to get a ride downtown to the office. Tim Manheim, a friend from work, who as a proper computer nerd would be at home on a beautiful summer Saturday, said he'd be glad to do it. Tim said he'd be glad to wait while Frankie met with someone at ODNR, then take him to Cedar Point to get his car, and then back again to get Sheila's car.

The meeting at ODNR did get serious when Frankie finally pulled out the tooth. The officer's eyes nearly popped out of her head. She was dark-haired, medium height, thin, late 20s, he decided. She was an attractive young woman, but was already showing signs of sun damage on her hands and face. Her name tag read M. Neubacher. The "M" was for Marilyn.

"May I touch it," she said, almost tenderly, as if it were alive. She was sitting behind the same desk Officer Mylett had been sitting behind the night before.

"Be careful," he replied. He did not want to strip the tooth of its organic material. He also did not want her to cut herself.

She looked at it as though she was holding a white diamond. Her eyes were totally focused on the tooth.

"Well, we know this didn't come from any indigenous species," she continued, holding the tooth with her thumb and index finger, and moving it in small circles, her eyes always on the tooth. It was a weird feeling, but it reminded Frankie of the way various characters in the *Lord of the Rings* movies reacted around "The Ring."

"Officer Neubacher, there will be a record of this meeting, correct?" Frankie asked?

"Yes."

"And in your summary, you will write that I was here twice, last night and this afternoon, to report two different shark attacks at Kelleys Island Shoal, one about 5 p.m. on Friday and one about noon on Saturday. In the Friday night attack, the shark ate most of my dog, a black lab named Priscilla. In today's attack the shark tried to eat my girlfriend, Sheila Piersall. She went for a swim off the boat and was attacked by the shark, but working together we got her back in the boat just in time. Both of her feet were injured in trying to get her back in the boat to escape the shark, one foot severely. She is at Firelands Regional Medical Center as we speak."

"Here," she said suddenly, sliding a pad of paper across the desk toward Frankie. "Just write it up like you described it, and add anything else you can think of, and I'll attach it to the report. And while you're doing that, I will take some pictures of the tooth, with your permission, of course. I'm a Division of Watercraft officer, but I have a degree in the biological sciences, "She smiled and said: "Part cop. Part scientist. What can I say? Only in the Buckeye State."

Frankie nodded his consent. Then he added: "The parts of Priscilla I gave to your colleague yesterday, where are they now?"

"They are in a baggie, in a pouch, in the refrigerator in the back room."

"When does Priscilla go to the lab?"

"Monday morning. With me. I'll be driving her down to the state lab, or over to Stone Lab on Gibraltar."

"I want her to be treated with respect," Frankie said. I want whatever is left of her to come back to the lake. She had a short life, but Pris was a great dog. She was my friend."

"She will be treated with dignity." She would be, Officer Neubacher said silently. She would be.

Frankie visibly relaxed. He felt he could trust her.

"You know," Mr. Visidi, "it might just be easier if you gave me the tooth. It would be easier all around. I'd make sure you got it back. You can have closure with Priscilla sooner."

Frankie's face tightened again. "No. The tooth stays with me." He said it again, "The tooth stays with me."

Officer Neubacher backed off. "Understood." She thought Frankie was more than little stressed. Something had happened at Kelleys Island Shoal.

———————∧———————

"There is another thing, Officer," he said. "You've got to warn people. They've got to know the risks when they get into Lake Erie. The *Sandusky Register* needs to know what's going on. Social media. All that stuff."

Officer Neubacher played it out in her head: *ODNR, Division of Watercraft, warns boaters and swimmers in Lake Erie that a large shark, of unknown species, has been reported near Kelleys Island Shoal in the western basin of the lake. The shark has killed a dog and severely bitten a swimmer in the past 24 hours.*

Yeah, right. Her boss would roll his eyes and want real evidence before walking down that street. Even if the remains showed there was shark DNA mixed in with dog DNA, that's not proof there was a 10-12 foot-long shark zipping around Lake Erie. Frankie Visidi could get the DNA from a basement aquarium. This was going to be the boss' call.

There was a large chart of Lake Erie's western basin on a nearby wall. "Mr. Visidi, could you show me on the chart exactly where all this happened?" Officer Neubacher stood up and started toward the wall. Frankie stood up, too, and together they looked at the chart. Kelleys Island Shoal is an extension of the northeastern tip of Kelleys, rising about one mile from the island and extending for a half mile until the deeper water takes over. It is relatively narrow, about a quarter mile wide. In low water years the least depth might be only three or four feet. The shoal bottom was gravelly, mostly limestone, and there are many small cavities in the rocks for walleye to deposit their eggs.

"I have the coordinates in my GPS," Frankie said, "but I can pretty much show you where we were both times." He put his long index finger on the chart and tapped it on the northeast portion of the shoal. "Right here," he said.

"What direction was the shark coming from yesterday, Mr. Visidi? Do you remember?"

"It was coming from the northeast, from the open lake. My theory is the shark was running the length of the shoal, looking for walleye. Instead, he found Priscilla."

"I am sorry for the loss of your dog, Mr. Visidi."

"Treat her with respect."

She told herself she really needed to call Firelands hospital and try to find out what she could about Sheila Piersall. The last name was familiar to her. Huron family.

"Same direction today?"

"No. The shark came from the opposite direction, from the southwest. "

Frankie moved his finger down and over several inches until it rested on Kelleys Island State Park. The Lake Erie Islands had few beaches; most of the shorelines were essentially rocky outcrops. But the north shore of Kelley was an exception.

"It's a short swim for that shark to get to the beach at the state park," he said. He paused a moment, then asked: "What kind of shark is it, Officer Neubacher?

"Assuming this all happened exactly as you describe it, there is only one shark species it could be. Take a guess," she said, almost coyly.

"Maybe tiger shark?"

"No, but you're close."

"Great white?"

"No. It was a bull shark. Had to be. Bull sharks can live successfully in fresh water, even thrive in it. They routinely swim up rivers in Australia, and in other places, including the Mississippi in the U.S. They have been found as far north as Illinois. And they do eat humans, or at least attempt to do so, when they get the opportunity. "And they do get to be as big as the shark you describe. Maximum length is about 11 feet, weight about 700 lbs. That's a pretty big fish."

Frankie thought about what he saw just as he bent forward to reach for Sheila's' hands to bring her into the boat. The fish was essentially on the surface. It was incredibly big, the huge wide mouth, its body seemingly filling his entire field of vision.

"How did it get here, Frankie?" Sheila was hungry, the aroma from the kitchen was wonderful. He was her first serious boyfriend who was good in the kitchen. He was not a foodie, and his range was limited, but Sheila appreciated what she had. His mother had taught him not to be afraid of the kitchen. In her experience, too many men were just afraid of being surrounded by so many variables.

Sheila eased herself into the comfy chair in front of the TV and watched Frankie bring out the plates and silverware.

"I say again, Mr. Visidi: How did it get here?"

"I have two theories," he said calmly, "the first, which I arrived at over the past few days as I read as much as I could about sharks, is that somehow a shark swam up the Mississippi to the Illinois River and then into Lake Michigan and then via the Detroit River into Lake Erie. All that water is connected. However, the invading shark would have to somehow get past the electrical barrier where the water goes into Lake Michigan, in Chicago. In theory, this should be impossible to do. Just ask all those Asian carp. They have been trying for years without success. Millions have died trying.

"Or they arrive via the east, from the St. Lawrence Seaway and the Welland Canal. But I don't think they come over Niagara Falls,

"The other option is that they are here because somebody wants them here." He shrugged and turned back to the stove.

"You mean the Mad Scientist theory."

"Sheila, you can't rule it out."

Frankie let the shrimp cook a little longer, but he did lower the heat. The key to the dish was the shrimp—no, it was not the key, there was no key. All was important. The shrimp had to be completely deveined and not too big and the tails cut off at the right place. The pasta had to be fresh, still alive, more alive than the shrimp. He preferred angel hair with shrimp. Got to hit the sweet spot with the sauce. Watch the butter. Careful. Careful. This is for Sheila. He glanced at the asparagus, always high risk but also high reward. People gave you a break—they hoped for the best but had had too much bad to mediocre asparagus not to let expectations get out of line. He bought this asparagus from a roadside stand out in the township where he had had good luck in the past. It looked good and goddamn it had better be good. This was for Sheila. The sauce again. Always pay attention. He added a bit more oregano. Frankie liked to be alone when he prepared food. He did not want helpers, even knowledgeable ones. He did not clean as he went unless he knew he would use the item again.

"Almost starting time," he called over to her.

The table was set, his good dishes, two wine glasses that had belonged to his grandmother and had first graced a table in a tiny port town in Poland on the Baltic Sea in 1875.

The dessert would be Key Lime pie, one of her favorites. He was not at the dessert-making stage of his culinary life, not yet anyway, and this pie came from Vine and Olive, a Mediterranean food store in the township.

The appetizer was walleye bites. It was a local favorite, easy to prepare. He made his sauce from scratch; dipping sauce made all the difference. So, it was all there: walleye bites, asparagus salad, pasta in a light white sauce with shrimp and mushrooms, key lime pie, fresh bread. Frankie was nervous now, even breaking some sweat as he orchestrated the last few minutes. The kitchen was a disaster, but Sheila thought it was charming.

"What would you like to listen to?" Their tastes in music met in the center, but there were serious differences getting there. She often teased him about his love for Taylor Swift.

"Oh, let's hear from Ms. Swift," she said, smiling.

They talked about her injuries, the shark, her time in the ER, the craziness of it all.

He thought she looked beautiful, pretty beyond description, sitting in his big TV chair. He invited her to sit down at the table. She got up gracefully, as though the bandage did not limit her at all. She was a good athlete. You could tell by the way she got in and out of the chairs.

"Here I am eating this walleye, and this shrimp, and I'm feeling something strange." The color drained from Frankie's face. "No, not that, it tastes wonderful," She reached out and took his hand and squeezed it. "Oh, it's something else, something I don't know how to talk about. I mean I say 'strange,' but I know the feeling very well. We are good friends."

He lifted the bottle of chardonnay and she nodded.

"Try me," he said.

"It was just a fleeting thing. I'm alright."

"Tell me what it is, Sheila. Is it the shark?"

"It's the shark and everything else. And I mean everything else. Frankie, I sometimes get these little mystical moments. I can't control them, they just happen. I feel super connected to everything that ever was and is. But not to what will be. They don't last long, less than a minute, maybe even less than that.

"And Frankie, I am not a witch.

"I guess getting almost eaten makes you pay attention. It is impressive how so many of us spend our time trying to eat each other."

Sheila lifted her fork as a prelude to stabbing a bit of shrimp, but then put it down.

"Frankie, I'm probably freaking you out with all this mysticism talk," she laughed, and squeezed his hand again quickly and firmly.

"No, not at all," he lied. He thought about Priscila. Pris was alive somewhere. Maybe in one of Sheila's mystical moments.

"Frankie, you are the only person I've ever talked to about my mystical moments. No one knows about them except you and me. I mean no one."

"Not mom and dad."

"Not mom and dad."

"No old boyfriends."

"God no."

"When I was working the COVID-19 floor of the hospital, I had some mystical moments. A few. It was not a prerequisite, but I never lost one. I mean I had mystical moments with patients who lived, but not with all that lived, but none

with people who died. I have no idea what that means."
She shrugged.

The food was splendid. He had to admit he was good in the kitchen. He got lucky with asparagus. The shrimp had just the right amount of garlic.

The condo had good natural light. He could see and feel it in the room. The evening softness was starting to creep into the condo. He could see single shafts of light.

"Frankie, I want to marry you."

CHAPTER 15

It started with a long voice mail. The caller identified himself as Paul Gutten, a friend of Eric Vankirk. He was also a European neighbor of Mr. Vankirk. He had business in the States to attend to, in Chicago, specifically, and then in Cleveland, but he would have a day or two between appointments and Mr. Vankirk had been after him for years to see his hometown and his museum. This seemed a perfect opportunity. He would be in Sandusky on Tuesday and staying at the Hotel Breakers at Cedar Point. He would have a car and a driver. Mr. Vankirk had told him he had spoken with you and you would be expecting his call.

The voice was polished, precise, and hard to place. Susan thought it sounded European certainly, but it did not scream German or French or Polish. It was professional but still friendly enough. She had no idea how old he might be; there were no giveaways in terms of word choice or pronunciation. He was in the wide period: he could be late 20s or mid-50s. He did not sound young, and he did not sound old.

She Googled him, of course, but there was not much to find out. He evidently kept a low profile in all things, especially social media. He had dual citizenship: Germany and Switzerland.

She found a few pictures of Gutten. She was not surprised that he was very good looking. He had an angular face,

what back in the day was called chiseled. His company was privately held.

Susan returned the call in the early afternoon. Gutten answered after one ring. They exchanged pleasantries. He would arrive at Cedar Point before 6 p.m. Would she join him for dinner and a walk around the amusement park? Erik had told him that he had to see Cedar Point. Susan was mildly surprised at his apparent interest in Cedar Point, but she knew from personal experience that amusement park fans are hard to categorize.

Paul Gutten stood at the west-facing window of the Presidential Suite at Hotel Breakers. He was looking out from the 10th floor, approximately 120 feet above the sand. He had changed into a pair of high-end jeans (Europeans did not favor shorts) and a long-sleeved linen shirt, rolled up to his elbows. He had showered and was drinking some bottled water provided by the hotel.

Gutten liked high things. His home was a castle, and he lived in a country on the edge of mountains. He enjoyed driving mountain roads. He was not bothered looking out from the tops of tall buildings, even very tall buildings. He always smiled when he saw the iconic photograph of construction workers on the Empire State Building sitting on a metal beam eating lunch almost 100 stories above Manhattan. He understood their apparent nonchalance.

This was his first view of in-person Lake Erie, and he was impressed. It was not unlike a view of the ocean, at least from this vantage point. In the late afternoon sun, the lake was shiny and new, more blue-like than green-like, though not the deep, full-throated blue of the ocean. There were a great many boats. To the west, he could see the Perry International Peace Memorial on South Bass Island, a 352-foot Doric column, the highest in the world. It was 17 miles away jutting up on the far horizon, fronted by a thin ribbon of green. The beach below was wide and long. He was less than 20 lake miles from Canada.

His driver, Regina, was also his bodyguard. She was in the room next door.

Cedar Point had been in operation since 1870, the second oldest park in the United States, and the Hotel Breakers, since the summer of 1906. Only a portion of the original hotel still existed, but it had been beautifully updated.

They met in the lobby, in the midst of dozens of family groups checking in. Susan was almost run over two or three times by gaggles of kids, suddenly free of their parents' cars after five-hour drives from Grand Rapids, Indianapolis, and Pittsburgh.

Susan saw him at once. He was not a fellow Midwesterner; he seemed to be a different species. He was one of the best-looking men she had seen in a very long time. He was tall, over six feet, and slender, but the kind of slender that still said strength. Dark wavy hair, perhaps a bit too long. Perfect features, model material. He reminded her of the Mediterranean men she often saw in perfume ads, or Olympic swimmers. He would stand out in any crowd. He did not seem to be scanning the room for her, more that he was waiting to be discovered and knew that he would be.

Susan had just enough time to dash home and shower and change into something more casual but still professional, which meant high end sneakers, khaki shorts that she thought fit her butt well, and a bright yellow blouse.

She came in for a landing.

At the last moment she decided to address him as Mr. Gutten instead of Paul, even though they looked to be age contemporaries.

He smiled easily, flashed bright brown eyes, and held out his hand.

"You must be Susan," he said. "Thank you for coming out this evening to show me around the famous Cedar Point."

The chemistry was right. She knew that instantly.

They started with the lobby. She knew the hotel well. She walked him down the corridor to the car entrance and showed him the two beautiful Tiffany stained glass windows designed by Louis Buser, the artist responsible for the stained-glass work in the Mormon Tabernacle in Salt Lake City and St. John the Divine church in New York City. She walked him back into the lobby and pointed out the antique chandeliers, also from Tiffany's. As they walked back through the lobby, he mentioned to Susan that he had given his driver the night off, "I've sent her off into the park. I think she'll find plenty to do."

They walked into the Rotunda.

"Paul, this is my favorite space in the hotel," she said, gesturing up with one arm. The ceiling was five stories up, each floor marked by a white gingerbread railing. Natural light flooded the room and the tan-colored wooden floor. Your head was jerked upward by an invisible lift of the chin to take it all in. It was not a large room, perhaps 2,000 square feet. Susan told him about the New York Metropolitan Opera visiting Cedar Point in the early 1900s.

"The guy who made all this happen, George Boeckling, ran Cedar Point for 30 years. He built Hotel Breakers and many other things, basically put the place on the map. He was larger than life in many ways, equal parts marketer and operator, genius at both, which is exceedingly rare. He considered himself an impresario, loved opera. In those days, the New York Metropolitan Opera made a summer trip to Chicago. Boeckling somehow convinced the opera to stop the train and get off in Sandusky and spend the night. He'd meet them at the station and escort them to the Cedar Point dock and then over to the Point by boat. The principals all stayed in suites just off the Rotunda. The great ones—Nellie Melba, Madam Schuman-Heink, Caruso—all stayed here. Boeckling cajoled them to give impromptu concerts, which they did, standing on the floor you are standing on now."

As she finished, she looked at Gutten, who was still looking up into the Rotunda.

"Very impressive," he said, but I am not much for opera."

"Now to the beach." Susan led him through the doors, and they were outdoors, greeted by a slap of warm Cedar Point air.

"I love the smell," she said, "but not everyone does," she laughed, looking toward Gutten for a reaction. She got a mild reaction, a slight smile.

"It's composed of many things. Sand. Fresh water. Lots of it, as much as you can imagine. Add in a walleye or two. Some insect life. Sunscreen. Cedar Point fries. Cotton candy. Coal smoke from the Cedar Point Railroad. It's intoxicating."

The beach was almost 75 yards wide and nearly a mile in length. The section in front of the Hotel Breakers was filled with beach chairs and umbrellas and cabanas. There were several sand volleyball courts. The Breaker's beach had two outdoor pools and several fire pits. The outdoor sound system was high quality and was programmed to play beach music, summer music, classic rock, current pop, new country, and island music. It was half past six, so the sun was still strong and bright, but it was sliding inexorably toward the western horizon. There were people everywhere, most of them from Ohio and neighboring states: Michigan, Illinois, Indiana, Kentucky, West Virginia, New York, and Ontario. It was the heartland. There were an increasing number of guests from outside this marketplace, which Susan could confirm from visitor surveys at the museum, but the core of the park's visitors were from Cleveland, Toledo, and Detroit. Cedar Point was their Walt Disney World.

Gutten stopped to look at two historic markers, one recognizing the 1910 Glen Curtiss flight, the first long distance flight over water, from Euclid Beach near Cleveland to the Cedar Point Beach, a distance of 60 miles; and one recognizing the contributions of Notre Dame football coach Knute Rockne, who with teammate Gus Dorais perfected the development of the forward pass while working as lifeguards at the Cedar Point beach in 1913.

"Do you know anything about football?" Susan asked.

"Not much," Gutten replied. "I have had opportunities, but I have never been to an American football game. The players look like Roman gladiators. It seems to me they are prepared to wage war."

Susan laughed. "We have a saying: you can't fake football."

When they came to a ramp, Gutten suggested they walk out to the water. "This is beautiful sand, and the beach is like Switzerland: clean." There were still people on the beach, but it was easy to see the day was waning. Gutten led her to the water's edge and kicked off his shoes. "I must feel the water for myself," he announced, as he rolled up his pants to calf length.

The wind was from the southwest and was very light. The water in front of the beach was nearly flat. The sound was very light, too, an on-again, off-again kissing as the water touched the land.

"It's warm," he said, letting his feet get covered by Lake Erie.

"I haven't been swimming on this beach in 20 years," Susan laughed," but you are right—it feels good. It is a very long slope to deeper water, I remember that."

"Do you ever have the algal blooms here at Cedar Point?"

The question surprised her, so she defaulted to her standard comments on algal blooms. She explained the short answer was no, that even in bad years the blooms stayed in the western half of Sandusky Bay or out on the lake; currents, wind patterns, and the Cedar Point break wall all helped to protect the beach.

"It is a beautiful place. It should not be defiled." Gutten did not speak to her but looked out to the lake and the blue-green horizon. Susan could feel the emotion in his voice.

"Time for Cedar Point fries and a ride on Millennium Force," Susan said.

Susan had two tickets—every year Vankirk purchased and then donated 50 park tickets to the museum for situations like this. At the end of tourist season, he expected a strict accounting as to how each ticket was used. A former employee, Susan always felt she was going on stage when she entered the park, even though she hadn't walked the midway wearing a name tag in twenty years. It stuck with you if you were lucky. Her historical knowledge of the area was impressive, at least on the surface, but there were certain subjects where she felt herself expert, and one was Cedar Point history. Another was the history of the War of 1812 in western Lake Erie. And another was the story of the three cholera epidemics that hit Sandusky in the mid-19th century.

Although he asked her many questions, she could not be sure if he was really interested or not. He certainly liked the Cedar Point Fries. Susan explained the fries were the park's signature food item. They made it from a very specific kind of potato, cooked in peanut oil, and cut thick. The local tradition was to douse them with vinegar and catsup. Susan indulged once or twice a summer.

Gutten asked a lot of questions. He wanted to know about her family, how she got into the museum business, what she liked most, and least, about it. He did not ask many history questions, either about the park or the area. She liked walking with him. Sometimes she caught women on the midway checking them out, wondering what the back story was.

"I doubt Cedar Point has any Swiss food," Susan said as they finished their fries. "What would you like?"

"I invited you, Susan. You must decide. I have an international stomach."

"Then we will have some barbecue," she said quickly. "Follow me."

This was the time of the best light. The sun was still the bigger force, but losing quickly to the dark. Midway and ride lights flashed and flickered, more and more visible as the sun retreated. It was the time when the remaining light often cut itself into shafts as it entered the windows of offices and restaurants, ride platforms and retail shops. It was beautiful, it truly was.

As they walked toward the back of the park, Susan looked for trash and looked for sweeps. Trash was minimal. She explained to Paul that she had worked two summers as a sweep.

"In many ways, best job I ever had: outdoors, lots of guest interaction, well defined expectations, immediate gratification— and occasionally I'd sweep up the random $20 bill."

Susan and Paul arrived at Millennium Force at sunset.

"We have to ride it, Paul. This is the best roller coaster in the world."

"No."

"Yes."

"No."

"Yes!"

"I've never ridden a roller coaster."

Susan looked startled, she stared at him in disbelief. "Look, I know they have roller coasters in Europe."

"They do. There is a big park not far from where I live, a place called Europa Park. They have lots of roller coasters. Big ones. Like here.

"I am not afraid of heights. That is not my problem at all. Nor is the speed. It's the fact that I am locked in and I have no control over what happens to me. I don't like that feeling at all. Also, I do not like going upside down."

Susan worked him hard. She was flirty and giggly—the situation required it, though not her style. Eventually, she wore him down and he agreed to ride. She had not ridden Millennium Force in two or three years. It always scared her, especially the climb to the top of the 310-foot lift hill. It was always the anticipation that made your butt pucker. The ride was pure speed, pure exhilaration, a ride like that cleansed you, body and soul. You came into the station with all the accumulated debris floating in your brain washed away, at least for a while. And without going upside down.

The wait was about 45 minutes. Gutten did not object, which surprised her. It was a warm night, but not particularly humid. They talked to a few people in line just ahead of them and just behind them. Friendly Midwestern park-goers. They were mostly younger. Lots of tanned skin and tattoos.

"This ride is German-designed, I think," said Susan, as they entered the station. The level of anticipation increased once you were partially undercover and the music, the screams, and the voices all increased in intensity.

"We should go in the front row," she said. "You have to wait a little longer but front row is the only way to fly. He stuck his thumb in the air, a very American gesture. And so, they waited. There was a couple just in front of them, probably in their late 20s, who needed to talk to stay calm. It was the female's first time on Millennium Force. They were from Michigan. They were an attractive couple. The woman asked where he was from, obviously smitten by his Gutten's accent.

"Where are you from?" she cooed. "We know it's not Michigan."

"Or Ohio," Susan offered.

"Well, that is true. I'm not from Ohio or Michigan." Gutten looked right past the man to the woman. "Take a guess?"

She didn't hesitate. "You're not French. You're not Italian. You're not Spanish. You are from somewhere in central or eastern Europe."

"A fair guess. My native tongue is not Latin-based."

The Blue Train rolled into the station to load, which triggered the strobe lights and the techno music. The Michigan couple stepped into the first row. The woman yelled back, "So where is it?"

Gutten just smiled.

Then the train was dispatched, and it started up the hill.

Susan had forgotten how steep, and how fast, the ascent was. There was barely enough time to take in the beautiful sunset panorama of Sandusky Bay in summer. The ride seats were designed to provide the least amount of cover possible; by design, the rider felt exposed not enclosed.

Gutten felt Susan's hands grab his arm. Her fingers dug in as they reached the top of the hill. It seemed to take forever to finally crest the hill and begin to point down. At first, it was slow, then as the back end of the train crested the hill and the law of gravity clicked in, the speed increased exponentially as they hurtled down toward a tiny opening on the ground. Gutten had to acknowledge it was a unique and powerful feeling. The rest of the ride experience consisted mainly of big sweeping curves and high speeds. The thrills were delivered smoothly, effortlessly it seemed.

"This is an engineering masterpiece," he said to Susan, who was still screaming. She did not take her hands off his arm until they came into the station.

The last stop was the Coliseum, an iconic Cedar Point structure which opened in 1906. Visually, it dominated the front of the park and the main midway. The exterior featured two large domes flanked by supporting cupolas. "This is the historic Cedar Point," Susan said as she led Gutten up the wide steps and through an unlocked door into the second floor Grand Ballroom. In style it was Art Deco, the floor original, recently refinished, so it had a bit of golden glow. The ceiling was almost 50 feet high. At one end of the room, the end closest to the lake, was a large performance stage, and at the opposite end was a raised viewing area with built in tables. Susan explained it wasn't used much, mostly group events, the occasional wedding, employee training. In the fall, it was headquarters for HalloWeekends makeup and costuming.

"Susan, it is marvelous space," Gutten said quietly. It was the kind of place where you whispered or shouted, nothing in-between.

"This place was at its peak in what we call the Big Band Era, roughly 1937-1947. That's when what was called Swing music—a form of Jazz—dominated popular music. Frank Sinatra supposedly sang here. Nearly all the Big Bands played here— Tommy Dorsey. Jimmy Dorsey, Guy Lombardo, Les Brown, Glenn Miller. I'm not sure how well known they are in Europe."

"Some more than others, but they are all known."

"I've got to admit the music doesn't do much for me," she said. "I'm good for three or four songs—I mean who doesn't like 'In the Mood' or 'Take the A Train'—but that's about enough for me."

They were standing in the middle of the room. They were alone, but there were lots of park sounds drifting into the building, including the almost continual beep-beep-beep, from one of the kiddy rides. Every few minutes they could hear the Raptor train as it flew down the first hill. It was a steel-on-steel roar, but filtered by other rides, the park's midway music, and the thousands of guests who were walking the main midway.

"You've got to see this look, feel this look," she said, and led him to the side of the stage. Susan walked across the stage to the podium, stopped, and then beckoned him over. Together they looked down to the floor and then up to the seating area which looked a mile away. The space was vast.

They met behind the podium and immediately began to kiss. There was a bit of fumbling, but things got sorted out and he pulled her tightly to him and she felt his hands on her back. It was mostly lust, and she was ready to sin.

"This is a very romantic place," he half whispered. "Thank you for the tour. Let's have a drink in that beautiful place you called the Rotunda."

They left the park holding hands, like 18-year-olds. It was about 10 p.m., The hotel boardwalk was full of guests enjoying a beautiful summer night. There were many strollers, some empty with mom or dad holding the child in their arms. They saw sunburned faces and bags full of souvenirs; Ohio State and Michigan t-shirts; Millennium Force hats.

"I am very impressed with the landscaping at Cedar Point," Gutten said, as they passed the floral displays on the boardwalk. "So far, I have seen wild blue indigo, butterfly weed, delphinium, cardinal flower, corn flower, coreopsis, cone flower, lily. All are well cared for."

"I did not picture you as a flower child," Susan laughed. She added the park had always had a focus on landscaping, even going back to the 19th century.

Susan was glad it was dark, and her face and eyes would not show clearly. Her mind was racing. Lust was gone, replaced by fear.

A few moments later, Gutten released her hand to get a device, she assumed a phone, from his jeans pocket.

"I need to check in with my assistant," he said cheerfully. "She might be in line to ride Millennium Force." Gutten stepped to the side of the boardwalk.

"I will go ahead and get a table" Susan said, grabbing his hand and squeezing it quickly. She walked on ahead. When she had about a 15-yard distance between them, she ducked in front of a big family group and started to run. Run. Run. She remembered the closing words of the John Updike novel, *Rabbit, Run*. "Run" she said to herself, "Run. Susan run. Run."

CHAPTER 16

She had to lose him quickly. Her one significant advantage was that she knew the landscape, and he, or they, did not. Gutten had been smart enough not to introduce his "assistant," to her so she had no idea what she looked like, if in fact she was a she. She could not run forever—she was in her early 40s—and her body would likely give up before theirs. Susan bobbed and weaved through the crowd, nearly hitting several people, and receiving lots of looks. They did not know her car or where it was parked, but for now she had to get someplace safe and figure things out. She passed the entrance to Friday's and kept on running. She knew she couldn't sustain this pace. She had to hope Gutten never saw her break into a run, that he was just now walking into the Rotunda and heading for the Surf Lounge and that the assistant was getting out of the Millennium Force queue line and hurrying back to the hotel. She thought about just running into the hotel office, but she didn't want to back track.

She always carried a small knife in her purse, but it was locked in her car as the park did not allow knives of any kind into the park.

Maybe there were more assistants? Maybe they were going to cover all corners of the parking lot. Maybe she should just run until she saw a Cedar Point Police Department officer. She should be safe then, but what would she tell them?

Then a strategy came to her. She ran between two wings of the hotel and then crossed over behind a barrier of shrubbery to the park's maintenance complex. The big doors were open, and inside was a labyrinth of ride pieces and parts, plus break rooms, carpenter shop and paint shop, lots of places to hide; and she knew from her time as an employee that there would be ride mechanics in the break room getting ready to start their shift. She slowed down to walk. Her heart was racing, and she was sweating in the humid air. She knew the Maintenance chief a little—his name was Rod Culver—his son had played Legion baseball with Jeremy. She could drop his name. She did not see anyone. She tried a door along a wall, and it opened on a thin path between the maintenance building and the fence around the Corkscrew. She was somewhere she wasn't supposed to be, which is where she wanted to be. The Corkscrew roller coaster train suddenly flew past her. The sound was deafening, a quick roar of steel and air that seemed to press her against the building. Safety. No "assistant" was going to find her here. However, a ride mechanic might use this path anytime. The Corkscrew riders wouldn't notice her in a thousand rides, especially at night. Susan followed the path alongside the building until the building ended and she found a gravel lot with trucks and construction equipment. Perfect, she thought. She stepped behind a big dump truck and called her cousin.

Bill Cleary was at home, into a second Miller Light. He saw it was Susan. He was tempted to be flip—he was off duty—but at the last moment he decided to play it straight.

"What's up, Susan?"

"Everything is goddamned up. I think I know who killed Krupp. And the people who killed Krupp are trying to kill me. I'm at the park. In fact, I'm hiding behind a dump truck by the Maintenance complex. It's a long story. I think Vankirk might be involved. There's another guy, a Swiss-German guy. They both have castles. Come get me, just come get me. "

There was no choice but to go on.

"I can call CPPD and have someone to your location in a matter of minutes. Susan, are you being followed?"

"I don't know!" she said in a loud whisper. "I took off running from the boardwalk in front of the Breakers. I've never looked. I wish I had a gun; I just wish I had a gun."

"No, not really, Susan. You should wish you had some good bear spray."

He remembered a case in Cleveland several years ago. The killer, an old boyfriend, had clipped a tracker to his girlfriend's coat and followed her into the woods. If his cousin was right, these people were sophisticated enough not to take chances. Tracking people was easy to do these days. He debated whether to say anything to her; she sounded near panic already. The park was not his jurisdiction. He could lose control. But the bureaucratic crap could wait. His duty was his cousin's safety. The only bottom line that mattered was that he got her involved in this crazy thing and he had to get her out safely. It was on him.

"Susan, I'm going to call Chief Rotsinger and ask him to get two bonded officers to your location. Stay where you are. When these guys get to you make sure they are wearing uniforms." Cleary didn't know which strategy was the safest: stay hidden or head for the hills?

He decided Susan's pursuers, if there even were pursuers, were not likely to have a tracking device.

Susan heard the door open at the spot where she had left the building and headed down the path by the Corkscrew. Then she saw two shapes. Then two flashlight beams. She was about 30 yards away and well hidden. They both seemed to be wearing uniforms, but she couldn't be sure. Then she heard a voice.

"Ms. Massimino, this is Officer Grumski of the Cedar Point Police Department."

When Chief Cleary arrived at the station, Susan was drinking coffee with the dispatchers. The edge was off, at least outwardly. He had made the trip to the park and then back to the admin parking lot in only 15 minutes. It always helped when you could go against the traffic flow. And it helped he was driving a police vehicle.

He hadn't said much to Chief Rotsinger, just what he had to. It helped that Rotsinger was at home. He told Rotsinger that Susan was assisting him in the Krupp case. While at the park on her own she saw someone, who might be involved. She got a little scared and decided to go hide, and then called for the cavalry.

Chief Cleary told Chief Rotsinger that Susan never actually saw anyone following her, which was technically true.

Susan looked happy to see him. The station also served as Lost and Found for the park and there was a steady stream of park guests coming into the tiny lobby in the hope a kind soul had found their prescription sunglasses, wallet, cell phone, purse, car keys, sweatshirt, backpack, camera, or beloved Millennium Force hat. Cleary had worked as a seasonal officer two seasons in college. This is where he learned to write reports. There was a lot to learn. Most people had no appreciation for how much narrative writing a cop had to do. He smiled inwardly remembering Sergeant Candreva, who reviewed his reports and told him more than once that, as written, his report was going to convict an innocent man.

Cleary thanked the officers who found Susan. He and Susan stepped outside.

"We'll walk to my vehicle. Then we'll drive over to yours. Then you'll follow me to the station. Then we'll talk about what the hell happened tonight."

No, we'll talk about it now, Chief, "This guy knew all the flowers we found scattered around Krupp's body."

"What do you mean?"

"He said they were all flowers he'd seen at Cedar Point. You tell me—what does that mean? How many people from Switzerland or Germany or wherever the hell he's from would know any of this? Detective Quick knows the list contained eight flowers. No one else knows this. Just us. He must be the guy who created the list. I think it was a test. I think he wanted to find out what I knew."

"I talked to Tim while I was waiting for you. He's not off until midnight, then he and some of the other kids are going somewhere to play video games. I didn't tell him any of this. I put on a good show."

Chief Cleary hated video games, even though given his age he should have been at least an occasional player. He did not have an ounce of facts to back himself up, but he was convinced that violent video games, which meant just about all video games, were too often prelude to murder.

CHAPTER 17

Officer Neubacher decided to take the specimen bag to the Ohio State University lab over at Gibraltar Island. The OSU Stone Laboratory had equipment sufficient for the first task, which was to determine what species they were dealing with: dog, shark, human. The ODNR manager in charge of their district did not feel it necessary to put out the word there was an aggressive bull shark swimming around in the western basin. He had no reason to doubt her, but there were no sharks in Lake Erie. Maybe a giant sturgeon, but not a 10-foot-long bull shark. Marilyn understood the position he was in, but if you believed there was a dangerous shark around in western Lake Erie you had to tell the truth. Marilyn covered herself with a memo to the file, including the information that she had discussed the whole situation with her supervisor. Sometimes there must be blood on the floor before anything happens. She decided to take the Jet Express to Put-in-Bay in the afternoon and spend the night, returning the next morning. She knew several faculty and the director. There was always an extra chair at one of the tables in the dining hall and a bed somewhere in the dorm or one of the faculty cottages.

The testing lab was part of the Ohio State operation which covered tiny Gibraltar Island. The island ran southwest to northeast only about five acres in size, ringed by 20 foot limestone cliffs on nearly all sides. It formed the northern curve

of Put-in-Bay harbor. In and around the trees and the limestone outcrops were several small buildings, including a dining hall and a dormitory. The largest building was a three-story brick structure which housed classrooms and the lab. On the northeast corner of the island was a shelf jutting out from the cliff, the spot, supposedly, where on September 10, 1813, one of Commodore Perry's scouts first saw the tops of the British ships appear as white specs on the northwest horizon.

But the most interesting building on the island was Cooke Castle, the summer home of financier Jay Cooke and family, from 1865 until 1920. A Sandusky native, Cooke made his fortune selling bonds to finance the Northern war effort. Cooke was one of the richest men in the United States in the years just after the Civil War. The Castle was his getaway place. The home did have a castle-like turret over the fourth floor. The view of the Put-in-Bay harbor was spectacular from the turret. Officer Neubacher knew that to be true, as she had been there many times the parts of two college summers when she was an intern at Stone Lab. Some of the students were housed in the old mansion. Access was easy to the turret, just a metal ladder and a trap door. There was plenty of room for a few lounge chairs.

She smiled thinking about one warm, wind-less night, when the lights from the Monument and all the bars and restaurants gave the harbor a watery glow. She and Preston Barker from Rocky River, Ohio, had taken an air bath together. It was Preston's idea. He said it was a favorite activity of Benjamin Franklin. It was wonderful for the skin. It was calming yet spiked with energy. Finally, after much negotiating, she had agreed to give it a try. They both removed all their clothing, each careful not to eyeball the other too much, and each sat back down on a lounge chair. They were very close together.

"Close your eyes," Preston said, "and you can channel Benjamin Franklin." What a crock, she thought, he just wants to have sex. She liked Preston, but she had no interest in having sex with him. But she enjoyed the air bath. It was mostly a sensual experience, not a sexual one, although she could see the possibilities if enjoyed with the right person. However, her mind did drift off to a few classmates who she would enjoy taking an air bath with. She loved the feeling of open, outdoor air on skin that never gets an opportunity to experience that feeling. But after five minutes her butt was starting to stick to the lounge and the mosquitoes had discovered them both. It was time to get dressed before some other students came up to the turret to watch the night. The next summer, when she took a class at Gibraltar, she enjoyed several solo air baths.

Officer Neubacher left the Jet along with dozens of tourists with backpacks, suitcases, bikes, fishing gear, and duffel bags. The dock was at the east end of the harbor, but only a short walk to the main drag through the village. It was a busy summer afternoon in Put-in-Bay. The marina was full; many boats were rafted two or three deep along the piers. The bars and restaurants were gearing up for another high energy night. There were golf carts everywhere. Too many, she thought. The downtown area was a high-risk environment for pedestrians. Marilyn got out her phone to call the lab, but before she could start punching the keys a young man, wearing an Ohio State ballcap and a Stone Lab T-shirt, addressed her, "Welcome to Put-in-Bay, Officer Neubacher," he said. "I'm your ride to the lab."

He was a handsome young man, she thought, no nerd DNA in this guy's genes. He was a bit too thin, but he had bright blue eyes. He looked like he needed a good air bath.

They exchanged introductions. He offered to carry the specimen bag, and she let him. She was in uniform and looked forward to getting to the island and dressing down. Everyone on the island was either a slob or scientist casual, depending on your perspective. They walked a short distance to a dock with a very intimidating sign warning would-be dock space thieves (docks were always at a premium) the full wrath of The Ohio State University and State of Ohio would descend upon them.

It was a very short ride, mostly spent avoiding all the boats, mostly sailboats, anchored in the harbor. It was high summer, and the harbor was filled.

Professor Joe Churchwell met her at the dock. He offered her a big smile. He was a short, thick black man with a doctorate in limnology and a magnetic personality. They had met her senior year at OSU. She was taking an elective in public administration (or how to be both a scientist and a PR person). He was doing the same, though just short of getting his doctorate. They were assigned to the same study group. He was clearly smarter than she was, something she discovered early on in their relationship. Marilyn had a high opinion of her own intellectual abilities, but she knew she wasn't in Joe's class. In addition to the brains, he had immense physical energy. He breezed through the doctoral program. He would be a full professor at a very young age. He was not an athlete— he did not play sports in a serious way—but he was not a non-athlete, either, unlike many of the kids in science programs. He could even preen a bit, telling people he was going to be the next Kirby Puckett, the famous Minnesota center fielder who played in the '80s and '90s. She did not follow baseball and was not impressed with the comparison until someone showed her a picture of Puckett. The comparison was on target, down to the smile. He had always liked her. She knew he would have an opinion on the Lake Erie shark.

"Welcome back to Gibraltar," Joe said, keeping his hands on his hips. It was post-pandemic time in America now, but the new habits still hung on. "You are all set up in the Duncan cottage. You know the drill. Great view of Rattlesnake Island."

"Still have those damn water snakes around?" Officer Neubacher replied. Scientists working in the life sciences could hate certain animals if they didn't take it very far and kept their feelings to themselves. The Lake Erie islands were teaming with snakes. The Native Americans even called them the Snake Islands. Early settlers all commented on the number of snakes as well. The rattlers were all gone, off the islands by 1940, but other snakes had moved in to take their place in the food chain.

The population of the northern water snake had exploded the past 20 years, helped in large part by the unintended introduction of the non-indigenous or "invasive" fish called a round goby. Small, the size of a small perch, gobies hung out along the shoreline and on rock bottoms in the lake. It was a tough competitor for bass, perch, and walleye. The water snakes all liked to eat them, but basically the snakes would consider eating anything that was smaller than they were. The goby homeland was central Europe. They booked regular visits to the Great Lakes in the ballast tanks of freighters. The price was right.

"There are water snakes everywhere," Churchwell laughed. "But let's get to the lab and see what you've got."

The three-story building in the center of the island housed classrooms and a lab. The lab was on the ground floor.

"It's a wild story, Joe. Wild. Wild. Wild. But let me get out of this uniform first. Joe took her to the small cottage where she would spend the night. She gleefully took her uniform off and pulled on baggy shorts and a polo shirt.

When they got into the lab, Joe took the package from Marilyn and opened it slowly. It was fishy smelling, but not as bad as she expected. Joe was all business now as he worked up the specimens. He worked and Officer Marilyn Neubacher talked.

"He's got a tooth, a beautiful tooth. I tried to get it away from him, but I had no chance. He's a dog guy. Big time. This is all that's left of Priscilla, or so he claims, and he's not letting it get away from him. Can't blame him, I guess." Joe nodded in agreement.

"He let me scrape some tissue from the back side of the tooth. Here it is," she said, reaching into her pocket and pulling out a baggie with a few strands of pinkish tissue. "I have pictures of the tooth on my phone."

"Beautiful," he said, smiling, as he thumbed through the images.

Joe Churchwell flew through websites and sorted through online references. Finally, he cranked up the big guy and looked through the scope.

"Dog, yes. Human, yes. Shark yes."

It was quiet in the room. There was a purple glow coming through the tiny window that looked across to the harbor to the Village of Put-in-Bay.

"So, Joe, that means—assuming I believe him—that there is a bull shark in the western basin of Lake Erie. There are "

"It would appear that is the case."

"I'm calling my boss," Marilyn said. "He can decide what to do next." She knew, instinctively, that her boss would do nothing. He would want more information. He'd want ODNR to talk to Frankie Visidi, try to verify his story. He wasn't going to go to the media with what he had now. The decision to go public would be made by the director, ultimately.

"So, Joe, if we accept Mr. Visidi's story, how did this big fish get here?"

"My first thought is that he, or she, swam up the Mississippi River, then took a right turn and went into the Illinois River and swam northeast to Chicago. There's a barrier there with enough electrical power to kill anything in this hemisphere, or the hemisphere below us. It's what keeps out all the undesirables, especially the Asian carp, the kind the news media love to cover because one species likes to jump into small boats and smack whoever is nearby. Great visuals.

"They are Public Enemy Number One. Their DNA keeps showing up in water samples from the Great Lakes, but so far, no fish.

This barrier was not designed to stop sharks. Electro-shockers work best on bony fishes. All bony fish have air bladders. Sharks do not.

"The most likely way for bull sharks to get to Lake Erie is to go up the Wabash River, a tributary of the Ohio River. In fact, it is the northernmost tributary of the Ohio. Go up about 400 river miles and you get to its source, a spot in Ohio about 1.3 miles from the Indiana line. Here, I'll show you," he said, getting off his stool next to a group of specimen jars of Lake Erie fish. Joe walked over to the wall which had a cluttered, and torn, map of the Great Lakes watershed. He began to trace the Wabash with his finger. "No, let's start at the beginning." He dropped his hand to where the Ohio flowed into the Mississippi. "He's already about 1,300 river miles from the ocean, but something pulls him north and into the Wabash. It's early spring. The river is high. At this point, he's big by river standards but not a monster, maybe one to two years old, and there's enough smallmouth, catfish, and fat bluegills to keep him, or her, going upstream. Maybe he, or she, is not alone.

"He finds himself at the headwaters. There is a big storm, a huge storm, buckets of rain. Then more rain. The field ditches fill, then get pushed into bigger ditches which are sometimes combined into new streams which carry fish in different directions. There is a great deal of new mixing. Our fishy friend is clueless—where to go? He senses there is no flight schedule to adhere to. He, or she, does not know it but he is now in a new watershed, the Great Lakes watershed. But it is now a long way to the North Atlantic. First there is the Maumee River, which flows northeast for 137 miles until it empties into western Lake Erie by way of Toledo, Ohio."

"If I can interrupt—"

"You just did," he snapped back, but smiling. "Sharks are born alive. No eggs. For this to work you need a female."

"It would have taken a longtime to get to maximum size, perhaps two years, and with lots and lots of walleye. I don't think there is any way a growing bull shark could stay hidden that long.

"The Central Basin is very big, plenty of water—"

"But not enough natural food," he said. Plenty of water but not enough food. But there are other issues as well, primarily the temperature of the bay and lake. Lake Erie is just too cold in winter. Bulls qualify as a sub-tropic fish species. They can handle colder water if they must, but not without some benefit. In the late fall and early winter, they would welcome the water around the intakes at the nuclear power plants. But I don't think you're going to have bull sharks butting their heads through the ice. Any bull shark that found itself here in November or December would not be a happy camper. And he, or she, would be a dead fish swimming. The shark would never survive the winter."

"I got to use your Cedar Point-clean bathroom," she suddenly said. They both laughed, thinking about what the bathroom she was about to use was likely to look like. It was bad, but she had used worse.

"Aliens?" she said.

"No," Joe said. "Definitely not aliens."

"This guy with the dog, he didn't make this up, Joe. I had the tooth in my hands. It wasn't an old tooth; you could just tell. It seemed alive."

Joe looked back over the lab. "I just don't see how a shark that big could make it into Lake Erie on its own." He looked back at map. "Even the scenario I just talked about is a huge—I mean a *huge* stretch. No fish the size of a cow is going to swim through a drainage ditch from the Wabash to the Maumee watersheds. No way. Now, technically, a big fish could get through the barriers in Chicago, but it's a long haul from Chicago to Kelleys Island." Joe walked back to the map. "I quickly calculate about 700 nautical miles. And Lake Michigan is not exactly known as the fish basket of the Great Lakes. Could he get enough to eat?"

"Got anything to drink around here?"

Joe laughed. "This is The Ohio State University. There's no alcohol allowed on campus, and Gibraltar Island is technically part of the campus. But never separate a biologist from his beer." I'll see what I can do. Back in five."

It was warm in the lab. Her body was getting wet under her clothes. She had to do a quick hard pull to get her panties out of her wet butt crack.

She liked Joe. She knew he was a good teacher. But this wasn't a teaching moment. Marilyn wasn't buying the "Nature finds a way" theory, the best line in the movie, "Jurassic Park."

Joe was back with a small cooler bag with a big Ohio State logo on one side.

"I got us two each. Saves the hassle of a return trip. Two is my limit," he said as he pulled out a cold and wet Labatt's longneck and handed it to her.

"God, it tastes good, "she said, after taking a long pull. "So, I've thought of lots of possibilities. Marilyn was off and running, starting with the mad scientist whose experiments have created a new kind of shark that grows to maturity in two years; a rich guy's fantasy of having the most dangerous pet imaginable; domestic terrorist plot; foreign terrorist plot; a secret government project; a secret alien government project.

They took a break for dinner. The dining hall was on the high point of the island on the open side. The view was to the north and west, a lake view, but Rattlesnake Island was clearly visible, just three miles away, and Middle Bass to the north even less. It was cafeteria food, but the price was right. Occasionally, they would get some fish donated and the staff would put on a feast for the students. The average age in the dining hall was about 22. More men than women, but many more women than she remembered.

Joe introduced her to everyone they ran into. Marilyn felt like a prized football recruit. She would have preferred he not go into much detail, any detail, about the purpose of her visit, but Joe was not the type to keep his mouth shut. It was not in his nature. He would hold up a slide specimen that contained some of Priscilla's DNA for a student and then begin a game of 20 questions.

Joe was indeed the whole package: young, articulate, ambitious, attractive, tireless, smart.

They talked into the night, into the beautiful summer darkness. The pink blemish on the horizon didn't drop beyond the horizon until almost 10 p.m. There were lights on now in most of the buildings, but you had to watch your step because the ground was uneven over the whole island. It was all that dolomite; it was not to be trusted. They migrated out of the lab and over to a small flat area with a few Adirondack chairs. The view was impressive, including in one sweep Perry's Monument, the Downtown, and the boat docks near the fish hatchery. Ten years ago, when she had been a student here, she sat in these same chairs, and looked out over the harbor.

They were into their third longneck, and she knew this needed to be her last. A few students stopped by to sit for a while. Joe introduced her to several. Scientist to cop; she was on a strange journey. Her dad had been with Highway Patrol, an uncle and a first cousin were cops. When she was adrift after college, wondering what the hell to do with her life, her dad encouraged her to look at the ODNR and the Division of Watercraft. She loved being outdoors. She loved being on the lake.

She wondered if Joe was attracted to her, or if he was just friendly. He was married, she knew, and had at least one child.

"I like it here," Joe said, as if reading her mind. "And we are doing important work here. Really important work." For the next several minutes Joe rattled off the list of research projects running through OSU and Ohio Sea Grant program. "I know it's the beer talking, but sometimes I feel my role is to be a guardian of Lake Erie. I just use science as my weapon. You get to use your gun," he laughed.

"Fortunately, not much call for that."

"Science nerds are not supposed to get emotional, but I do. I love Lake Erie. I love the water and the fish and the freighters and the marshes and the history and the wineries and those damn water snakes and the people and the boats and these beautiful islands—and I hate the barbarians trying to breach the wall and do her harm, which means zebra mussels, and algal blooms, and Asian carp, and global warming, and sewage, and wind turbines in the wrong places. I am a guardian of the lake. That is what my students—well, some students—call me: The Guardian of the Lake," he laughed,

He switched to another channel.

"You ever think about coming back? You could do it. It's not too late. You've got a degree in the biological sciences. You've taken enough post grad courses to be a third of the way to your doctorate. You're a good communicator. You're self-confident. No one is going to give you any crap."

It was probably the beer talking, but Marilyn said quickly that there was no way she could make up the time she'd already lost. She was 29. No one starts in a doctoral program at that age.

"There's nothing I feel passionate about. I like science. I like to answer questions and I like to collect information." She laughed and said: "I do like knowing things, proving things, but I don't see devoting my life to the study of one thing, as so many of you do. I don't want to be the world's leading expert in zebra mussels."

Joe laughed loudly. "Well, I happen to know that person. His name is Louis Loudon. He got his doc from U of M, but he's on the faculty at Northwestern. Good guy. Likes Canadian beer... just like us," he winked. He got up from his stool. "I've got two left. I'll be right back." He was at the door before she could object. What the hell.

The bottle was very cold. The beer had just about been robbed of its taste. Too much of a good thing. Some cold water was what she needed. She had decided to quit at three but there was a part of her that had already said yes when Joe went for the fourth. But this absolutely had to be it. At the very least a mild hangover was going to greet her in the morning. But she wasn't quite ready to stop talking.

"I like what you said about a being a guardian of the lake, a defender. I feel that way, too," she said. She did feel that way. For her, it filled the space occupied by religion or a quest, or family for others.

"I am a card-carrying member of the Guardians of Lake Erie." She said, lifting her bottle. "I am a cop. You are a scientist. Together we defend our beautiful watery world."

"Marilyn, I know a guy who knows a guy who knows a lot about sharks. He's at Florida State. I'll get his contact information and zap it to you. But I don't think this could have been a bull shark. There's got to be another explanation. It wasn't Bigfoot, either everybody knows he doesn't' know how to swim." They both laughed.

"What about aliens?"

"Same deal. They don't swim, either."

"Visidi" is pretty convincing, Joe."

"So are the hundreds of people every year who claim to have experienced alien abduction."

"What about the tooth?"

"Based on the picture and the bits of flesh you gave me we know it's a shark. But it might have come from the Cleveland Aquarium."

"You haven't met this guy, Joe. He saw a shark."

"Officer Neubacher," he laughed, using his best officious delivery, "everybody knows there are no sharks in Lake Erie."

"Joe, you laugh, but this guy saw a shark. Not only that, but the shark ate his dog and tried to eat his girlfriend. He almost got her, she almost lost part of her foot."

The pathway was dark and uneven. Marilyn had to walk slowly and carefully. There was little if any lake breeze. She could sense as much as see all the swallows and other birds working above her slashing through groups of insects. They were efficient hunters. They ate untold numbers of insects every night.

They reached the turn-off for the Duncan House, where she was staying the night.

"There are bits and pieces of the Milky Way up there tonight," Joe said, stopping, then looking. He was right. It was spectacular—white on black sprinkling the night sky—a beautiful blanket of light.

Instinctively they hugged. She was tall and he was short.
"We are guardians," he said.
"We are guardians, "she quickly replied.

CHAPTER 18

The Jet Express was advertised as the quickest way to the islands, and the advertising was a legitimate statement; it was the truth. From the dock in Port Clinton, the small town on the mouth of the Portage River, the 12 miles to Put-in-Bay, in good weather, was a 20-minute ride. A high-speed catamaran with three decks, the Jet could ferry up to 150 guests a trip. Strictly passengers, bikes, and strollers—no motor vehicles. Top speed: 40 mph.

The Jet had been introduced in 1988 and had been successful from the start. Proof enough was that there were now four boats in the fleet, and it connected Sandusky to the islands as well as stops at Kelleys Island. The Jet even went on charter to Cleveland and Detroit for sports events or casino visits.

Officer Neubacher was on the 9:45 a.m. Jet. It was a beautiful high summer morning on Lake Erie. Winds were light and variable from the southwest. The sky was bright with patchy white clouds. Marilyn was back in uniform, but she still planned to go back to the condo and dump her stuff before heading to the office. She felt like she was in uniform. She always did, even when she was not. Boats were her business, her professional life. She knew the young captain of the Jet, Lou Barbera. He was a good-looking guy, late 20s, blue eyes. Marilyn usually always flirted with him, as she defined flirting, which meant she talked

to him, looked him in the eye, and smiled. He would make a good Guardian of the Lake, she decided.

As soon as she got aboard, Marilyn walked up to the mostly glass wall that separated the pilot area from the passenger space and looked to make eye contact with the captain. She didn't have to wait long. He recognized her and smiled back. He waved his hand, inviting her into the pilot room. It was a professional courtesy, offered even when she was out of uniform. They made small talk as the boat continued to load passengers. Marilyn wanted to tell him what was going on, but there was no time. He had a boat to operate. The Jet would be more than three quarters full for the trip to Port Clinton.

The morning return trips to Port Clinton or Sandusky were always more subdued than the trips out to the islands. Even on a weekday, there were lots of hangovers, including hers, on display. They were easy to spot: eyes closed, bad posture, sunglasses, heads in hands. Not all were tourists, there were others going to the mainland for dental appointments or to visit friends and family.

The Jet moved out of Put-in-Bay harbor and passed Gibraltar Island on its portside. The route would take the Jet around Peach Point, the northwest corner of the island, then a pretty much straight shot along the island's west shore, passing tiny Green Island on its starboard side.

———————∧———————

The group of kayaks, ten in all, were headed north along the island's western shore. The tour originated at the state park about a quarter of a mile down the shoreline and was on its way to Peach Point and then to Put-in-Bay harbor. There were two guide kayaks, eight customer kayaks including two two-person boats. The guides were experienced kayakers. As the group paddled, they took turns sharing the history of the islands, their geology and natural history, and information on Lake Erie. The flotilla of kayaks, in several different hull colors, were paddling about 200 yards offshore. The shoreline was a series of short cliffs, 10-15 feet above the level of the lake. In many places the dolomite had broken off into huge boulders. Beyond the cliffs were private homes, some the nicest on the island. Many were cottages originally built in the early 1900s. The houses were mostly small and swaddled in green. The cottages all faced west, the direction of the prevailing wind, which made it difficult for outdoor living at times, but it also meant they could watch the sun disappear on a clear horizon anytime there was a sunset, which occurred more nights than not in the summer months.

The kayaks were spread out in convoy style, but still close together, close enough that the lead guide didn't have to shout to be heard.

Schools of fish patrolled the shoreline, mostly white bass, and smaller baitfish. But there were smallmouth bass as well, and walleye.

The surface water temperature was 76 degrees, a subtropical to tropical temperature. The water depth about 15 feet. This was an algae-free year, and the water was clear, visibility 3-4 feet under a bright mid-morning sun. The kayakers looked up as the Jet came toward them, its white rooster tails shooting up beyond the stern. The wind was from the southwest, and light, just enough to give the surface character.

There were three sharks now, rivals for food and territory, usually solitary, but not today. All were females, Alpha 3, Alpha 2, and Alpha 5.

The lead tour guide, a young woman from Rocky River, Ohio, saw something dark and large in the water ahead of her and coming toward her. For a moment she thought it was a rock, but she knew there were no rocks there and she knew rocks do not move. Maybe a big tree limb, washed into the lake in the nasty squall they had last week. Seated in the kayak, her eyes were only 18 inches above the lake. Then she saw the fin break the surface. She knew it was not a dolphin.

Officer Neubacher was looking at the kayakers. She had a kayak she used infrequently. Probably half the passengers on the Jet were watching the kayaks, too, especially those on the portside, facing toward the island. The fin broke the water 50 yards in front of the lead kayak. It was unmistakable.

Stop the boat!" she screamed. "Stop the boat! Lou, stop the boat!" She pulled the captain's arm and pointed down to the lake and the kayaks and the huge shape heading directly toward the lead kayak.

Reflexively, though he had never done it before, Captain Lou lowered the speed as quickly as he could, hopefully without causing injury to the crew and passengers. Passengers still went flying, adding to the confusion. Others, who had a grip on the rail, started screaming it looked like a shark. "Shark! Shark! Shark!"

Parents grabbed their children. Even more grabbed their cell phones or cameras.

The great fish dropped below the surface for a moment then rose toward the bow of the kayak. For a moment, the guide looked directly into the mouth of the fish, saw the teeth, saw the eyes. She had the paddle in both hands and screamed "Fuck you!" and slammed the paddle on the shark's snout. The bull shark's bite, measured as the strongest bite of any shark at 5,914 neutons, pulled the bow under and sent the guide spinning into the lake.

The shark dove to the bottom. The guide splashed around. She saw the Jet, only 50 yards away, and the beach, only 100 yards away. Her group was in between, some closer to shore and some closer to the Jet. Most of the people were screaming.

"Captain, blow the horn." Marilyn screamed. "Blow the horn!"

Then another fin arrived, this one closer to shore. And a moment later a third fin popped the surface behind the last kayak. The first fin was back and closer to the main group of kayaks. It hit the side of one kayak, a tandem, with a middle-aged couple on board. The shark shook its head as it backed off. The couple was in shock, confused, as the big shark swam away. The remaining kayaks were moving quickly toward shore, but there were at least four people in the water.

Tim Massimino was on the first deck, leaning on the railing and daydreaming about going back to school when he felt the boat suddenly slow. He heard the crowd noise. Then he saw the fin and a dark massive object to go with it. People around him were shouting and screaming. The Jet was leaning to port there were so may passengers fighting to see what the hell was going on.

Tim didn't hesitate. He kicked off his boat shoes and dove off the Jet and began swimming toward the couple thrashing in the water less than 50 yards in front of him. He swam hard but it seemed he was making slow progress. He did not see the fish or feel the fish; he did not know the fish was agitated and confused and down on the Lake Erie bottom getting ready to return. The fish could sense the presence of the other two sharks and did not like it.

Tim got to the woman first. She was screaming "Art!" in staccato bursts. Tim grabbed the back of her life jacket and began pulling her toward the Jet. He could look backward as he swam, and he saw the man's head on the surface and in the middle distance two other kayaks about to reach shore. He could hear people shouting from the Jet. The man with her was 15 yards away, splashing furiously. Tim knew he couldn't' bring them both to the boat. He tried to make eye contact with the man. The woman was heavy, dead weight. "Kick!" Tim yelled. His head kept bobbing below the surface, and he kicked frantically. For the first time, he noticed there was blood, a bit of pink, in the water around them. He took in air in big gulps. He knew he must be close. The boat's engines were off; it rocked and bobbed with the small Lake Erie swell and towered above him. With his right foot he kept hitting the woman's lower leg and foot. He knew it didn't feel right; he knew some of her leg was gone.

Officer Neubacher pushed and shoved her way to the first level. It helped that she was in uniform. She made it to the gangplank portion of the deck. She looked for another crew member—there should be two—to help lift the section of railing to get them into the boat. A 30-ish man came up to her and said he was an EMT. He was holding the first aid pack that had been mounted on the wall nearby.

"Help me clear the area," she asked. He nodded acknowledgement and began to move people back. At first, the crowd did not respond, but then, sensing they must, they began to move back, clogging the steps to the second level.

Tim knew he was there. He had to be there. He looked up and saw the hull in front of him and faces and bodies behind it. The woman was no longer talking.

From the third deck the captain could see everything, including the massive shape that was moving just below the surface but moving toward Tim and the woman.

Tim touched the metal hull and reached up. He felt several sets of hands pulling him out of the water. He did not let go of the woman's life jacket. Then he was on the deck and there were many hands and arms and faces around him.

The crowd was close, and it made noise, much of it indistinguishable, but he heard shouts of encouragement. There were several children on the boat. Some of them were crying.

The woman's leg beneath the knee was mostly gone, just shreds of flesh. The other deckhand, a retiree, tried to push the passengers away.

Tim looked for the man who had been in the kayak with the woman. He did not see him.

The captain knew he had to decide quickly. Go back to the dock at PIB, haul ass for Port Clinton, wait here for the Coast Guard. This was not in the book, he said to himself, this was not in the fucking book.

"She's lost a huge quantity of blood, she's in shock. We've got to get her out of here right now!" the EMT yelled, as he began to apply a tourniquet above her right knee. Her face was ashen. The EMT didn't say it but he didn't think the woman would survive much longer.

Other boats were starting to converge on the area. He did not see any other swimmers. The captain could see knots of people on the cliffs above the lake. Suddenly, a fin broke the surface about 20 yards off the port bow. He had to make the call. He looked around. All the kayaks were either on shore or approaching it. He saw no swimmers.

"We're going back!" he yelled down to Marilyn. She gave him the thumbs up gesture.

It seemed every passenger on the boat was either taking pictures or frantically making phone calls. The shark attack on Lake Erie was already a news item in New Zealand. Marilyn called 911. They were already aware. She identified herself on the phone to the officer in charge and calmly—though her heart was racing—told her they were bringing in a severely injured middle-aged woman who needed life flight to Toledo. She described the woman's injuries as best she could, then passed the phone to the EMT.

On the rocky shore the tour leader kept scanning the area and counting heads. Three kayaks had been attacked: hers, the middle-aged couple, and one other. The fins were gone, but she did not trust her eyes and kept scanning and scanning, just as she had been taught when she was training to be a lifeguard. By her quick calculation, they were missing two kayakers.

"Scramble the bird" Marilyn said. Get the ambulance to the Jet Express dock and get the bird to the Put-in-Bay airport." Everything was in motion to save the woman's life. She was still breathing, but it was shallow. Marilyn wondered who she was, where she was from. She looked to be about the same age as her mother.

CHAPTER 19

Peter Newcastle had a favorite bar in most Great Lakes ports. He had spent 15 years creating and then refining his list. In Cleveland, his bar of choice was Big Bend, named for the big twist in the Cuyahoga River just before it empties into Lake Erie. The bar was tucked away on the west side of what residents called the Flats. The bar catered to people who worked the docks or the boats or the small manufacturing operations which lined the riverbanks going south. But it sold beer to just about everyone, even college kids who wanted to slum a bit. It was a dark place, both by design and God's law.

Peter was slowly drinking a second Great Lakes Brewery pilsner, hoping to catch the local sports news at noon, when the TV announcer said there has been what some are calling a shark attack on a group of kayakers near Put-in-Bay, earlier this morning. It was the lead story. The anchor threw the story to one of the general assignment reporters, who was standing in downtown Sandusky with the bay and the lake as background.

Earlier this morning, at approximately 9:30 a.m., a group of local kayakers were attacked by what witnesses claim were at least three sharks. The attack occurred just on the west side of South Bass Island and was observed by the passengers and crew of the Jet Express ferry, which had left Put-in-Bay just a few minutes before.

Robyn, the Ohio Division of Watercraft reports several vacationers were hurt in the attacks. A woman has been life-flighted to Toledo Hospital. The woman's husband is also seriously hurt. There are reports of other injuries as well. And, Robyn, there is at least one kayaker missing.

The Marblehead Coast Guard, the Ottawa County Sheriff's Office, and the Ohio Division of Watercraft are all on the scene.

Robyn, Channel 9 will be here all afternoon gathering more facts on what exactly happened at Put-in-Bay this morning. I should add Channel 9 has been inundated with pictures and video of the attack.

There are no sharks in Lake Erie, but maybe there are now...

"I know it was a goddamned shark. It was a shark! Just like the one I saw from the bridge of the *John Byrne* two days ago at 0700 between Pelee Island and Point Pelee in the heart of the Northwest Passage." Peter spoke to the TV, but also to anyone in the bar who would look at him.

"He was trolling for gulls. I watched him come up behind and swallow a goddamned herring gull that was as fat as a Thanksgiving turkey."

The bartender stared back at him, a rather pretty woman in her 40s, then went back to the TV, then looked back again at Peter.

"They don't have sharks in Lake Erie," she said, aiming her words at Peter and to everyone else at the bar. "Sharks live in salt water, not freshwater." She added: "I learned that in high school biology."

When the segment ended, Peter began telling his story in more detail. But there wasn't much to tell. What he saw took only 10-15 seconds from the time he saw the fin until the surviving gulls suddenly went airborne.

One guy at the bar, also a lake man, told Peter he should get off his ass and report what he has seen and what he knows to the TV station. "They need new stuff to talk about all the time. What we just saw begs a thousand other questions. Go for it, my friend. Just don't tell the skipper until after it's aired. "

Peter thought more about what the guy had said. Peter had never been inside a TV studio. He'd never spoken to a TV news reporter. This was an opportunity to do both. What the hell— he was feeling that second beer.

Peter took the bait. Peter got out his phone and called for a taxi. He assumed the station was located somewhere in downtown Cleveland; it had to be close. Turns out, the station was only 10 minutes away. He was going to tell the driver to wait, but then decided against it. It was a beautiful summer day. He didn't have to be back on the *Byrne* until 11 p.m. He could walk back if he wanted to.

He announced himself to a receptionist.

"I've got some information on that shark attack in Lake Erie story you were just talking about." He could tell she was not up to speed on the story, but she asked him to take a seat while she checked with the News Department.

While he waited, he looked through the internal glass wall that opened on a huge room filled with desks and TV monitors. He could see what looked like a set in the back of the room. He was about to sit down when a tall woman in her 20s came out to greet him. The shark story had come to them, and she was excited about what that could mean for the news cycle.

With a smile, she quickly identified herself: Amy Vorkapitski, news producer.

"I saw the shark eat a big fat seagull yesterday morning," he announced, as she led him back to her cubicle.

Her desk was full of notes with names and phone numbers of people who witnessed the kayak attack (that's what they were calling it) and her computer was drowning with emails and Facebook posts. The regional internet was in high gear. She figured the story in some form was going to pop up on the MSN or Fox News home page at any moment.

Peter told his story. The producer took a few notes, including the name of the freighter. He knowingly added a bit of drama to the story, estimating the length of the fish from 10 feet to 12-15 feet. He was tempted to add a second bird attack to the story as well, but at the last minute decided not to do it.

"You see a lot from the wheelhouse of a laker," he said. "We are trained to be observers. And we see a lot of strange things, but I have never seen anything like this."

"We'd like to have you talk to us on the air," the producer asked. The fact that he had come to them made it certain he would talk. She wouldn't have to sell him on going on air.

"Let me get a reporter," she said. "But worst case it will be me." Peter nodded agreement.

She left her office and asked him to wait just outside in the hall. She told Peter she would return in a few minutes. Peter took the opportunity to think about what he was going to look like on TV. His self-inventory was a disappointment. He needed a shave. His polo shirt was wrinkled and dirty and it had a Rock Hall logo over the right breast pocket. His hair was longer than it should have been.

He had to pee. The second beer had kicked in. He was about to go look for a bathroom when the producer arrived with a female reporter and a cameraman.

"So, this is quite a story" she said, smiling. It was a big, professional smile. She introduced herself as Melissa Morenzo, news reporter. Her voice was clear and strong and Peter was half in love already. "Peter, tell me what happened. What did you see? "She led them across the hall to a furniture grouping and motioned for him to sit down. She flipped open her reporter notebook.

Peter walked her through seeing the shark two days ago. He felt his voice was uneven and kind of shrill, but he couldn't control it.

"This is the first time for me," he told her. "I have never been on TV before,"

"Oh, it's not so bad," said the reporter.

The producer walked over and joined them.

"Let's go outside," she said to the reporter. "We've got time."

"I'd love to go down to the boat and get some B-roll of the boat." The reporter and the producer went back and forth on whether they should take the time to go to the boat. Ultimately, they decided to do it from the station on the back lawn where they could have the waterfront and the lake itself as a background.

"I know we've got lots of file footage of lake freighters, said the producer. "I'll get on it."

The reporter led Peter and the cameraman out the back door to a patio and a lawn area. The Rock Hall and the Browns Stadium were below them, the open lake in the background, about a half mile away.

"Let me wire you up," the cameraman said, and attached a clip-on microphone to the front of his shirt. He asked Peter to run the cord under his shirt, then to his hip where it was attached to a battery pack.

Peter had to pee really bad. He wanted to ask the reporter where there was a bathroom, but she was busy writing a few notes and talking on the phone at the same time. The cameraman was setting the camera on a tripod.

"We're going live," the reporter said. They love the story. They are going to break in after the next segment. We go in six minutes."

"But I gotta go now," Peter implored. I've got to use the bathroom." The reporter looked irritated, but said "Go for it. Just inside and on the left." Peter took off like a rocket. When he got to the bathroom, he was so nervous he couldn't handle his zipper very well. He was conscious of each second. His relief was instantaneous. He ran his hands under the faucet and wiped them on his jeans as he ran out the door.

"Okay, Peter, we are going to do this," said the reporter, positioning herself a short distance away from where she had positioned Peter. Then she looked at the cameraman.

"Bob, they are going to throw it to me. I'm going to do a brief intro, then we'll switch to Peter.

Peter noticed there were several people gathered on the edge of the patio, the result of word getting out in the building they were going to interview someone who had seen a shark in Lake Erie.

"Peter, look at me when you talk, not at the camera," She said. A moment later the cameraman was gesturing with his fingers: three, two, one...

Thank you, Roger. We're here overlooking Lake Erie trying to make sense of what is happening in Lake Erie. Peter Newcastle, a crewman on the lake freighter, John Byrne, *claims to have seen a huge shark attack a seagull while he was on the bridge of the ship. This happened early yesterday morning in western Lake Erie near Pelee Island. Peter, can you share with us what you saw.*

"I was on the bridge. It's my job to look for things. I saw a big group of seagulls off the starboard bow. Then I saw a dark shape

trailing behind them. It was huge, and it was right behind them. It was a fish, a huge fish, a shark. Then it submerged. But then a few seconds later it came up and just opened its mouth and swallowed one of the gulls. As he spoke, Peter made a motion with his right arm and hand simulating the shark attacking the gull.

I couldn't beieve what I was seeing, but I knew I wasn't dreaming."

Peter, how big do you think the fish was?

"Well, it looked like the shark in Jaws, *maybe his little brother. I'd say it was 12-15 feet long. It all happened fast. The* Byrne *was moving at 15 knots.*

Peter, you're aware of what happened at Put-in-Bay this morning. What do you think is going on?

Peter shook his head. *"I think maybe there's a new guy in town. I just wonder who invited him in."*

The reporter did a quick wrap and then sent it back to the station.

The cameraman helped him take off his microphone but first asked him to look at the camera and state and spell his name, the name of the freighter, and his position with the crew.

Peter felt a vast sense of relief.

The reporter, Melissa Morenzo, thanked Peter for coming to the station to tell his story. Her voice was pleasant and sincere, but Peter could read in her eyes she was off and running in her head to her next assignment.

As the producer walked him to the lobby, he asked her if there was a way he could get a copy of the interview.

"It's already posted on the website," she said quickly. "You can see it there."

When they got to the lobby, the producer thanked him again. She also offered to get a cab to take him back to the freighter or wherever he wanted to go.

"Well, I'd like to go back to the bar, if I could. The Big Bend, down in the flats." She laughed. "Been there."

He walked into the bar as a conquering hero. He did high fives. He was a major celebrity. Everyone was all smiles. Everyone told him how good he looked, how well he sounded. They had all seen it on the big screen behind the bar.

"Here," an attractive woman said, thrusting her phone into his face, and he watched himself perform for the world.

About 120 miles west, in a Toledo hospital, Andrea Hazeltine, 54, drifted in and out of consciousness, absorbing painkillers. Her right leg had been amputated just below her knee. She called for her husband, Art, but he could not answer her.

CHAPTER 20

Chief Cleary decided to have a car at Susan's house for the remainder of the night. He wasn't convinced this exotic friend of Vankirk's, Paul Gutten, was necessarily everything Susan thought he was, most specifically that he was a murderer.

They sat in Susan's kitchen. Kitchens are intimate places. He found his eyes would wander from the bowl of fruit to the magnets on the refrigerator to the stack of unopened mail at the end of the counter. Tim was asleep upstairs. It was pleasantly cool in the house, the air dried and cleansed by the marvelous machine that made living in places like Houston and Miami possible. On nights like this it was worth a million bucks. He had never seen Susan like this, but he had seen it in others. Her face was flushed and her voice, despite her best efforts to control it, was higher and thinner than normal. She had the look of someone who had just survived a car crash or had just escaped from a burning house. Whatever happened at the park, his cousin wasn't faking it.

"This guy, Gutten, he knew about the flowers," Susan said. "He just mentioned it in passing, but he rattled off the names of every flower I saw at the scene."

"Every flower?"

"Yes, every damn flower."

"In your report, you listed every flower."

"Chief, who has seen that list?"

There was a pause, as Cleary ran through the possibilities.

"Well, it's in the case file. I have access. Detective Quick has access. Sandi has access. Nothing leaves that case file unless I know about it. You have a copy of the list, but you're not authorized to view the case file. BCI has their own case file, I'm sure. "

"One of the *Sandusky Register* reporters keeps calling and asking a lot of Krupp questions I can't answer, and one of them is when are we going to release the list of flowers."

"Chief, what matters is he knew the list, the whole list. How could he know that list unless he got it from you or Quick, or Sandi or BCI, or me. We've just run through the options. Let's just assign probabilities. It's obvious the scenario with the highest probability is that he knew the list because he created the list—which means he's our killer." Oh, there is also the possibility of coincidence. The list of flowers he mentioned seeing at the park just happened to be the same species that someone scattered all around Bill Krupp.

Chief Cleary looked down, eased his chair back a little. His eye drifted to the calendar on the wall next to the refrigerator. Then he looked at his cousin.

"What's the motive? Why kill Bill Krupp?"

"Why try to kill me!" Susan yelled. She said it again: "Why kill me? She was shaking again now, on the edge. "He must think I was going to figure it out and tell the cops. That means you, Bill. He wanted to find out what I knew—and he certainly did. I took off like a damn rabbit."

"He doesn't know you took off like 'a damn rabbit ' He just knows you disappeared. There is something we need to consider, Susan."

"Which is—"

"He's sweet on you."

Her head was reeling, she thought back to the Coliseum.

"No," she said quickly. He's a wealthy guy, looks like a model; he can have a roomful of 25-year-olds every night. And every day."

"Don't sell yourself short, Susan." He paused, waiting for a reply, but she let him keep talking. He was here on a date, at least in his mind. He certainly wasn't planning to kill you. But now you've got a problem. We must assume he thinks you think he's a killer. And let's just assume he is the killer.

"He must think I was going to figure it out and tell the cops. You, I mean. And he didn't want me around to corroborate what you knew. He wanted to send a message to somebody somewhere that Krupp had done something awful to this world we live in.

"You don't understand, Chief. I haven't been on a date in almost two years. This is complicated."

The Chief rolled back in his chair, raised both hands.

"Immaterial," he said.

———————∧———————

The next day, on his way to the station, the Chief got a call from the FBI, specifically his FBI buddy, Zamboni. There was no fishing banter to begin the call. This was business. This was an official call. In fact, Zamboni stated it upfront: "First business, Chief, then walleye," he said. The fact that Zamboni addressed him as "Chief" said it all. Cleary wondered if there were other FBI people in the room and/or on the line.

"Chief, one of our guys came up with something. They say computers do all the work, but sometimes they come up with things that make you think there's a miniature person, a human brain, a very smart guy, hiding inside. I will get to the point: we think your victim, Krupp, was killed by members of a secret society that executes people who have committed environmental crime. We think they've branched out from environmental crime to becoming an almost Murder, Incorporated or Terrorism, Incorporated, and will take on jobs for a variety of clients, including some nation states. This society operates internationally. They have been around at least five to ten years. We don't know much about their relationships with other terror groups. They don't seem to be affiliated with any of the Muslim groups. We have no evidence they are into cyber attacks, but I'm sure it's on its way.

"What we do know is they have a calling card. That's what the people working AI came up with.

"Keep going" said Cleary. "You were right to notice the flowers."

"The flowers are the key. Chief. There have been flowers at the crime scene at all these deaths. Sometimes they are on the victim's body, sometimes within two or three feet; other times the flowers are across the room on in a vase on a dresser, something like that. Sometimes the flowers are fresh, sometimes not."

"How many deaths? Cleary asked.

"We think about a dozen. We're sure of 10. I think there are more. About half took place in the U.S., all in the West, at least until now. This is the first in the Midwest. . . I should add there have been no arrests or convictions to date."

"What do they call themselves?"

"Well, we don't know. But we know what some of the other groups call them."

Zamboni was working him over a bit, and Cleary didn't like it.

"Which is?"

"They call themselves Father Earth."

"What?'

"Father Earth." He said it a third time: "Father Earth."

"So, the dark side of "Mother Earth?"

Cleary could sense a shoulder shrug on the other phone.

"Maybe. Who knows? There was a murder in Brazil two years ago, a rancher who had done some despicable things to the rain forest to get more land for his cattle. As I recall they found him hanging from a tree about 100 feet in the air holding a bouquet of flowers."

"A hundred feet?" Cleary said quickly. "They must have some big trees in the Amazon."

He turned his SUV onto Columbus Avenue. He would be on station in a few minutes. In the parking lot he waived from his car as employees began arriving for the first shift.

Cleary knew the drill, and he knew what was coming next.

"Chief, as soon as a certain piece of paper gets signed—it is one floor down from us as we speak —your role in this is going to change. The FBI is going to be the lead investigative agency on this case."

"Screw you," Cleary replied to himself.

CHAPTER 21

Tim was groggy, but he understood this was important. His mother never woke him up, even from a nap, unless it was important. A few days ago, everything was crazy-crazy. Now, there really were sharks in Lake Erie, specifically in the western basin. The blue-green water was now carrying millions of tiny bits of cells directed to create monsters.

"I got this text from your brother," Susan said, sitting at the bottom of the bed and holding up her white iPhone. I'm going to read it to you. Actually, he texted this to both of us."

Tim pulled up the covers. He felt, what was the word: lethargic. The pillow felt good. He never wanted to move again. He could just stay here in the warm bed with the soft pillow and talk to his mother.

So proud of my little brother. You are the best and the bravest. You've done something that validates your life. Thinking about you. Can't wait to see you and Mom.

Susan read it with emotion, as a performance.

"How's the lady doing?" Tim asked, his voice muffled by the pillow. It was several days after the attack.

"I spoke with Officer Neubacher from the Department of Natural Resources earlier this morning. She's sort of our liaison on everything involved in the attack. She's alive. They

195

had to take off her right leg just below the knee. She's an older lady, mid 50s, and this was very hard on her."

"Is she going to live, Mom?"

"I don't know. I don't think Officer Neubacher knows either."

"Mom, there was a lot of blood."

"Sometimes it looks worse than it is."

"The EMT saved her, Mom. It wasn't me. If he doesn't do a spectacular job with the tourniquet, she dies. I am no doctor, but I know that much."

"I spoke with her husband. He wants to talk to you, thank you for what you did. He's with her in Toledo. He got separated from his wife after the shark flipped the kayak. He ended up on the shore. One of the onlookers reached out, helped him get to shore. There are relatively few spots where you can easily climb out. Long and short of it, he couldn't get to the hospital until almost two hours after the attack. Can you imagine what that would have been like?"

The adrenalin had fueled him to the woman, and adrenalin had fueled him back; but what made him jump into the water. No one else did. All those people just watched it all happen.

"Mom, I don't want to talk about this to anyone else. I don't really want to talk to the lady's husband."

Tim sat up in bed. The walls around him reflected who he was: Metallica, LeBron James, Baker Mayfield.

Susan put her hand on his shoulder and squeezed. It was hard muscle now. She remembered when he was a child, and it was like squeezing a loaf of bread. Not anymore.

"You need to talk to your dad. I called him yesterday. I wanted him to get the news from us, not from the news media or some random acquaintance. He's very proud of you, very proud of you."

"Okay, Mom. I know. Dad is going to be all charged up."

Tim's bedroom had a kind of womb-like feel, she had to admit. It was bright sun outdoors. The drapes were closed. It was still except for the sound of their voices. It was gray light.

Tim had reported for work at the Sandusky dock the next day. There were TV people everywhere. His boss told him he could leave if he wanted to, but he stayed. He didn't believe he deserved a day off to enjoy being famous. He was in uniform and he saw people pointing at him. He didn't like it at all.

CHAPTER 22

Alpha 1 was near death. It could sense the transformation was at hand. It was dark in the truck.

The trip by plane was a little over two hours, but the shark had no sense of time as we know it, so it did not matter how long the flight was. She could feel a sense of being crushed, as her internal organs sank down inside her body.

The situation would always be delicate. She wanted to go home to the warm waters off the Florida coast.

It was 11 p.m. The night was barely an hour old in this latitude and at this time.

Z watched intently, standing to the side in an observer's role as the two primary scientists began to supervise the crew as they prepared to release the fish into Sandusky Bay. This was easily the most expensive operation he had ever put together. It had taken nearly two years and millions of dollars to get to this point. However, he did not begrudge the investment at all. He was proud of it.

The ground was soft near the edge of the bay. The plan was simple, in theory. The sleeves which held the sharks would be disconnected and one by one the sleeves would be pulled to the back of the truck and then connected by cables to two small boats just offshore, perhaps 30 feet into the bay. They needed to be as close to the shore as they could be without grounding their propellers into the wet muddy shoreline. The two boats would

each pull a sleeve with a shark. When they were perhaps 25 yards into the bay, another crew member would walk in behind the sleeve and pull the bolts which held the sleeve together and it would fall away and, in theory, the sharks would be able to swim on their own, totally unrestricted.

The water in the sleeves was salt water. A pump in each sleeve had pushed water through their gills. For the past week, each shark was injected with ascorbic acid (Vitamin C) to reduce stress.

The impact of all this would be anticipated and unanticipated challenges to the sharks. Z knew this was the moment of truth. Just before they began the procedure to put the sharks in the water each fish received an injection of a stimulant to get them going. It was a high dosage, but Z had been counseled to err on the side of too much. The sharks would die quickly if they did not start swimming on their own.

The site had been well scouted, and Z knew that the water depth would increase quickly to about four feet, which would be enough for the sharks. From where the sharks were introduced into the bay it was about a half a mile to the confluence of Sandusky Bay and the Sandusky River. If the fish would turn right, to the south and west and start swimming upriver there would be problems and it would be doubtful if they could ever get them to turn around. It was hoped that when the sharks reached the confluence, they would angle a little north and east and catch the current from the river and then ride it all the way through Sandusky Bay passing under the Edison Bridge into the main bay and then out into the lake.

That had been the plan.

Each shark had been fitted for a transmitter that would allow his team to follow the sharks as they moved around Lake Erie.

Alpha 1 did not hesitate. As soon as the bolts opened and the sleeve dropped down, she began to swim, almost on cue, and in the direction they had intended her to take. The fish did not wait for the others. It kept swimming, its massive body settling in to a smooth and constant bending and returning as it headed out to the bay.

The launch site was deep in a 100-acre woods that bordered the far western end of Sandusky Bay on property owned by an exclusive duck hunting club. The club was only active two or three months in the fall so there was no one to disturb. There was only a caretaker on the property at night, and he spent most summer evenings at a local bar in Port Clinton. Z had put in place a plan to monitor his whereabouts the evening of the shark launch, the club had built many dikes in the area to create and protect the marsh. They had a road network, with hard beds to allow a semi and trailer to get close to the water without sinking into the marsh.

It was hot and sticky, a classic mid-summer night along the lakeshore. Everyone on the ground was sweating and swatting. Fortunately, the woods were very thick which would only help Z and his team. In Sandusky, no one went wandering around the marshes at night. It was not comparable to the South, where the dangers from alligators and four or five different species of venomous snakes were real, but it just was not a smart thing to do. Though rare, there were massasauga rattlesnakes in the marsh.

Z had stationed guards wearing lightweight jackets and vests which read "Great Lakes Fishing Station" at the entrance of the two gravel roads that led back into the woods just in case someone got curious. Most of the land that bordered the highway and fronted the woods was planted in field corn which by this point of the growing season was head high. They kept light to a minimum, using flashlights. They had practiced the unloading sequence many times. The sharks, of course, did not bark or growl or hiss or howl. If they splashed it would be a good noise and would not carry very far through the barrier of insect noise. The engine motors were an indigenous sound. This was the time of the team's greatest vulnerability. If someone had alerted the local police or the federal authorities, all they would have to do is control the gravel road access to the marsh at any point, especially where it met the state highway. They were not going to get far driving a big truck through the cornfields to escape. Working in their favor was the fact that without sharks there was really no evidence of wrongdoing. It was private property. When the truck left, it would not have to go too far, only a few hundred miles into Michigan. Six months previously one of his companies had purchased some property in the Upper Peninsula on a side road and built a small steel building where they would park the truck and its contents for as long as needed. The building was certainly vandal-proof, but there would always be a way to break in if you had the right equipment. The most important thing was to keep it off the road. Z felt the secret would remain safe for a very long time.

Buying the truck was easy enough. There were lots of trucks available, and it was easy enough to find people who would sell their equipment without asking many question if you offered the right price. His team was adept at that sort of thing. The tougher part was modifying the truck to fit their needs. The process took several months.

After Alpha 1, came Alpha 2, and in order until it was time for Alpha 6. His team had gotten better with each shark, the process smoother with each shark. One of his scientist's walked up to him with an iPad and showed him the track of Alpha 1. She was following the Sandusky River current, moving slowly but steadily toward Edison Bridge and the main part of Sandusky Bay. Z was pleased. He shook his fist in the air. It had been his dream to do this for years. He was not a demonstrative person, but he kept shaking his fist. Everyone in the world would know about Lake Erie very soon.

CHAPTER 23

Chief Cleary had respect for the FBI. They often did brilliant police work, but they could also be aloof and condescending and patronizing without ever knowing they were doing so. He envied their resources: all the smart people; all the equipment; the contacts; the awesome people held them in; the fact their calls were much more likely to be returned first; the fear some public officials felt when they were in the room (even the innocent ones), their pay, their benefits, and their pensions.

Detective Quick put them on a pedestal. He was young. He would learn the FBI were just cops, too.

There were FBI offices in Cleveland and Toledo, but their field agents were mostly young and did not have much experience in Erie County. They assigned the case to one of their domestic terrorism units. The agent in charge was a man named Timothy O'Brien, a California guy by birth, late 30s, a strong work ethic. Cleary liked him. He was tall, probably six foot three, on the thin side, and had thin reddish hair. He looked a little like the actor, David Caruso. Cleary's FBI friend, Peter Zamboni, had asked for a temporary assignment to the unit. He was in the meeting, too, along with the Erie County Sheriff, Darius Sampson.

The meeting room served many masters including service as a break room. Cleary thought it always smelled of something, sometimes good and sometimes bad, from fresh-made coffee

to day-old pizza hot from the microwave to the unique smells of barbecue and certain Chinese dishes. The walls were covered with fliers, maps, sketches of bad guys, various bureaucratic postings. Township Hall and the Perkins PD shared a building on a side street not far from the fairgrounds. In the warmer months, if you took your break outside you could easily hear the traffic on Route 2 about one mile north.

They had started with a long session where Chief Cleary and Detective Quick downloaded everything they knew about Krupp's murder. In short order, they had all decided, with varying degrees of certainty, that this was a case of domestic terrorism.

"The flower thing puts it all together," said Cleary. Chief Cleary and Sheriff Sampson were the only ones in uniform.

"This group wants the world to know they have a footprint everywhere," O'Brien said.

"It's personal with these guys." O'Brien said, taking a sip of black coffee. "They want you to know who committed the terrorist act, but they don't care if the rest of the world knows or not."

"How big a group?" the chief asked.

"Big. Certainly, big enough to pull off some very sophisticated attacks. And all over the world. Keep that in mind. But again, the acts are not directed at broad subjects, but at people, like our guy Krupp." O'Brien looked directly at Chief Cleary. "They are executions. We think that's important. This isn't a plea for clean water. This killing was payback for dirty water." The chief nodded in response. He had no facts that would lead them down another road. He and O'Brien essentially agreed to agree. It would make the investigation less stressful all around.

"We have been working our sources hard the last several days. What comes out of the funnel is there exists a group that is taking the lead in these 'punishments.'"

"Who might they be?" Quick asked.

"Don't know," he said, trying to look at both Detective Quick and Chief Cleary. "We have no one on the inside, or anywhere close to it. "I can't even tell you what continent is home base. But I suspect Europe or North America. And they are well funded. But this is not likely Mideast money."

"Chief, you a fan of James Bond?" Agent O'Brien asked with a smile. "Books or movies or both?" he quickly added.

"I am," he replied. His favorite was *Goldfinger*.

"Count me in," said Quick.

"Well, we think—I think—the guy ultimately in charge is cut from the same cloth as Ernst Stavro Blowfeld. Throw in a little *Goldfinger* or *Dr. No*. However, much better looking than any of these guys."

There was a collective laugh in the room.

"You remember SPECTRE?"

"Special Executive for Counter-Intelligence, Terrorism, Revenge, and Extortion," said Quick. He was on a roll. He had every Bond movie ever made and every Bond book written by Ian Fleming. For some guys it was Frodo and the gang, or Spiderman and his fellow Masters of the Universe. For Quick, it was "Bond, James Bond." He was a throw-back.

"This group is the model we think we are dealing with," said O'Brien. "I don't think they are political, but they do have a focus on environmental crimes—or what they say are environmental crimes. They work for both sides."

"Where's the money come from? "It was Quick being quick the chief laughed to himself.

"A variety of sources, I think." It was Agent Zamboni, his first comment. "A very wealthy guy who believes in the cause. A *group* of wealthy people who believe in the cause. Drug cartels. Organized crime. Political or cause-based terrorists, who buy their services as needed. For the most part they are not political, it's strictly a financial consideration. The one exception is what they perceive as environmental crimes.

"I'm sure there's a law firm or two in there," said Quick.

They all laughed.

For Agent O'Brien's and Agent Zamboni's benefit, Chief Cleary summarized the life of the deceased in about five minutes. He had a pile of newspaper clippings and other documents that Sandi had pulled together over the past several days. As usual, she had done a good job as an internal librarian. She Googled Krupp from every direction. She had a gift for it, Cleary knew, and he never missed an opportunity to sing her praises publicly. Cleary slid the big pile of documents across the table. The cover sheet was the copy of the *Sandusky Register* the day after the killing.

"What we know is that he made a lot of money—at least by local standards—buying and selling farm property. A lot of this buying and selling took place within the extended family. He was active politically, very conservative, but not a nut job. He didn't belong to any militia or anything like that.

"His relationships with the state regulators weren't the best. They didn't trust him. His big environmental crime was being on the wrong side of the algal bloom issue."

"Walk us through that, Chief," It was Peter Zamboni.

"I got to tell you guys from the jump that I'm on the side of the greens on this one," the chief said. "The last ten summers or so we've gotten huge algal blooms on the surface of the lake, mostly out here in the western basin. It's shallow here. The water gets very warm in the summer—high 70s maybe low 80s by the end of July, almost tropical. The lake is a very fertile place. But when you add lots and lots of phosphorus—a key ingredient in most fertilizers—the lake goes crazy. The phosphorus fertilizes the algae that are already in the lake the same way it fertilizes lawns and crops. The problem is that this kind of algae also produces toxins that are more toxic than cyanide."

He smiled inwardly as he saw their heads pick up when he said "cyanide." It always got a reaction.

"This stuff is nasty, can kill dogs and make people get pretty sick."

"The phosphorus comes from the fertilizer. It also comes from all the cow, hog, turkey, and chicken shit. If you get a lot of rain in the spring, or if you spread fertilizer or manure on frozen ground, the runoff will be loaded with phosphorus."

The Chief knew he was on a roll, but he didn't care. O'Brien was from northern California and Zamboni was from suburban New Jersey. They didn't know jackshit about Lake Erie. He would be their teacher.

"Ever hear of the Great Black Swamp?" Cleary asked. Both FBI guys shook their heads. About 50 miles west of here , the Maumee River flows into Lake Erie. It drains a large area, even parts of Indiana. In fact, it's the largest river that flows into any Great Lake. The drainage area is mostly swamp and marsh. Back in the day, it was impassable except in winter. It was the last area in Ohio to be settled, a lot of it was wilderness until the 1870s and 1880s when they finally started to drain it. The land is incredibly rich, flat, and is ideal for agriculture. It's the best farmland in Ohio and arguably among the very best in all of North America."

"North America?" It was Zamboni.

"Yes, North America," Cleary replied. He knew he was going to lose them all if he didn't wrap it up. "We are on the edge of it right here in Sandusky."

The sheriff stood up and walked over to the wall. There were several maps on display, the largest a map of western Lake Erie, and with one arm he outlined the historical border of the Great Black Swamp.

"We have been lucky this year," the sheriff announced. "Dry spring, no real big storms when it did rain, and the water temperature is at its historical average. No algal blooms of any significance. We are probably home free—for this year."

"I take it Krupp bought a lot of fertilizer and put it out on his terms," O'Brien said.

"That would be a true statement," Cleary said. "But it's not so much that he broke the law. There isn't much law to break. There are guidelines farmers are supposed to follow to help control the blooms, but not many laws. Farmers have a lot of clout in this state. Krupp led the charge to let farmers be in charge. He testified at several Ohio legislative hearings. He liked being the enemy, I think."

"So, someone decided that he should pay with his life for that?" Agent O'Brien said. His instincts, after 20 years on the job, told him there had to be more to it. Yet, when had read the material the bureau had on file about the other "flower power" murders, some were pretty over the top as well, like the rancher in Brazil. There was the owner of a strip mine in West Virginia who was beaten to death with baseball bats. But there was never a message, never a phone call or a letter or any kind of online communication. No one took credit. It was bizarre.

"I've talked to enough farmers in the area the past few weeks to know they are all scared to death," the chief said. "Maybe that means mission accomplished—if you're the killer."

"I will ditto that," said Detective Quick. "They all think they might be next."

Chief Cleary had the bad feeling they were going to gather lots of information but never going to charge anyone with anything, a prospect he hated to think about. An unsolved murder was a raw wound.

O'Brien asked how the local press were handling it.

"The guy covering the story is the best the paper has, but he's young and from Dayton so he doesn't always pick up on stuff. They all love the Sheriff," Cleary laughed, jerking his head in Sampson's direction. He tells stories and he loves the limelight. The media love him. Besides, he's a local guy, born and raised here in Sandusky. Sports hero, too. "

Zamboni perked up. "What did you play?" he asked.

"I played a little of everything," the sheriff smiled, "but mostly baseball."

"He's too modest," Cleary said. "He threw two no-hitters as a senior and set the all -time Sandusky High School record for home runs in a single season as a senior. He hit 11 home runs."

They were drifting off course. Agent O'Brien brought them back.

"How do we break this case? What haven't we checked out yet? We live in the dawn of the digital world. There is a number connected to everything. It's hard to hide. This homicide had to involve several people, maybe more. As the Chief has pointed out, it would have taken 3-4 strong guys to carry the victim from whatever vehicle he was into the horse stall. When and where was Krupp killed? Who lured him to wherever and then they killed him?

"I'm sure you've gone through his phone records?"

"We have," said Quick.

"His computer?"

"We have," said Quick.

"No leads on the truck?"

"Nope. It's disappeared. And he drove a nice pickup, a 2019 Ford 150 loaded for bear," said Quick. "You'd think it would show up somewhere. It's got value."

"But let's assume he was killed by professionals, by terrorists," said Sheriff Sampson. If someone came here from Spain or Argentina, or wherever, they wouldn't worry about getting the value out of the truck. They just want to get rid of the truck. It's a cost of doing business. Economic benefit was not an issue; they just wanted it to disappear forever. Why not just drive it into the lake or stick it in the woods? You know, it would take a big damn hole in the ground if you wanted to bury a full-size pickup truck. I know what I'd do if I were in their shoes. I'd arrange to sell it to some bad guys and wash my hands of it. Make it someone else's problem. The car people know their market, and they know how to break a vehicle up the right way to erase the VIN, all that sort of thing. There's plenty of operations in Ohio and Michigan that can handle it. Hell, by now it's down in Oklahoma somewhere being used as a ranch truck, no license required. But if you are from Argentina and aren't a criminal except for executing the occasional polluter how do you find the right chop shop in Detroit. How do you find it?"

Agent O'Brien looked over at Chief Cleary. "Have someone start checking every public camera capture operation within 50 miles. Let's not be intimidated. These guys aren't all geniuses. Just because you are a terrorist doesn't mean you're good at it.

There was no money to launder, no jewelry to fence, no witnesses to intimidate or kill. No bribes to pay. They did have to get rid of the truck. Once Krupp's body was delivered to its spot in the horse barn, getting rid of the truck was the highest priority.

———————Λ———————

It was easy enough to lure Krupp to the right location. The caller (from a burner phone) dangled a juicy section of farmland in front of him, 300 acres was big enough to make it worthwhile, and he agreed to meet them at the spot, in the southeast corner of Erie County. He had not mentioned his call about the property to his two dinner friends, Gil Radtke and San Munchhausen. They were friends but they were competitors, too.

It was still daylight when Krupp got to the property. He did not know the farmers on either side of the property for sale, but he did know the Weingartner family who lived a half mile west. This was decent land, not quite as rich as the land where he lived, about 20 miles northwest. As he drove up to what he decided must be the barn associated with the property for sale he was already thinking about what he would plant there next spring. He compared the height and apparent health of the corn on both sides of the road. The ground here was starting to roll in gentle waves, leading to the Vermilion River, ultimately to the Black River and then onward into Cleveland. The flat earth he had just driven through in Huron Township was the flattest he had ever seen anywhere. You either loved it or you hated it. He loved it.

The caller had identified himself as Josh Weller, a friend of the family, and they had been given Krupp's name as a potential buyer based on Krupp's track record for acquiring farmland. Krupp noticed the red sedan and the sign alongside it which read: 300 acres for sale. Two men stood on either side of the red sedan, waving him in.

Krupp pulled his truck in next to the sedan and got out of his vehicle. The two men approached him, both smiling.

"Anyone else coming with you?" the taller man asked. Krupp heard something vaguely European in his accent. But he didn't have long to think about it. The same man reached one hand behind him and almost instantaneously brought it back, this time holding a small rifle. It was a tranquilizer gun. The gunman didn't hesitate. He pointed it at Krupp's chest and from about 20 feet he shot him. The dart hit Krupp where the shoulder joins the chest. The dart was designed for a larger animal; Krupp was on the ground twitching and grabbing for his throat and talked some gibberish.

"We just watch," the Shooter said.

"Just watch," the second man repeated.

The process of watching Krupp die didn't require a lot of talking. In less than two minutes he was face deep in the earth he had called home for more than 60 years. The Shooter told the second man to get on the radio and tell them to bring up the other vehicle. Krupp was nearly dead. A few minutes later another pick-up pulled up and parked next to Krupp's vehicle. Two men got out. They walked over to look at Krupp. He was motionless. The Shooter thought he could feel Krupp's soul seeping into the earth. He had felt it once or twice before. It did unnerve him a bit, but he refused to let it make a difference and it went away quickly.

"What kind of wattage did you use?" one of the new men asked.

"Just enough to almost kill him," The Shooter said. "Let's get him in the truck." The gate was opened and with each of them taking an arm or a leg they lifted Krupp up and carried him a few yards to the second truck. They laid him on a stretcher.

"Time for the juice," Shooter said to one of men, who immediately went into the trunk of the sedan. He returned with a small bag and gave it to Shooter. He opened it and took out three small vials of liquid. He uncapped one of them, held it up to look at it, then stuck it into Krupp's arm and pushed the plunger. "Welcome to the green world, Mr. Krupp," he said solemnly, "and enjoy some clean water."

The Shooter was beginning to relax just a little. He returned the spent needle to the bag and reached for the second needle. First dose is in, now it's time for the second dose he said to the group, though he looked at no one. Now, for number two. And I have something special for dessert. He picked up the last needle. The liquid was greenish. "Here goes," he said, plunging in the last needle. "All done, Mr. Krupp," he said, pulling out the needle.

Krupp started coughing. He wasn't quite dead yet. Blood and mucous was starting to dribble out his mouth. His eyes seemed to be popping like ping pong balls. The goal was to shoot him up with just enough juice so that it would take him several minutes to die. They needed that time to get the poisons into his blood stream. They needed his heart to work for a few minutes.

Five minutes later he stopped breathing.

The manner of death, the location, had all been planned by Z. It was a sophisticated approach. The Shooter preferred shooting. He had been a sniper in a European army.

Not a single car had passed down the road while they were there. But the Shooter was nervous. It was nearly dark, which was good, but they had to get going. The horse barn had been picked for a reason he did not know. It was his job to execute the plan, not to create it. He observed as two of the group put a light tarp over Krupp's body, which in turn was covered by the truck's regular bed cover. Together, they were a real cavalcade: Krupp's pickup, the team's pickup, and the sedan.

And now was the tricky part, the drive to Oakland Cemetery. It was 10.6 miles. No cell phones allowed by design, but they did have hand-held radios they could use for communication. It was in the middle of the tourist season, at night, and there was always the possibility of a delay or an accident or some other reason that resulted in getting pulled over by the local police. Something would happen, there would be some reason the officer wanted to look in the bed, and if that happened, he had his orders: kill the police officer, which is why he had his Glock in his front pocket.

Cemeteries were rarely victims of theft. They contained little that was commercially valuable. In the case of Oakland Cemetery, the most valuable resource was the timber. There were a great many mature oak and maple trees. The biggest reason for a surveillance system was as a deterrent to vandalism. Still, it was a rare thing to find a defaced grave marker. The Shooter had a Plan B, and it was to enter the cemetery by cutting a hole in fence in the northwest corner of the cemetery behind the Erie County office building and the Erie County jail. It was a dark corner and at 11 p.m. clear of office workers. The Shooter had thoroughly scouted the fairgrounds and the cemetery. There was a surveillance system, but it was relatively easy to compromise. The Shooter confirmed that the camera watched the main entrance and the service entrance. The plan was to enter through the service entrance. The main entrance was on the main highway leading into Sandusky, U. S. 250; it wouldn't do. The service entrance was back in the far corner of the cemetery. The main problem was that it was close to several residences. It was high summer. Windows would be open. It was a Friday night.

The Shooter worked through several alternative plans, but ended up disabling the camera at the service entrance.

He cut the lock with his bolt cutter and walked back to the truck. He was getting nervous. So much so he changed plans again; now we were going to execute Plan C. The shooter cut the fence and quietly entered the cemetery. There was a service road along this back side of the cemetery, wide enough they could turn the vehicle around, which was a critical consideration. Just inside the fence was a strip of grass. Then the service road. It was quite dark; the sunset had gone to yellow to red to purple to black. The Shooter could see the grandstand ahead and various outbuildings, and of course there were some lights. But no people. Only the horse barn was in use. They walked about one quarter mile to get to the spot where they were quite close to the horse barn. He supervised turning the truck around. If they had to make a fast exit, it would be much easier this way. He gave the signal and the driver cut the ignition.

Now it was time to deliver the goods. He went to the back of the truck and got out the bolt cutters. It was a heavy tool, but with some assistance from one of the men he cut a big enough hole in the fence to drive a snowmobile through it.

It was only 25 yards from the entrance to the horse barn, and they covered it easily and quickly though the Shooter was glad there were four of them. The dead guy was heavy.

They stopped at Stall 11. No rationale, only perhaps they felt safer inside the barn than outside at the corners. It was a warm summer evening and the smells, the insect noise, all paraded around in his head, looking for love. The Shooter waved his hand and two of his crew helped him to roll Krupp off the gurney and onto the floor of the stall.

The last thing the Shooter did before he left the stall was take off his backpack and reach in and pull-out wads of flowers. Some had been picked very recently, perhaps today, and some had been minus soil and water and sun for a long time. The latter were starting to wilt, edges browning, and flowers themselves starting to curl into fists.

The Shooter had a quick but silent debate as to whether he should distribute some of the flowers on top of Krupp's face. He was starting to look grotesque. His face was multi-color and the dried blood and vomit spilled from his mouth down onto his chin and finally to his shirt. Once when he was arranging the flowers, he thought he heard a moan, but he knew that was impossible.

The Shooter was not in favor of using flowers as a calling card. Assembling them was always harder than it should be. It was risky business.

The Shooter took a few pictures and then nodded to the group. Their response was immediate and seemingly in seconds they were through the fence, including the gurney. As he did going in, the Shooter walked ahead while the three others rode in the truck. He could clearly hear the big trucks on route 250. In a few minutes, they were at the northwest corner of the cemetery. Krupp's truck and the sedan were both still there. It was goodbye time, perhaps forever. The Shooter would take the sedan to the Cleveland Airport and return it to Hertz. Then get on an early morning flight to New York, and from there to Rome. His assistants would drive the two pickups to the chop shop in Detroit that Central had found. Their business complete, they would go to the Detroit Airport and disappear into the wider world.

CHAPTER 24

Ohio Route 2 is really an extension of I-80. It separates from the Ohio Turnpike at Lorain/Elyria in suburban Cleveland and rejoins further west at Oregon just east of Toledo. At some points it is less than half a mile from Lake Erie. Route 2 bridges several rivers and creeks, among them the Vermilion, Huron, and Portage. In the early 1980s, a bridge was built across the Huron River in an area where the river and the land created a large estuary. As a joke, one of local habitants, whose home bordered the estuary, built a model of a sea serpent (the type common to European mythology and representations of the Loch Ness Monster) and stuck it in the muddy bottom of the estuary so that the only body parts above water were the head and neck, a bump in the middle, and a bump at the tail. From the highway at 65 mph, it looked very realistic.

The Lake Erie Monster is a staple of Lake Erie folklore. Most scholars feel the myth was created around the actual existence of freshwater sturgeon, which were quite common when Europeans first came to the Great Lakes. Lake Erie sturgeon can live more than a century and grow to 10 feet in length. They're long and relatively thin, ugly, and spend their long lives on the bottom of the lake.

Children, of course, loved seeing "Lessie" as he (or she) was called. For many years, children and many adults had craned their necks to spot Lessie as they headed west on Ohio

Route 2 and crested the Huron River bridge and looked down into the estuary.

Only three days after the Jet Express disaster someone had put a shark fin in the spot where Lessie had been. It was a large fin, proportional for a 20 or 25-foot Great White or even an Orca.

Frankie felt vindicated. Now, he knew he wasn't crazy. This was more than one of Sheila's magic moments, too.

"Do you think we should tell our story?" he asked Sheila. They were at her condo, near Plum Brook Country Club.

"I don't care, Babe." He really really loved it that she called him Babe. "Who would you tell it to? You mean like one of those Cleveland TV station people, or do you mean somebody from *The New York Times* or *Scientific American*?"

"Not sure," he said.

"You don't have to tell anybody. You've done your duty. You reported everything to two different ODNR officers. Who else knows? "

"Probably more people than you think. The news is everywhere now."

"Did you tell your mother?" she laughed." Frankie's mother was in her late 70s and lived in a retirement home on the west side of Sandusky. She was in the middle stage of dementia. His father had died when Frankie was in high school.

Frankie wanted the world to know about Pris. He wanted another dog, but he wasn't done grieving.

Frankie and Sheila went downtown to the *Register* and told them their story. However, they did leave out the part where Sheila was naked during the shark attack. That would be their secret forever, they decided.

Frankie had his first nightmare a week after the attack. He had thought that he was going to get out of the whole experience psychologically unscathed, but that was not to be. Everything was a bit hazy, but in most of his dreams he was in the water with Sheila when the shark appears from a distance, and starts scouting them out, trying to see if they are worth eating. Sharks hear, but they do not speak. In his dream, he and Sheila swim to the boat. They arrive at the same time as the fish. The fish grabs the bottom half of the outboard and pulls it off the boat and then spits it out, his mouth pinkish from all the cuts from the metal outboard. They turn and swim in the opposite direction toward the reef. The water is low and in some places the rocks and stones break the surface. They scramble up one of these ridges. They stand up, naked, and the water is only up to their ankles. Will it stop the fish?

Then he wakes up.

"Do I thrash about or say anything?"

"No, Babe,"

Sheila pulled him closer and kept her hand and arm on his chest.

"That fish ate my dog. That fish tried to eat my fiancé, tried to eat *you*!"

"He's a fish, and not a vegetarian fish. Besides, I'm here for you, Babe."

"I never would have let you get in the water."

"I know, Babe."

"But you're beautiful."

"So are you."

The media blitz was unending for several days. Every network, both major and minor, continued to follow the story, but there was not much new to report. The fish—it was confirmed from video—numbered at least two. There could be more but there were at least two. But they were gone for now, which frustrated everyone.

Tom Churchwell became the primary scientific spokesperson on the story. He became the face of Ohio State University for all things shark related. Marilyn watched it all happen and was glad for it. He was the right person for the job. He had the credibility with his Ph. D, and he had the camera skills for TV. He was a natural. The good ones like doing it, and she could tell he liked doing it. He knew when to look out and when to look in, when to smile and when to look concerned.

He stuck to the science for the most part, and he bought into the need to keep the public aware of what was going on as well as pointing out there was no need to panic. One of his favorite lines was that you aren't going to meet a hungry bull shark in the basement or the garage, or backyard; if you don't go in the water, if you don't swim or water ski, you literally had nothing to be afraid of. The western basin is about six million acres in size. To our knowledge, he would say, there are only two sharks. In a comparable area on the Gulf of Mexico or on the Florida coast there are likely to thousands of bull sharks in the same area. So, he would say, we have them outnumbered.

Of course, the bull shark attacks brought lots of general craziness out in the sun: people reported seeing Bigfoot swimming along the shoreline not far from Middle Bass Island. It was reported he switched back and forth from the breast stroke to the back stroke.

The scientific community was desperate to get hold of one of these fish and study them.

The Canadians, of course, own half the lake and were not always pleased with the way things were handled.

One of the bestselling souvenirs in the region was a line of merchandise built around the message: *The Great Lakes (or Lake Erie) – Salt Free and Shark Free* or *The Great Lakes – Unsalted and Shark Free*. Within days of the Jet Express attacks, there were t-shirts with the message: *Lake Erie – Unsalted and Shark Free (not).*

Who "owned" the sharks? The state of Ohio? The federal government? The Canadian government? No one?

August was the peak month for boating activity on Lake Erie. For the Division of Watercraft, it was a crazy time. The shark attacks had made it much worse. All reports of shark sightings were to be reported to the Sandusky field office, and at that point reviewed and organized. Marilyn's office was the lead for further investigation. Marilyn put up a large map of the western basin on a wall in the office and put in a pin at the approximate location and put a pin at the point the shark was observed. She shared this information with Tom at Gibraltar. He had one of his students create an electronic version of the map, which he then shared with Columbus and made available to media outlets statewide.

The news media kept coming up with different angles for the story as the public seemed to have an insatiable appetite for more shark information and shark speculation.

The working assumption was that someone had brought the fish from somewhere else and introduced them to Lake Erie. It was the only logical assumption. No one in the scientific community believed they had arrived in the Great Lakes through Chicago, or had crossed over from the Wabash watershed, or had arrived via the Welland Canal and the St. Lawrence Seaway.

The sharks were sharks. One person was dead. One person was missing. Two people were seriously injured. A dog had been killed. This was serious business. The sharks were still out there.

The scientific community was in consensus that the water temperature in Lake Erie would be too cold for the bull sharks and they would never last the winter. The sharks could function, perhaps even reproduce, in the Great Lakes, but the bull shark favored warm water like the Gulf of Mexico, the Australian coast, the Carolinas.

And what would they eat? The western end of Lake Erie was a bonanza of fishes, but the other sections of the lake not so much. Given the relative plenty in the western basin, there was room at the top for another apex predator, but that didn't mean we should introduce one. Lake Erie already had its share of invasive species—sea lampreys, zebra mussels, and the round goby.

Still, the signs went up on public beaches warning swimmers about sharks.

Officer Neubacher took some solace that millions of people lived alongside some very fearsome sharks and in climates where year- round swimming was a way of life. Sharks were respected in these communities, as Tom Churchwell and others explained at every opportunity, but sharks and people had very different agendas and had co-existed for a very long time.

CHAPTER 25

It was indeed a castle. Not overwhelming in size, but the biggest home Jeremy had ever seen. In the U.S. he had been to Biltmore in North Carolina, which claimed to be the largest private home ever built in the U.S., but it was built as a residence, not a fort. He had not been to Hearst Castle in San Simeon, California, which was a close second in size, but he had seen pictures. This structure was clearly a fort first, built as a military necessity, not primarily for corporate retreats or hosting parties and wedding receptions. It was built as a military requirement. The exterior was smooth, a kind of plaster overlay, something most likely added in the past two centuries. The plaster had been painted white, but there were accents of black around the battlements and other areas where the white was flooded with stronger colors. The castle did have a moat and a black iron gate. It was located at the base of a forested ridge south of Munich not far from the Austrian border. Over the years the growth of Munich and the other small towns, helped grow the area around the castle to the point it seemed it was a signpost for the German post-war recovery. The castle had a name—Schloss Hohenwald—which means high woods in German.

Schloss Hohenwald had long ago been modernized. Vankirk did not purchase the property to restore it. Rather, he saw an opportunity to put his business operations in a unique setting; it would also be a great place to maintain as a residence in Europe,

particularly in Germany. The idea for creating an American restaurant experience on part of the ground floor was his ex-wife's idea. The idea had worked, too, despite much skepticism from all quarters, including his own. Madeline had become obsessed with making it successful, and in Vankirk's opinion it usually took someone to take on a significant project body and soul to make it flourish. This rule applied to most human endeavors, in his opinion, not just restaurants. There was always a true believer somewhere, at least one obsessed person, to make things work. If there was not, hold onto your wallet.

In addition to the restaurant, offices, and their private residence, Vankirk also operated a small boutique hotel within the castle. Its clientele was mostly business guests. There were only 12 guest suites, a small conference room, and a public area around a modest-sized front desk.

The hotel kept a low profile. It avoided listings in regional magazines and brochures. Guests had to work to find it. In terms of décor, theme, and atmosphere it was German, not American.

The entrance to the restaurant, called Yellowstone, was at the interior side of the drawbridge. The bar area had a distinctly Native American theme including a massive wall map of North America behind the bar which identified the traditional homeland of all the major tribes and most of the minor. The main dining room was dominated by large screens which rotated classic North American images, both historic and contemporary, urban and wilderness, stills and video. She understood that most Europeans loved the American West.

In addition to the bar and restaurant, there was a gift shop which sold quality North American gift items, including craft items made by Native American artists: blankets, pottery, and jewelry. The book section had a variety of cookbooks featuring regional American cuisine, from the South Carolina Low

Country to the salmon culture of the Pacific Northwest to barbecue and TexMex.

Yellowstone had a taste of Walt Disney World in its concept and its execution. Critics of the restaurant—and there were many—accused it of more "show biz" than fine dining. Yet, Yellowstone was more; in Madelaine's mind Yellowstone was first a wonderful place to eat, and second, a wonderful place to be entertained. She brought in first rate talent for both the kitchen and restaurant. The food was prepared and served with great skill. She understood that great chefs do not duplicate, they create. The menu was limited considering it represented a continent.

Madeline was French-Canadian. She was aware that about half the European population was to some degree anti-American, especially the urban elites, who had nothing but disdain for American cuisine. In fact, they would argue that there wasn't one. Almost everything was derivative of another food culture: Italy, Germany, France, China, Japan. Her counter was that America was blessed with an amazing number of regional food traditions.

Yellowstone had been open for three years and revenue was steadily climbing. Madelaine felt almost vindicated.

Jeremy had not grown up on caviar or smoked eel or white asparagus. He knew English beer and that red wine went with meat loaf and white wine with fried chicken, but that was about it. He and Alexis had been eating street food for several weeks. Street food in Italy or France is quite good.

Jeremy had called the number Vankirk had provided to his mother a week before. Surprisingly, Vankirk had answered the phone himself. He was very friendly and Vankirk had again offered to let them stay in one of his guest rooms. He insisted on it. Jeremy finally agreed, but decided not to tell his mother until after the fact.

He did not know much about his mother's business. He was not a fan of history and only read what history he was forced to read. He knew Vankirk and had met him several times at museum events of various kinds. He knew he was rich, that he was a big fan of Germany and that he made his money in financial services, in particular a kind of software that allows investors to do specialized comparisons. After several weeks of England, Italy, and France, he was ready to see some of Germany and then get the hell home. He would be applying to law schools in a few months. He and Alexis spent some of their rain day money in Munich to buy some clothes for dinner. He didn't think stained and wrinkled jeans and a t-shirt would be appropriate for Yellowstone and a boutique hotel.

The castle was impressive, no question, for a Perkins Township, Ohio kid. The hotel was a new experience. They were in a suite. There were white cotton robes in the closet with the logo of Vankirk' s company. There was a fruit basket, ice, glasses, a refrigerator with complimentary beverages of all kinds. They were in a castle, but the room smelled and felt like a June morning. The shower could accommodate three or four people and there were two sinks. And a bidet, of course. On the nightstand was an envelope addressed to Jeremy and Alexis, confirming their dinner appointment with Eric Vankirk. He would meet them at the restaurant. They had 45 minutes. They spent the next 30 minutes in the shower in a marginally effective effort to keep Alexis' hair dry.

"So, what are we going to talk about with this guy?" Alexis asked as she started to dry her hair around the edges.

"My guess is he'll do most of the talking. He's a business guy, and according to my mother the smartest person she's ever known."

"Smart, we'll see. But based on the picture in the Welcome to Schloss Hohenwald book, I know he's cute."

They both laughed, remembering the game they played in Paris at the train station waiting for their train to Munich. They took turns rating all the men and women who walked past them, everyone but children and nearly all people over about 55, a game you can safely play only when you are convinced that the person you are with is as smitten as you are.

A covered walkway led from the hotel entrance to Yellowstone. Vankirk was standing next to the hostess. He glanced their way and immediately recognized them, breaking out into a nice smile.

"My ex-wife, Madeline," is going to join us," Vankirk announced. He quickly added they remained good friends and were in business together on several projects, including this restaurant, Yellowstone. "She has a remarkable commitment to succeed at whatever she chooses to do, and she has chosen this restaurant."

The server came to the table, a tall and elegantly dressed middle-aged man. He spoke heavily accented English, but did not get a single word wrong; he was easily understood. He asked if Herr Vankirk's guests would like something from the bar, shifting his gaze back and forth from Alexis to Jeremy. Neither was much of a drinker. Each looked to the other to lead the way.

Eric expected this reaction and said, "Jeremy, I'm guessing you appreciate American lagers, as well as uncounted local craft brews. We have a good sampling." Jeremy knew most American lagers were from northwest Europe, but of course he could only think of Miller, Pabst, and Budweiser. "I'll have what you recommend, Mr. Vankirk." He looked at Alexis next. She just replied she would have the same as Jeremy.

"We are a long way from Sandusky, Ohio, Vankirk said. "He looked at Alexis. "Your friend Jeremy and I went to the same high school. He would have been much later than me." He laughed. "We didn't know each other then. But back to beer. I recommend what in Perkins Township would be termed the house draft. In southern Germany especially, every brewhaus makes its own. Generically, it's called Karst. In style, it is much like a lager, but on the light side. It is customary to drink it in special seven-ounce glasses."

Vankirk was a good salesman. Jeremy could taste the beer.

"We should toast something?" he asked.

"I know," Alexis said, "let's toast Ohio University."

"But let's do it in German," Vankirk said. "In German, it would be '*Prost Ddve die O-*' " Vankirk was right about the beer, Jeremy thought, and Alexis seemed to like it, too.

A moment later a striking woman, black hair cascading to her shoulders, walked up to them smiling the All-American or at least All-North American smile.

"I am Madelaine," she said directly, before Vankirk could start his own introduction. Jeremy remembered his manners and stood up. Jeremy was smitten. She was tall and slim. Her jewelry was impressive but understated. She was dressed for summer in light colors. Dark eyes, intelligent eyes. He decided she was the kind of person who got what she wanted more times than not, a person who could easily charm, or not. Jeremy wasn't sure how to address her, but she did use her first name when she introduced herself, so he decided to stay with Madelaine.

Jeremy remembered what his mother had told him more than once: get people to talk about themselves. In most social situations, this was easy enough. He started out by asking questions about the restaurant. She was off and running with kitchen details, the demography of her guests (primarily German but spread across western Europe); the process for determining what images would be used and where); the skills of her head chef, Gregory Loccacio, who had created a truly marvelous menu. Jeremy guessed she did not work well with partners, but she could manage investors well.

When Vankirk decided she had had center floor long enough, he started asking Jeremy questions about the shark attacks.

"I realize you are here, not there, but what do you think is going on? He laughed and said: "I grew up in Erie County. I still have a home there. I am a local voter. I know there are no sharks in Lake Erie."

"All I know is what my brother told me. He was there. He was in the water with the people and the sharks."

Alexis jumped in: "Everybody on that boat, the Jet Express, took pictures and video. Something happened. It's crazy. There were dozens of people on the boat. Jeremy's brother is a true hero. He dove into the water and swam to one of the kayakers and dragged her back to the Jet Express." She paused for a moment, as if to catch her breath. "I saw this morning while checking my voice mail that there was a different attack maybe a week ago on a local woman. This woman and her boyfriend were out fishing off Kelleys Island and the woman was swimming off the boat and got attacked—and she survived. So, the bill is adding up: a dog, a middle-aged man, and who knows who will be next."

Vankirk decided Alexis was a very determined young woman. She didn't look to be the type, but she was.

"So, there's at least two big, scary, dangerous creatures swimming around the islands in Lake Erie. What do we do?" Alexis said.

They all had the look of not really knowing what to do.

"I grew up outside of Quebec City, on the St. Lawrence," Madelaine said. "You would occasionally get some strange fish washed up on the beach, usually a whale. But nobody ever goes into the water because it's too cold. There could be a great white shark every 100 yards and it wouldn't make a difference in people's lives."

"Well, it's a no-brainer the sharks didn't get there by themselves. They needed help, lots of help," Alexis said, "from somebody like us, that is homo sapiens."

"Or aliens," Jeremy said.

"Yes, of course. Aliens are always a possibility," Madeline said. Jeremy felt she believed what she said.

The first dishes arrived. The first were walleye bites, served with a red sauce of some kind. The second was a sample of wings with the option of various sauces. It was all good, Jeremy thought.

A second beer arrived.

"Your hometown is certainly in the news these days," Madelaine said. "I was told a prominent citizen was murdered there recently, a farmer." Jeremy and Alexis both nodded their heads in agreement. "And this shark business at the same time. Do you think they are related in some way?"

Vankirk excused himself to take a phone call. Madelaine took the opportunity to talk to Jeremy about his mother.

"Eric is a big fan of your mother. It's more than business, much more than business. Don't be surprised if he looks for ways to spend more time in Sandusky and starts hanging around his museum. I am not a museum person, not at all. But he likes all that old crap. She must as well."

Alexis laughed. "How do you say "old crap" in French?

Discussion at the table flowed easily and they covered a wide range of subjects. Vankirk wanted to know what Jeremy and Alexis thought about what they had seen thus far in Europe, and what they had liked and disliked. So far, they had been to Italy, England, and France. They were due to fly home in three weeks. Alexis was most impressed by St. Peter's in Rome, which surprised both Madelaine and Vankirk. They had been there on a day when Pope Francis had greeted visitors in the Square. They had picked the right place and the right time, and they were able to see Pope Francis from only a few feet distant. Alexis was sure they had made eye contact.

"I was raised Catholic," she added.

"For me," Jeremy said, "It was Stonehenge."

Both Madelaine and Vankirk shook their heads in understanding.

"I know this sounds a bit strange—and understand this is a different perspective, which means it's coming from a person from a small town in Ohio on Lake Erie—but my overall impression is that Europe, so far, feels like a theme park."

Vankirk laughed. "Explain."

"Based on what I've seen so far, Western Europe anyway, is neat, clean, well-manicured. Everything is painted. The towns and villages look like movie sets. The countryside, especially, looks idealized—at least compared to most of the U.S. Very few junky almost falling down barns and out-buildings, junked cars and trucks, roadside litter. There aren't billboards every ten feet. I realize there are historical and cultural reason for this."

"You are a very observant young man," Vankirk said. "This is a very beautiful place. And it is becoming even more beautiful. I find the history, the context of what you see all around you, fascinating. Many buildings have been occupied for more than a thousand years. There are so many stories. I keep a house here. No, I guess you would be closer to the truth if I were to say I keep a castle here."

"And none of us can even begin to appreciate how badly the towns and cities were wrecked by the War. Fortunately, as Americans, we have never had to experience anything like what happened in the Second World War to Germany and Russia and so many other places."

"Did your family have a connection? Alexis asked.

"Well, yes. Both my grandparents came to the U.S. in the 1950s. My great grandfather was an engineer. He was never in the Wehrmacht. He worked in a factory where they built tanks. I was told by my father that he contributed to the design of the Panther. That name probably wouldn't mean much to you, but Panthers were very good tanks. My great grandfather was born in 1900. He served in Russia in World War I. I don't know what he did, but he did survive. My maternal grandfather—his name was Detwiler—lost two sons; they would have been my great uncles. They died in Russia. One was a fighter pilot. The other was a regular soldier. I was told he was in the artillery. He died at the Battle of Kursk in 1943. It was not a good time to be alive, at least in Europe."

Jeremy felt a bit of chill in the conversation. It was time to move on. A moment later the first of the small plates arrived: barbecue St. Louis style. Madelaine launched into an explanation of the different style of barbecue around the U.S. The war discussion went away. After the barbecue, came a slice of Chicago style deep dish pizza, then some New England clam chowder, then some deep-fried Lake Erie perch. Each dish was the best he'd ever had.

Suddenly, Erik turned to his left looking back to the restaurant. He was smiling. "Look, Maddie," he said, "there's "Paul Gutten." Jeremy's head turned as well. Gutten was standing by the hostess stand, looking in their direction. Jeremy saw him as he said something to the hostess and then began walking toward their table.

Vankirk stood up and greeted Gutten warmly. "What a nice surprise," he said. "Can you join us?"

"I will join you briefly," he said, in near perfect English. "I am meeting with a few associates here shortly. Please introduce me to your guests," he said looking at Jeremy and Alexis. Alexis was instantly charmed; Jeremy could tell by the look on her face.

Another chair instantly appeared at the table.

"Paul, this young man is Jeremy Massimino. I believe you met his mother not long ago—Susan gave you the tour of Cedar Point. And this is Jeremy's friend," Alexis Kraus. Gutten held his smile for Alexis: "Kraus. A good German name. Do you know what it means?"

"I have no idea," she said, which was certainly the truth.

"In German, it means curly-haired." She blushed slightly. Her hair was, in fact, what would be described as curly.

"Unfortunately, I was unable to see the museum. I had to return quickly to Europe to deal with a minor emergency. However, I did get an excellent tour of Cedar Point, courtesy of your mother. And I will be back to see the museum, possibly in the next several weeks."

"Well, I know how much my mom likes to show it off."

"Your mother is a great museum director," said Vankirk. "I really enjoy working with her. The museum is her passion, and we are all the beneficiaries of that passion."

It felt strange to have two very rich and successful men talk about your mother like that. True to his word, Gutten did not stay long. Jeremy saw him take a seat at a table in the main restaurant and then pull out his cell phone.

Madelaine kept the food coming and Vankirk kept the beer flowing.

———————∧———————

"I'm drinking my after-lunch coffee at the Jackson Street Pier," Susan said. "So, where are you calling from?" She thought of it as a basic business call, that Vankirk had some museum issue to discuss, until Vankirk said to Susan, "Say hello to Jeremy and Alexis," he said enthusiastically. Inwardly pissed off, she tried to make the best of it. She greeted Jeremy with all the enthusiasm she could pull together.

Susan was in limbo. She had not spoken to Vankirk since the night she ran away from Gutten at Cedar Point.

"So, how's the restaurant? I assume you are at Yellowstone?"

"Just an amazing place, Mom. You would love to come here. I was going to send you an email about the last few days in Germany before we—he stumbled slightly on the word "we"—before we went to bed." Spoken like a true married couple, Susan thought, not liking it much.

Susan tasted bile in her throat, something that had happened only once or twice before in her life. She didn't know what to do as she sat there looking out over Sandusky Bay while the man who killed Krupp and who tried to kill her was having dinner with her son, who knew none of this, and was thousands of miles away. A mother's first instinct, above all others, is to protect her child from all enemies, foreign and domestic, and her innocent child was in the lion's den. Her fear started morphing into anger. She wished she had a gun.

"We also just met Mr. Paul Gutten. He stopped by the table and said to say hello."

CHAPTER 26

Although the land is largely flat, caverns and caves are common in Erie and Ottawa counties. The geology of the area favors their creation. Most of the bedrock is one of a variety of limestones, but all are porous. There are underground streams which drain the area, especially in western Erie County, which eventually flow into Lake Erie in some cases more than a mile offshore.

Seneca Caverns, south of Bellevue, has been an important tourist attraction for decades, a crack in the earth which leads down to a stream that never once sees daylight, ultimately mixing with the waters of the western basin. The Blue Hole, now closed, but for many years a popular tourist attraction, was a beautiful pond that was advertised as having no bottom, or at least an unknown bottom, but in truth it was connected to an unnamed underground stream which drained into Lake Erie.

The Lake Erie Islands have caves as well, most notably Perry's Cave, which rests 52 feet below the level of Lake Erie and was ostensibly discovered by sailors from the fleet of Commodore Oliver Hazard Perry in 1813. Tradition holds they were looking for a source for drinking water.

William Krupp had discovered his cavern by accident in the late 1960s. The entrance was in a small woodlot that had never been farmed because the ground was rough and uneven

and there was so much available cropland there was no need to make this area cultivatable. At the far edge, it merged into very wet soil that eventually became a legitimate wetland, a taste of the Great Black Swamp. He was young then, just starting out, and he was poking around the woodlot just curious about the trees and found his own crack in the earth. He pulled rocks apart and dug around the immediate area and quite suddenly his feet gave way, and he was in something. At first, he was badly frightened, and blasted out a chorus of curse words. He scrambled back out. Curiosity was a stronger factor than fear: he returned with a shovel, a flashlight, and a lamp and began digging. It was not a big cavern as caverns go, but when he got down about ten feet, he found himself in a space that was more than ceiling height and stretched to both his right and left. The air felt damp. He thought he could hear dripping somewhere. It was relatively flat where he was standing. He had a distinct and disconcerting feeling that he was not alone. However, he brushed the feeling aside and began to explore the interior. In one corner, he noticed something irregular on the wall. He walked closer and put the light on it. There were scratchings or scribblings on the wall at about eye height, obviously manmade. So, he wasn't the first person here, but most likely the first European.

Krupp told no one about his find. He did not see it as a spiritual place, a place that was a transition between two worlds, a sacred place. He was a practical man, a modern man, and the cave to him was an ideal place to hide things or store things you perhaps didn't want on the driveway. It started slowly, but over the years the cave was the final resting place for a lot of nasty stuff, including solvents of various kinds, insecticides, fertilizer, herbicides. Krupp did share the existence of the cave with a few fellow farmers and his son,

Richard. Occasionally, he would be asked to help people get rid of dangerous chemicals. It was an underground effort.

Krupp believed the answer to everyday trouble was an empty 50-gallon drum.

CHAPTER 27

Chief Cleary did not think Eric Vankirk was a murderer. His firsthand knowledge of the murdering type was limited, he knew, but like all good cops, he relied on his instincts and his track record was way better than average. Vankirk's German buddy was another story. He didn't know this guy at all, only what his cousin had told him, which, he had to admit, sounded creepy. Eric Vankirk was too smart, for starters. Anyone might kill for passion, but it is a tiny subset that would kill over an issue like an algal bloom.

But they were apparently buddies, Vankirk and Gutten, two rich guys who shared a love of castles and perhaps had an interest in his cousin. He had to take some initiative. The case wouldn't solve itself. And now he was surrounded by his friends from D.C., which meant it was a competition. He had to do better than the Feds. This was his township. Krupp was his guy. But if you pull it altogether, he was dealing with something potentially very big and very dangerous. And thanks to the shark hysteria, his part of the world was in everyone's crosshairs.

He set up a meeting with the FBI guys and Susan. Susan was key. They met at the chief's office in Township Hall. Another blistering hot day, the kind of day that had him dreaming about those crisp October days to come.

"Vankirk checks out," O'Brien said, lifting his Styrofoam cup of black coffee. "We've looked at him 16 different ways and he seems to be clean. He is who he is, no secret life we can find anyway. He doesn't appear to have a motive—he's not a crazed environmentalist. He was in New York City the night of Krupp's death. His businesses seem to be legit. He's not politically active. He's a registered Independent. He's one of those quiet I-like-my-privacy rich guys." No social media accounts, amazingly enough; he doesn't do Facebook, or Instagram, or Twitter. None of that. It takes discipline."

That's the only way to fly, Chief Cleary thought to himself, the only way to fly.

"There's only one mysterious circumstance," O'Brien continued. "his relationship with Paul Gutten."

"So, we've got to talk about this," said Cleary. "Vankirk set up a tour of the museum for his friend, Paul Gutten. Gutten is in the U.S. on business. Susan meets the guy at Hotel Breakers over at the park. The plan was that they'd walk around the park that evening and the next day he'd get his tour of the museum. Then he'd zip back to Cleveland and get on his private jet and head back to Europe." He looked at Susan. "You take it from here."

"We spent the evening in the park. He told me he had an assistant—I assumed a bodyguard—but he gave her the night off. It was just the two of us. We had a lot of fun. He's a charming guy." She added: "I assume she, or he, or them, were following us throughout our time in the park, which was about four hours.

The chief jumped in. "You've seen his picture. He's a good-looking guy, a stud."

"We're walking back to the hotel. The park has just closed. We are on the boardwalk with a thousand other people, and he suggests a nightcap. Then he makes a comment about the landscaping at the park, especially all the beautiful flowers.

Then he ticks off a list of the flowers he's seen: Corn flower, butterfly weed, blue flag iris, delphinium, day lily, cone flower, cardinal flower, coreopsis. This is the list, the exact list, of the flowers we found in the horse barn with Krupp."

"So, you knew he was involved in Krupp's death?"

"The instant he ticked off the names of the flowers, I felt he had killed Krupp, or that he had set it up to kill him. In the second instant I felt he was going to kill me since I had figured out what had happened so far. He might think he has to kill me. It gets complicated.

"All I knew it was flight or fight mode, and I chose flight. He got a phone call. He answered it. I walked ahead and got in front of a big group all wearing Michigan t-shirts and his view of me was blocked, and I took off. I just started running. I ran like a crazy woman. I ran around the corner of the hotel and out into the parking lot and kept running and didn't look back. When I was in college, I worked at Cedar Point, so I had an idea of where to go. I decided to run into the back side of the Maintenance complex and hide in a kind of alley behind the Corkscrew where there was always lots of junk."

"That's when she called me," Chief Cleary offered.

"I admit I was pretty wound up."

"She was," the chief added. "I called the Cedar Point PD—they are a functional police department—and asked Chief Motsinger if he'd send a couple of guys over to the Maintenance building and find Susan and bring her back to the station until I got there to pick her up. I told him she was helping on the Krupp case and might have been spotted by a bad guy. Of course, I am out of my jurisdiction at the park. He did me a favor, didn't press me on anything. But I'm sure there's a report on what happened."

O'Brien sat back in his chair a little. He had made a few notes in a notebook while Susan had been talking. He kept the pen in his hand.

"I'm assuming he didn't show up for his museum tour the next morning?"

"You assume right," Chief Cleary said quickly. "I asked the CPPD to find out if he was still there."

"When did you do this, Chief?"

"As soon as I got to Susan's house. Turns out he was already gone. He left the key in the room and left town. His personal jet was waiting for him in Cleveland."

O'Brien's face said it: you messed up.

"In hindsight, maybe we should have asked the CPPD to start checking cars, but Gutten and his assistant would have been smart enough to give the hotel a phony plate number and car description when they checked in. No hotel checks that shit. All this assumes Gutten is a bad guy."

"Back to the flowers," O'Brien said, looking at Susan. "You and Mr. Gutten are the only people privy to your conversation?'

"Yes."

"He made no threats against you, nothing—outside of this list of flowers—that you would say was criminal in any way."

"Nope. He was a perfect gentleman, a real charmer. He seemed to like being in the park. We even took a ride on Millennium Force."

"I think this is a big deal," O'Brien said, looking at Zamboni first, then Chief Cleary, then Susan. "I think this guy Paul Gutten leads a double life. He's a successful businessman by day and he heads up an international criminal organization by night. This will not be easy, but we have a way in now."

"What do you mean?" Susan asked.

"I mean as a practical matter we can't arrest him and prosecute him for the murder of William Krupp. We don't have any physical evidence, nothing that really ties him to the crime. You're on the stand. You're asked about the list of flowers. What flowers? He will say in rebuttal. "We never talked about flowers."

"The people who did the deed are long gone, probably back in Europe by now, or maybe South America. Who knows?"

O'Brien pounded the table with his fist. "But now we know who the son of a bitch is. We can try to get someone inside his organization. We can—with the help of our friends in Europe—dig into Paul Gutten's life. He's not God, although he thinks he is. He's made mistakes. We can surveil him. Maybe we find he's got a rival, an enemy, maybe we trap him. Maybe we get lucky, and he drops his guard."

"Why flowers?" Susan addressed the group. "I mean why a calling card at all? Isn't leaving a calling card something out of the movies, like the 'Water Bandits' in *Home Alone*?"

"Great movie," said Zamboni, "Pesci stole the show." They all nodded, smiling. They all needed a little break.

"Actually, if you are a student of these things, you realize that leaving a calling card is fairly common," said O'Brien. "It's dangerous if you're the perpetrator, and usually it's not required to get done what you want to get done. It's ego. It's wanting others to notice you and appreciate you."

"So why did he come to Sandusky?" Susan said to the group. "There was no need for him to come here. All that should have mattered was that Krupp was dead. He could declare victory and move on" In her heart Susan knew the answer.

"That's simple," said O'Brien, "it's the 'King Kong' syndrome. He wants a date with Mary Susan Massimino, and he is willing to risk a lot to get it."

"So, that means at some point I'm going to be bait."

"You said it, Susan." It was Chief Cleary. "You already are."

"He doesn't want to harm you," said O'Brien. "My guess—no, my belief—is that he has no intention of hurting or threatening your family. He wanted to impress you, flirt with you." There was a pause, then he said: "He probably wanted to have sex with you."

"We'll, if he hadn't mentioned the flowers, he probably would have," Susan said.

"So, I am safe to say there was no physical contact between you and Gutten?"

"This sounds like high school."

"Maybe it does, but it's my job."

Susan wasn't planning to share the kiss on the ballroom stage with anyone. Certainly not her first cousin and two FBI agents.

Susan laughed nervously. "Please consider. This guy has movie star looks and a Bill Gates bank account. You know that old saying—'He can have any woman he wants?'—well, this is the guy they had in mind."

"What about Eric Vankirk, his rich buddy?" said O'Brien. He stood up and walked over to the coffee pot. Susan liked coffee—a lot, as a matter of fact—but not in mid-summer when it's 90 degrees outside. O'Brien sounded awfully confident, perhaps too much so.

"We need to talk to Vankirk," O'Brien said to the group. But not in Germany, here in the U.S. Maybe they are just friends, or maybe they do business together."

"This is huge. I mean, I know it sounds like not much short term. But the fact we know who he is, that we know that Paul Gutten is the Father in Father Nature, means that ultimately, we are going to get this guy. Look, he's smart. As soon as he decides that he's been made he's going to disappear, go underground. Paul Gutten will be no more."

There was a long pause.

"We have another thing to talk to you about. Yesterday, someone called in a tip to both the federal and state offices of the EPA that there was a pile of toxic material in a cave on the Krupp property. The caller gave us specific coordinates. We had no trouble finding it. Lot of bad shit, at first look anyway. It could have been leaking stuff into Sandusky Bay or Lake Erie for years."

"Scary stuff."

"Very scary stuff," Susan added. "Let me know when you talk to Richard. I'd really like to be there."

CHAPTER 28

The great fish discovered the Cedar Point break wall and the riches it contained: mainly a plethora of fish and snakes, all good to eat. The break wall, built in 1914, marked the east entrance to Sandusky Bay, extending 5,000 feet into the lake from the tip of the Cedar Point Peninsula. There was no paved walkway or defined access from the land out to the lighthouse. The rocks, all limestone from local quarries, were 15 feet deep. In the summer months there was a lot of boat traffic into and out of Sandusky Bay. Daytime it was not an issue, but at night, in the summer months, it could be a dangerous place. There was no light on the break wall; it was a black blank from the lights at Cedar Point to the white light on top of Lighthouse. Over the years there had been many nighttime boating accidents involving the break wall, including several fatalities. It was a deadly mix: darkness, too many Brandy Alexanders, waves, too many lights and too few lights, inexperienced boaters, too many boaters.

The break wall was the best thing ever to happen to the Cedar Point beach. Although the prevailing wind on the south shore is west to east, the littoral drift is from east to west. Sediment, mostly sand, tends to move east to west, aided by strong spring and fall storms, which are often Nor'easters; the sand moves west until it hits a barrier, in this case the Cedar Point break wall. Some sand washes through the rocks,

249

but mostly the sand continues to pile up against this barrier making the beach larger and larger. The Cedar Point beach is constantly being renourished. The beach today is much larger than the beach of 50 or 100 years ago.

The break wall is its own ecosystem; home to a great variety of aquatic life from zebra mussels and northern water snakes to catfish, drum, smallmouth bass, perch, and even the occasional walleye. The rocks provide wonderful spots for ambush predators like water snakes but also great places to hide and to give birth. On the tops of the rocks hundreds of gulls sit in the sun and scan the lake for signs of baitfish.

Two of the sharks, Alpha 4 and Alpha 5, liked to hunt the break wall, working north or south or south to north, just below the surface where the water clarity was poor. As a species the bull shark had evolved to find food in dark water. Its sense of smell was very well developed compared to most sharks and its ability to use sound waves to locate prey was a further adaptation to the murky waters of rivers, estuaries, and lakes.

The Cedar Point beach stretches for nearly a mile from the tip of the peninsula past sections of the campground, water park, hotel, park, and parking lot. The section in front of the Hotel Breakers is the most used.

Along with length and width, the Cedar Point beach was known for its gradual descent into open water. Some years, you could walk out 50 yards before the water reached your waist.

On summer Saturdays and Sundays, the beach was home to hundreds of boats which would anchor just off the beach. Boaters spent lazy afternoons sitting in the sun and occasionally slipping into the water to cool off. Enterprising boaters grabbed a sponge or a brush and cleaned the exterior of their boats. Others walked ashore and crossed the beach to grab a drink at the Surf Lounge in the hotel.

The Cedar Point beach scene was family, relaxed, quiet, peaceful. The beach scene on what the locals called the Sand Bar, a sandy extension of the Marblehead Peninsula on the opposite side of the entrance to Sandusky Bay was a party scene, the home of "Booze, Bands, Boats and Babes," as one sign stated to all the world. On summer weekends, the Sand Bar was a crazy place, at times attracting more than a hundred small boats and jet skis, including a party barge with a band. The Sand Bar was just that—no bathrooms, no umbrellas, no buildings, no tables, no chairs, and not much of a beach. It was a more localized version of downtown Put-in-Bay. Lots of people, mostly in their 20s and 30s, drinking enormous quantities of beer. The Sand Bar was as much a state of mind as a physical place. The Sand Bar was only a half mile from Johnson's Island, now residential but in the Civil War a prison for Confederate officers.

Frankie and Sheila split time between the Sand Bar and the Cedar Point beach. They never went alone to the Sand Bar, only if invited to go with friends. Frankie really didn't like taking his boat there because no boat is safe in that kind of environment. There was too much risk of collision or running over a swimmer or someone falling off a boat. He preferred the Cedar Point beach, and so did Sheila, but this Sunday they got talked into going to the Sand Bar, only a 10-minute boat ride from the Cedar Point marina. Shelia was still mending and did not plan to get her feet wet. She told Frankie she'd go if they brought his boat, so they could leave whenever they wanted to leave.

The distance between Johnson's Island and the tip of the Sand Bar was less than a half mile and the water depth was only five to six feet.

Frankie and Sheila invited another couple to go with them, Bob and Linda Speer, but each went over in their own boat. They were in the area where Sandusky Bay meets Lake Erie.

The Sand Bar changed location nearly every year depending on the lake level, the timing of major storms, and underwater currents, especially the slight channel created by the Sandusky River, which effectively ended as it passed by the Sand Bar and was greedily consumed by the lake.

Sheila sat in the boat under the sun canopy. Frankie stripped down to his swim trunks and water shoes and stood in the water alongside the boat. The water came up to his mid-thigh. He had tilted the outboard up to make sure the prop stayed clean. There was little wind, it being August, and what there was came from the northeast and across Mosely Channel and the entrance to the lake, which meant the natural drift of a boat off the Sand Bar would be to open water and Johnson's Island. Still, Frankie did not want to be too close in where it could be a major inconvenience to other boaters if he decided to leave early. In any rafting scheme there are winners and losers.

The big feature story on their battle with the shark had run in the *Sandusky Register* just a few days before and they quickly realized they were now celebrities and considered heroes. The *Register* reporter, Tony Lindor, was originally from Tampa, Florida, and had grown up swimming at St. Pete Beach. He had been around sharks most of his life, including bull sharks. He asked Frankie and Sheila a lot of questions, and he shared some of his experiences with them.

"They are mean creatures" he said. "Other sharks are afraid of them. They will take on fish bigger than themselves. My brother and I were swimming once and a small bull bit him on his lower leg. He was about 12 years old. I still have the article that ran in the *Tampa Bay Times*. I'll send it to you. People up here have no idea how this place would change if they ever got a bunch of bulls in Lake Erie."

Frankie and Sheila attracted a minor crowd of the curious. Frankie had brought with him the shark tooth which he would occasionally bring out as a showpiece. But after a half hour of this, Frankie wanted to go home. He thought Sheila would feel the same way. He just had to pull her aside before she took up talking with someone else. He visualized being home snuggling with Sheila on the couch while watching Cleveland play Detroit. The AC would be cranked up enough that cuddling was desirable.

When they moved in together, which they expected to do in a month or so, they were going to get a dog. The plan was to move into Frankie's place. It was slightly bigger but more importantly it was on the water. Sheila wanted a house at some point, but she was okay with condo living for a while.

Frankie had not been able to shake his nightmares about the shark attack. The bad dreams were not every night, but it seemed that way. He liked it when Sheila cuddled against him and said it was okay that she was alive and well. He wanted to protect her. That was your job if you loved someone—you protected them from all enemies including sharks.

Sheila had spent a lot of time assisting on the Virus floor of the hospital during the pandemic. She performed her duties well and received many notes of gratitude from family members and patients, and physicians, too. She was still young and strong and had no family to go home to, so she just stayed at the hospital with her patients and her fellow nurses.

The scream rose above all the extraneous, unfocused sounds at the Sand Bar, up above normal conversation, and someone's boom box and the lapping of the water against the sandy edge of the shore and the low grumbles from outboard motors.

The scream came from Traci Moretti, 23, a recent Bowling Green State University graduate from Lima, Ohio, who was in Sandusky to visit her college roommate.

What she saw was the massive dorsal fin of Alpha 1 as she began to cruise parallel to the Sand Bar. The fin was perhaps 30 yards away and moving across Tara's front. She couldn't see the rest of the huge fish, but she could feel it. Alpha 1 was receiving a strong message signaling the possibility of food in the direction of all the sonic activity to her right; but she continued to swim slowly in the warm water.

Traci continued to scream, now waving her arms, and pointing to the shark fin. A moment later there was a second scream, then a third, then a cacophony of screams. A few people moved closer to open water to better see what was going on, but most scrambled for shore as fast as they could, or back into their boats. Cell phone cameras were popping up everywhere.

The fish made a slow, sweeping motion, turned, and headed back along its previous route, acting like it was a dog herding sheep back into the barn. A few minutes later, it started to veer right toward the open water and Johnson's Island and disappeared.

On the other side of Mosley Channel and the entrance to the bay, Alpha 4 was working the inside or east side of the break wall. She veered left, really her only option, when he approached the shore. He continued to hunt for food. That was what he did; that is how he spent almost his entire life. He did not play. He did not spend time with others of his species except for reproduction, which was minimal. He did not sleep as we know it, but instead slowed his movement during the nighttime hours, conserving his energy. He had to keep swimming, at least minimal movement, since he did not have a swim bladder and would slowly sink to the bottom and eventually drown. He and his brothers and sisters were apex predators in their world, kings and queens if they lived to maturity.

Cedar Point had posted signage warning bathers about the dangers of swimming in an area where sharks had been reported.

The park distributed a card which informed swimmers that there had been two documented attacks by sharks in the past two weeks and recommended swimmers stay inside a string of buoys just offshore, basically in water less than three feet.

The shark issue was discussed by most everyone using the beach. There were lots of mothers from Columbus and Pittsburgh and South Bend who would not let their children in the water. People speculated: it was fake news, a prank of some kind; it was the media's idea of a joke; it was a military experiment gone awry; scientists had succeeded in manipulating walleye genes to the point they grew to be the size of sharks; when Sea World closed, they left behind a little surprise; the sharks came from the Cedar Point Aquarium, which closed back in the '90s.

So far, the hunting had not been good. Alpha IV had not found suitable prey. It cruised in between boats in four to five feet of water. It had not gone far when it got tangled in an anchor line, a relatively thin one as it was for a 25-foot boat. Instinctively, the shark bit down and shook its head, though it kept moving. The boat owners were on the beach drinking margaritas. It did not take long for the shark to cut the line. Two 12-year-old boys, who were swimming on the forbidden side of the buoys, noticed that the boat was drifting right toward another boat. They watched the two collide. So did two couples in a 32-foot Sea Ray anchored nearby.

"What the hell is going on?" one of the men said to the others in the boat.

Then came the scream.

The boat owner scrambled up the ladder to get on the flying bridge to hopefully see what was going on.

Looking down, he saw Alpha 4 swimming alongside his boat, headed out toward the open lake. In his mouth was a man.

255

CHAPTER 29

Z did not know how much the FBI, or any other law enforcement agency knew about him, either generally or specifically. You could be surprised—you found out they knew a lot more about you than you thought possible. That was the rub, as an American might say. He enjoyed running the legitimate business owned in one way or another by Paul Gutten. Like the character in the American crime epic, *The Godfather*, the youngest son, Michael Corleone, who wanted to move one hundred percent into legitimate activities but in the end could not, sometimes Z felt he could make it work, other times, not.

The organization that had wanted William Krupp dead was based in South America. They had decided on a new strategy in the war for the future of the planet: go after people, individuals, not places or things and not large groups of individuals. Their strategy involved executing people who they believed deserved it and letting the word get out slowly that they were executed for cause. In this "gig," as the Americans would say, the punishment perhaps did not always fit the crime. But that was not Z's call. His job was to make it happen.

The flowers were his calling card. He had to have something. That was what made it fun.

The fish were a different call. He had been a fan of sharks since childhood. In fact, he was nearly killed by one on a

snorkeling vacation with his parents in Spain when he was 11 years old. He and his father were snorkeling on a reef off Majorca. A very persistent Tiger shark started to stalk him, twice coming so close he could look into his mouth. "The shark was trying to decide if I was food or not," he would tell people, "and to my good fortune he had decided I wasn't worth the risk of an upset stomach or diarrhea." People usually laughed when he said that, but it was always a nervous laugh as it was protection from the most primordial human fear: being eaten alive.

The effort to get the bull sharks to Ohio and Lake Erie was monumental. It took two years to put it all together. It had cost him a great deal of money. But it was worth every penny.

CHAPTER 30

Public attitudes started to change after the death of the young man, David Laurens, of Columbus. His body was never recovered. The total number of casualties in the Shark war was now two dead and several injured, two seriously injured. The public fascination with the subject was now changing to fear, frustration, and payback. The sharks had taken over the western end of Lake Erie. Most people wanted it back.

The Governor appointed a special task force to deal with the shark issue and serve as the coordination point for all state-related organizations. At the suggestion of the president of The Ohio State University, he named Thomas Churchwell, the Director of Stone Laboratory on Gibraltar Island, to head the task force. He was charged with finding out how the sharks came to be in Lake Erie and making recommendations as to what, if anything, the state should do about their presence, even their fate.

There was a side benefit to all this, as Churchwell told Officer Neubacher:

"This has really put Lake Erie on the map. I see it as a great opportunity for our efforts to guard the lake. Selfishly, we should hope the shark's situation lasts for a while." They were sitting on the white metal bench closest to the water at the Jackson Street Pier in Sandusky. The pier had been redesigned and refurbished two years previously and was a focal point for

activity in downtown Sandusky for both residents and tourists. Churchwell was returning to Stone Lab after a day of academic meetings at OSU, and a first meeting of his bull shark task force. After his talk with Marilyn, he would board the Jet Express at the Cedar Point dock next door and return to Stone Laboratory.

"You know, I'm still trying to recruit you for the doctoral program in limnology," he said, reaching into his bag and pulling out a ham and cheese sandwich. Officer Neubacher had her own chicken salad sandwich. Marilyn was in uniform.

"I am flattered, I really am, but it would be freaking hard work. At 29, it's hard to go back to being a starving graduate student."

"It's better now compared to when you were at Ohio State. I'm not saying it isn't academically rigorous—because it is more rigorous, without a doubt—but they like this program. They want it to succeed. I want it to succeed."

"Maybe better?"

"It is better. No starving graduate students. Our folks get a lot of support, little things and big things. I want our program for Lake Erie to be the best of its kind in the world."

Marilyn didn't doubt his determination. It was a worthy goal.

"We can't do it unless we have the best scientists. Marilyn, you could be one of them."

They had talked several times following the attack on the kayakers. There were lots of loose ends to tie up.

"Beautiful spot," Churchwell said, looking out over Sandusky Bay and the entrance to Lake Erie. Johnson's Island was in their field of vision, but so tightly secured to the Marblehead Peninsula from this distance it all seemed to be a low green wall on the horizon. There were plenty of boats coming and going, both sail and power. To the right of the entrance to the lake was Cedar Point, its skyline clearly visible; from this distance, about 1.5 miles, several of the larger rides were clearly identifiable. Neubacher's office was close by, housed on the Cedar Point dock in a unique building that had served as the park's winter headquarters in the 1920s and 1930s. The building's architecture was called "early amusement park" by the locals and Italianate by others. There were shoreline fishermen on either side of them. While waiting for officer Neubacher, Churchwell had engaged both fishermen in conversation. He asked them what they were catching, what bait they were using, how often they fished the pier, what was the best spot on the pier, what time of day was best. He could easily have spent the afternoon with them. He was interested in everything about the lake.

"You know, we've both got it good when it comes to work environments," he said. It was a clear day, the snap in the air due to high pressure from Canada which had dropped down overnight. The air was cool and dry, easy to breathe, almost an edible thing.

"No argument, Tom. We live at the apex of the beautiful and the sublime. Every day."

"Whoa, that's not very scientific," he laughed. "Let's see. How would we design the study to test that hypotheses?"

"I'm not leaving, Tom. Ever. You aren't, either. I can tell. Remember, we are guardians. Now, I realize checking boat registrations pales versus hunting for evidence of Asian carp DNA in Sandusky Bay or addressing the U.S. Senate on algal blooms in western Lake Erie."

They both started to laugh.

"You are good on TV," she said. "You've got the gift."

"Yeah, I know," he said, laughing again.

"You really look comfortable in front of people."

"So do you."

"Not like you."

"Back to our friends, the bull sharks," he said, taking another bite out of his sandwich. "Bulls tend to be solitary.

They are very territorial. Having two sharks at essentially the same place seems odd. So does the fact they attacked the kayakers at all. They are just not programed to think of humans as food. Sharks have gland in the back of their mouths. They taste things. They have likes and dislikes. I know bulls aren't very picky, but only the tiniest percentage of them have ever tasted human beings."

"The guy from Sandusky—the guy whose dog was eaten and who's girlfriend was attacked—"

"That would be Frankie Visidi."

"From what you told me, the shark hit the dog once, then came back to finish the job. Well, the shark came back because the dog tasted like food. Odds are, given another opportunity, he'd eat the dog again. The attack off Peach Point, the kayakers, it's hard to say. Maybe they saw those shapes in the water, big shapes, like what they sometimes saw in the Atlantic—"

"Dolphins maybe?"

"Maybe."

"It was chaos, Tom. I hope I never see anything like it again."

"The Sandusky kid, who dove into the water to save the woman, was by all accounts a true hero."

"He is paying a price." She gestured over her shoulder toward the Cedar Point dock where the Jet Express leased dock space. "I had seen him around this summer, but I didn't know who he was—except that he was a cutie. His mom is Susan Massimino, the director of the Museum of Lake Erie," gesturing over her other shoulder. "I stopped over a few days after the attack just to let her know how great her son had been. No question, he saved that woman's life. Everyone else was just frozen. It isn't in the job description to get in the way of a bull shark and his prey. But he did."

"Now, according to his mother, he is having head troubles. Can't sleep. Worries about everything. Not eating."

"Almost sounds like some kind of PTSD."

"Exactly. I hope he's okay. His mom seems clued in." There was a pause. "I turned in my report to ODNR in Columbus. I was generous in my praise of Tim Massimino."

"How are you doing? I know we've talked about it before. You still okay?"

"I'll tell you how I feel. I just told you that I never want to see anything like it again. And that's true. But, you know, I did okay. I didn't panic. I took charge. I think if it happened again, I'd keep my cool again."

"I think you are absolutely right."

CHAPTER 31

Dessert was key lime pie, Boston cream pie, and Lady Baltimore cake. Madelaine provided a short history of all three desserts. They were splendid. Well-made and well-presented desserts were not a regular part of Jeremy's college diet. Susan was not much of a kitchen person. She favored store-bought cakes and pies and cookies.

"There will be a driver here tomorrow morning at 8 a.m. to pick you up for your tour. I have arranged for a tour guide, a graduate student from Heidelberg University, who has been to the U.S. many times, speaks better English than we do. His name is Johann Schoen. He is studying American history, specifically the period from the Civil War through WWI." Vankirk smiled and said: "He knows a lot about the period, more than all of us put together. He will ask you lots of questions, but don't let him go too far. His job is to show you the city and some of the history of this part of Germany. I think you'll like him. I know you are headed to Berlin in two days, but I will do everything I can to make your stay in Munich fun—and a little bit educational."

Jeremy and Alexis thanked Vankirk and Madelaine profusely.

"Jeremy, we are fellow graduates of Perkins High School. I'm glad to do it. And I certainly want to keep your mother happy. She's a good friend as well as great museum manager. I would love for her to see the castle someday and visit Munich."

He added that he would be traveling to Paris on business the next day but hoped to be back in time to see them before they left for Berlin.

As they all got up to leave, Jeremy glanced over to the table where Paul Gutten was having dinner. There was a large group with him, probably six or eight people. They seemed to be having a good time.

———————Λ———————

Churchwell had to assess the potential threat to human life. No one knew how many bull sharks existed in the western basin. They only knew with reasonable certainty that there were two, but it was unlikely there were 200, but there might be 20? Could there be more bull sharks in the central or eastern basins that simply hadn't been discovered yet? What about the other lakes? There were already many reports of shark sightings in Lake Michigan and Lake Huron.

Thomas Churchwell had many questions, few answers. This was an invasive species story as Hollywood might tell it. He pulled together a task force of 10 scientists, including several associated with universities outside Ohio, and a Canadian representative. He wanted academics who knew sharks, and he wanted academics that knew Lake Erie.

Was there a circumstance where an adult bull shark could survive a winter in Lake Erie? To him, that was the ultimate question. It was not an issue of food. There were 130 million walleye in the western basin, enough to maintain a population of bulls, maybe even a moderate population. They would be at the top of the food chain, the kings of Lake Erie. The impact on the lake's ecology could be massive. As climate change continued, Lake Erie would get warmer and more temperature friendly for bull sharks (and a host of other fish species).

Without the assistance of people but aided by a warming environment, it might take only 5,000 years for bull sharks to make it to Lake Erie on their own. By that time Lake Erie would be ice-free in winter and sub-tropical in summer.

But almost no one thought this could be happening now. The sharks that attacked the kayak convoy would not live to see another spring. They would die and their bodies would sink to the lake bottom.

Churchwell pondered the logistical issue as well. How the hell do you get a mature bull shark from Florida or the Carolinas to Lake Erie without killing it in the process? Catching the fish would be a tough enough job. It would require considerable resources and considerable skills. And lots of people. Half the world now knew about the sharks in Lake Erie. Why hadn't someone on the inside stepped outside? You could make the job infinitely easier if you transported much smaller-sized fish. The bulls that attacked the kayaks were 800 – 1,000 pounds. A fish that was 200-400 pounds would be much more manageable. If you wanted to find out if bull sharks could survive here, you didn't need a bunch of big fish. But the decision maker must have wanted a man eater.

Maybe you gathered the sharks and transported them in the modified hold of a commercial ship and went up the St. Lawrence and down through the Welland Canal and then into Lake Erie. Then when you were in the western basin you opened the hold and let them go?

Or, you modified a truck trailer into a giant aquarium and transported the fish from, say, Jacksonville Florida, to Sandusky as quickly as you could. Could you keep them alive in the aquarium for 10-12 hours? Would you transport them one by one or all together? And where would you launch them into the lake? Lots of people and lots of equipment would be involved in any of these schemes, too many to keep it secret.

But someone had pulled it off. The sharks were real. The sharks were here. Hannibal had crossed the Alps in 323 B.C. riding an elephant. How do you get elephants across the Mediterranean given the technology available in that time?

CHAPTER 32

"I only know Gutten socially," Vankirk said. "He came to the restaurant frequently. I think he had a thing for my ex-wife, but he never said anything to me about it. It was just something I sensed. He's handsome, charming, all that and more, but Madelaine told me once or twice she sensed a real dark side. She didn't elaborate. I didn't see anything nasty."

The group was sitting around a table on the third floor of Vankirk' s home on the Cedar Point Chaussee. The third floor was mostly glass and deck. It offered a commanding view of both Lake Erie to the lake side and Sandusky Bay to the bay side. Cleary had never been to Vankirk' s home and was amazed at the wealth on display. And this was just a taste, as he had heard his homes in New York City, Key West, and the castle in Germany were amazing places. As Chief of Police for Perkins Township, he had been in a wide variety of residences. A good and careful observer could learn many things about a person by eyeballing his kitchen, or what was lying about on his desk or what was hanging on his walls.

Vankirk was not used to being interrogated. He was clearly uncomfortable.

"We got this guy," O'Brien said suddenly. We just got to get him here." In his heart, he felt this was going too easily. Paul Gutten led a double life. He wouldn't be the first terrorist or criminal to do so. If you had talent and resources, your ego

269

under control, and some luck, you could do it, sometimes for significant periods of time. If they got this right, it could mean a lot to a lot of people, including Richard Krupp's family. Gutten could be the key to unlocking a lot of open cases here and in other parts of the world.

Cleary was more skeptical, a reversal of what was typical for the local law enforcement group vs. the FBI.

They did have a plan. Given everything he knew about Paul Gutten, O'Brien was certain he would pay a visit to Sandusky in the near future to "visit" Susan. He wouldn't be able to stay away.

"We need to get him to admit to conspiracy in the murder of Krupp. It's our best chance. There's no physical evidence linking him to the crime, and, frankly, we have a much better chance of nailing him than nailing any of his team. They are all long gone to various continents.

The museum also had a sophisticated security system. There were cameras everywhere and an audio system as well, which could be activated from the executive director's desk, specifically a button on the floor, similar to what is used in banks.

As the group broke up, Eric asked Susan to stay for a few minutes to discuss some museum business.

They were alone on the rooftop viewing area.

"Susan, I had no idea Paul Gutten is a terrorist. I thought he was just another rich guy, a German or Swiss version of me. He was a guy who spent a lot of money at my ex-wife's restaurant. " I feel very badly about all this. I have screwed everything up."

"What kind of women did he bring to the restaurant? Susan asked.

Vankirk seemed surprised at the question.

"Well, no one memorable, but it was, as you would expect, a parade of good-looking women."

As they spoke several gulls flew over them heading to the open lake. "Three or four gulls in the right mood can generate quite a racket," Susan said.

"Susan, I have access to private security people. I would be happy to set it up so the boys are cared for until this thing gets resolved. Very discrete, of course, and we'd have to let your cousin and Agent O'Brien in on it. They won't like it, but it's your call."

"Book them, Eric."

Z would go back to Sandusky to see Susan. And he wanted to see his sharks, or at least one of them, to make sure with his own eyes that they were adapting to their own new world. Each shark had been fitted with a tracking device so Z could follow their journeys around the western basin. The scientist who developed the program was unsure how long the six devices would function, hopefully for many months but quite possibly only a few days or so.

Why had Susan disappeared that night at Cedar Point? She had determined the mention of flowers on his part signaled that he was somehow involved. She would have known of the significance of the flowers only if she knew they were calling cards on other murder investigations. And she would know that only from the FBI. He did not know if they were involved or not, or if they were involved to what extent. There was no physical evidence, of course, linking him to any of the murders.

Z had no one on the ground in Erie County, Ohio, so he was limited to what news he could pick up from the local news media and social media channels. There was little news now about the Krupp killing. It had faded from view in local and state media, and even in social media. What everyone wanted to talk about now were his sharks. That was fine with him.

CHAPTER 33

The idea started with Joe Dugan, one of Frankie's fishing buddies, who also kept his boat at the Cedar Point Marina. Joe was a hunter as well as a fisherman, a native Sanduskian who now lived in Columbus, where he sold copiers and office equipment. His boat did double duty as a weekend condo and a fishing boat. He was recently divorced; his newest girlfriend was a looker and knew it and enjoyed putting on a show for the boys on the dock. Beth seemed to have a different swimsuit every weekend.

Joe had fished for sharks numerous times in South Florida and the Florida Keys. He had caught several species: nurse, hammerhead, reef, bonnet, black tip, lemon. They fought hard, which is why they were prized. In the interest of maximizing fishing time and fishing success, Florida fishing guides used a chum line to attract bigger fish, especially sharks. Chum was the scraps of teeth, skin, bones, organs, eyes, and tissue leftover from cleaning fish for eating. The chum was frozen into blocks. Guides put the block into a flow-through bag and then, after anchoring, dumped the bag over the side, keeping it tethered to the boat, and then waited for the fish to investigate. Joe planned to use "Lake Erie Power Chum," which started life as gizzard shad harvested outside Lorain harbor. It was marketed as far away as Louisiana where it was sold to crayfish trappers.

Most freshwater fishermen would not approve of this method of fishing, but in saltwater fishing it was acceptable, honorable.

Why not try to catch one of these monsters? Joe did not have the kind of equipment needed to bring in a big bull shark. He did not have a fighting chair in the stern of his 33-foot boat. He had two heavyweight rod and reel set ups, but both were inadequate for what they were hunting. But what the heck, it would be an accomplishment just to hook one. For the hell of it, he planned to give it a try. If he somehow managed to land one, it would be the biggest fish ever caught on the Great Lakes.

Joe had a backup plan, which was to get the bull shark, or bull sharks, close enough to the boat that they could kill it with a gun. In Joe's plan, they'd then slip a line around the fish's tail and drag it to the closest marina for pictures. He mentioned to anyone who would listen the writer Ernest Hemingway's judgment that the only proper tool for dealing with sharks was a Thompson submachine gun.

It would not be easy to find the fish. By all the official accounts, there were at least two to three bulls in the western basin, but they could be anywhere within it. Assuming there were one or two more bull sharks, it was still going to be luck more than anything. But it was worth a try. Based on everything he'd heard, the bull sharks could not survive a Lake Erie winter, which meant they were going to die soon anyway and shooting them in advance probably saved them from the misery of starving to death or freezing to death.

Listening to the reports in the news media, the scientific community was desperate to get their hands on one of these fish to study them.

All of that said, it was still illegal in Ohio to shoot fish with a firearm. If fishing, there were lots of safer methods to deal with potentially deadly fish.

Joe did not have trouble putting a crew together. He went to Frankie first, who was hesitant for many good reasons. Joe was disappointed but felt renewed when four other guys jumped at the chance to go shark fishing with guns in Lake Erie. Joe didn't have to do much selling.

"I thought you'd jump at the chance to go," Joe said to Frankie. They were sitting in the back of Joe's boat in the Cedar Point marina. It was near sunset and the day had cooled from the afternoon. "More than anyone else, you have a reason to go after these sharks. They killed your dog. They tried to kill your girlfriend." He added: "And they have messed with your head. If I were you, I'd like to kill them ten times more."

"It's complicated, Joe."

"We're friends. We'll just leave it for now."

The afternoon of the hunt, Joe and crew looked like a squad of Army Rangers. They had more hunting than fishing equipment.

"Let's go get the bastards," Joe said as he backed his boat out of the slip. His crew all raised their rifles or shotguns and cheered. Beth blew them all a kiss and then took a picture. She was looking good, and Frankie resisted the impulse to flirt with her.

Instead, he called Sheila.

The shark, or sharks, had attacked or had been conclusively observed at six locations: Kelleys Island Shoal (twice); the Sand Bar; the Cedar Point beach; Peach Point on South Bass island; and Pelee Passage (Canada). Studying the chart, Joe thought he could see a pattern, a circle surrounding these locations, a big circle perhaps 60 miles in circumference with a radius of 15. Joe did some quick calculations based on these assumptions and concluded that the shark should be between Catawba island and South Bass island. At least it was a reasonable starting point. Any location was going to be a crap shoot.

They left the dock with plenty of killing power: a 45-caliber pistol; a .38 caliber pistol; two .30-06 deer rifles; a 300 Winchester magnum; two shotguns, both 12 gauge; and a modified semi-automatic assault rifle.

Frankie ran through the list of firearms with Sheila as he watched Joe's boat move out into the marina proper. It cut a fine figure. She was a beautiful boat with a flare bow and flying bridge. It was probably more boat than Joe could afford.

"Babe, they could invade Canada. The boys from up north wouldn't stand a chance."

It took Joe only about 30 minutes to get to his shark location. The area between South Bass and Kelleys Island on the north and Catawba Island and the Marblehead peninsula on the south was called the Southwest Passage. It was about 15 miles long and 6 miles wide. The mainland area was covered with small, and large, marinas, so there was always boat traffic in the passage, including lake freighters, which picked up stone from the Marblehead quarry. Joe found a spot off tiny Starve Island very close to the hole that marked the deepest spot in the entire western basin. It was 65 feet deep.

"This feels like the place," he said. They dropped anchor. There wasn't much wind, but there were so many boats in the passage that boat wakes created almost a steady chop. The waves hit without warning sometimes and rocked even a 33-foot boat for a short time. The surface water temperature was 77 degrees, the same temperature as the air. Filtered sunshine.

"Weapons check," Joe announced, and everyone checked their weapons. All weapons loaded, but safeties on. They were anchored in 25 feet of water, just west of the Starve Island hole.

As discussed within the group, two guys set up their poles to fish for walleye. The plan was to supplement the chum with hunks of fresh, bloody walleye to attract the sharks. Joe climbed up to the fly bridge to get a better vantage point. Now, just wait.

Most states have regulations forbidding the discharge of guns into water. There are plenty of risks for all involved. Light refraction from the water make fish appear to be in a different place than they really are. Water itself, its density, shortens the killing range of the bullet. But the biggest risk is a bullet ricocheting off the surface of the water and going in an unanticipated direction. Depending on the angle, speed of the bullet, etc., shooting into water can be very problematic, like shooting into concrete or metal. And the sound itself is very scary.

"Time for dinner," Joe announced and flipped open the first live well. He lifted the first chum block and secured it to the boat and then flipped it into the water on the starboard side of the boat. Then he did the same on the port side. While they waited, a couple of the guys started in on the beer.

The chum was working. There were lots of baitfish at and just below the surface of the water surrounding the boat. The baitfish would bring walleye, drum, white bass, which in turn would hopefully bring in the bulls. Joe kept checking the fish finder. It had been clear at first, but now, an hour into the chum fest, Joe noticed the dots on the screen which represented fish.

"Fish on," yelled one of the guys. "It's a walleye." Good fishermen could always tell the species just by the way they hit the bait. "Good size, too." The fish never broke the surface. Halfway through the retrieval the fisherman felt something hit the line, and then there was nothing. He reeled in just a fish head.

Joe was ecstatic." Boys he's here," he yelled down to the guys on the aft deck. "He'll be back. Look to your guns. Get ready."

But it turned into 30 minutes of beer drinking, though they did catch a few more walleye, all of which made it to the boat intact for a very short time before they met the mallet and the fillet knife.

The rule they all had agreed to was that only Joe could give the word to shoot. After he fired, the rest could fire.

Joe stayed up on the fly bridge taking in the view. He looked out over the stern. About 30 or 40 yards behind the boat, he could see what seemed to a gigantic dorsal fin. The fin cut through the water effortlessly, back and forth, swimming up closer to the boat where the chum smell was strongest.

"There he is!" he screamed. Dead astern. Coming right for the boat." All they could see was the fin. At some point the fish was going to break it off and swim away; they might never see his head and mouth.

When the fish was only 10-15 yards away and they were beginning to both sense and see his massive bulk, Joe said to stand by. "Safeties off. Remember, I get first shot." With a bull shark a few yards away and a loaded rifle in his hands, he did not notice the set of four large waves about to hit the boat, the wake from a big 40-footer that had passed by a hundred yards to the west of their boat. The first wave hit just as Joe squeezed the trigger on his 30.06, aiming where he thought the head of the fish was. The boat suddenly rocked severely, and Joe fell forward. Instinct took over and he tried to right himself holding the rail and holding the rifle as the four other hunters started firing, also in a tangled mess from the waves hitting the boat.

The sound knocked them all sideways. No one had thought to bring ear protection. The shotgun blasts nearly knocked them all sideways. No one had thought to bring ear protection.

The smoke, smell, kick, and sound was like being transferred to a battlefield. The fish was obscured by the water, but Joe was certain he saw clouds of red.

"Cease fire! Joe yelled.

They were all starting to high five when Joe looked down and saw Bob Steiner collapse onto the back deck. Joe had a sickening, nauseating feeling that when he fell forward with his hand on the trigger guard of his 30.06, he had fired the shot down and it had hit Bob Steiner.

Bob Steiner was dead.

Alpha 5 was dead, too.

Officer Neubacher was the first on the scene. She heard the radio call and could feel the fear and the panic in the voice. They were heading to the closest marina, which was Gem Beach next door to East Harbor State Park. She and officer Mo Burch were just leaving the harbor entrance in their patrol boat. They immediately turned back to the dock.

The U.S. Coast Guard had responded as well. They were sending their closest patrol boat, but it was clear they would arrive too late. Marilyn called the Ottawa County Sheriff's office and Magruder hospital in Port Clinton. As soon as they pulled into the marina, she sent Officer Burch to the marina office and told them to prepare for the ambulance.

Officer Neubacher was there when the boat pulled in. The four men were all ashen faced at midday on a beautiful summer afternoon. Their friend was laid out on the deck, his head on a boat cushion. They had put a beach towel over his body. The beach towel was as bloody as the deck. Officer Neubacher got off the dock and stepped into the boat and looked down at the man on the deck. She knelt and checked him out as best she could. He was indeed dead.

"What's his name?" she asked.

"Bob Steiner," they all said at once.

"It was an apparent accident, a ricochet, had to be. We were shooting at the shark."

"Did you kill it?"

"I think so. It was close range," said Joe. Then he looked directly at Marilyn.

"Somebody has to call his wife."

"Give me his information, his phone number. I will call," she said. "It's my job."

The ambulance was in the marina now.

"Who owns the boat?" she asked.

"I own it, " Joe said.

"I will call Mrs. Steiner. What's his wife's first name?"

"Sarah."

"Look, this boat is a crime scene. Don't touch anything, especially the firearms. I am going to need a statement from each of you. Go up to the marina office and wait for me. Don't leave the area." She told Officer Burch to gather the firearms and match them up with the owners. Then she moved off the boat and back onto the dock. She had to nudge several gawkers away. The EMTs brought a gurney and a green body bag. Two of the shooters were crying as the EMTs zipped up the bag. They were going to take the body to Magruder Hospital in Port Clinton for an examination.

Marilyn looked for a quiet spot. There were none. She thought about going into the ODNR boat but there was no privacy. The marina manager, reading her thoughts, offered the use of his office.

Marilyn's hand was steady as she gripped her phone. She was more worried about her voice. The woman would see ODNR pop up on caller ID, which would immediately put her on her guard, but of course she wouldn't think the worst.

The phone rang three times, then she picked up.

"Is this Sarah Steiner?"

"Yes."

"Mrs. Steiner, this is Officer Neubacher of the Ohio Division of Watercraft. I sorry to have to inform you that your husband, Robert, died this afternoon in a boating accident on Lake Erie."

"How? What? I can't believe what you're saying" the voice said, starting to choke.

Marilyn told her that her husband was with four other men shooting at what they thought was a shark. One of the bullets somehow hit her husband. It was an accident. He was shot in the chest and died instantly. There would be a complete investigation.

They talked a few minutes longer. Marilyn asked her to go to Magruder Hospital. A sheriff's deputy or a Division of Watercraft officer would meet her there. She repeated there would be a full investigation of the accident.

The next step was to call her boss. He lived in Columbus. It was Saturday. No matter, he would want to know about this. Officer Neubacher went through a mental checklist of all the things she had to do. The Division's media relations staff had to know about this too. They would need to be ready for the firestorm of questions. This was a man bites dog story. Social media would explode as well. It had probably already started. Right now, they had no idea who ended up shooting Mr. Steiner.

It took a while to get the full statements of each of the men. Marilyn looked at their faces. They were scared, sad, and worried. As the owner of the boat, Joe Dugan bore more responsibility for what happened. He would be explaining this for the rest of his life.

"Mr. Dugan, did you know that shooting fish is illegal in the State of Ohio?"

"No."

Later in the afternoon, while she and officer Burch were taking pictures of the firearms and the boat, she got a call from Tom Churchwell.

"I heard what happened, must be crazy for you right now." There was a pause. Marilyn didn't react.

"Marilyn, I want to try to find that fish. Can you help me? He's on the bottom of the lake. Where did all this happen? I can get a research boat there quickly and start dragging the bottom."

Marilyn understood. Tom was a scientist. He had to learn about things, he was driven by the need to learn things. She got the coordinates from Joe. Dugan. They had anchored just east of the Starve Island Depression, a small area where the bottom of lake dropped to 65 feet. It was the deepest spot in the western basin.

Alpha 5 did not have an air bladder. Like all sharks, when it died in went straight to the bottom. It did not linger. It sought its grave.

CHAPTER 34

From the air, banking in from the east, above the intermittent cloud cover, the western basin of Lake Erie was clearly visible. The islands were green and brown, the lake a gray to green as the plane dropped in altitude and began the descent toward the small but still jet friendly airport on Catawba.

It was the off-season now, mid-October. There had been occasional shark sightings in the western basin, but no confrontations.

At Z's direction the pilots followed the north shoreline, the Canadian side, then to the entrance to the Detroit River. He could easily make out the stacks at Monroe, Michigan, and then the Maumee River and Toledo. Out there all alone was West Sister, the island home to thousands of birds and not one human being.

Z felt it was all his.

It was mid-October and there were still a few small algal blooms off Toledo. Seeing them from the air for the first time, he felt revulsion. He had seen images from some of the bad years, including two of the last three, but it was a shock to see them for himself in real time.

Z asked his pilot to take another pass over the islands and Sandusky Bay before landing. The day was clear except for the occasional cumulus cloud, puffy cotton balls that hung down from the deep blue overhead. Z had a map with him, and he

opened it so he could orient himself to the spots where his sharks had been active. He also had a printout of where each shark had been the past two weeks, a series of lines that seemed to be helter-skelter. Only three tracking devices remained in service. Alpha 5's bullet-ridden corpse had been discovered disintegrating on the sandy bottom of Lake Erie between South Bass island and Kelleys island. Alpha 6's transmitter had stopped sending messages almost as soon as it had entered the lake, but there was no way of knowing if it was a technical problem with the unit or if the shark had died. As it was, he found it amazing enough that with his PC, iPad, or iPhone, he could track their movement in real time.

The Shooter was with him. The Shooter was trying not to be nervous. He didn't particularly like flying, and after these many hours in the cabin of the Gulfstream he was more than ready to get off. He thought it was crazy to return to the places they had just been. It was unnecessarily risky. They had a new target, a situation in Australia that would require a great deal of planning to execute properly. That's where their efforts should be focused.

The U.S. Customs review was perfunctory. It was a weekday in October. There was only one person on duty. All their papers were in order, as Z knew they would be. The airport was small, just big enough to handle small jets. Z worked on the assumption that five of the six bull sharks were still alive. Only Alpha 5 was dead. He assumed Alpha 1, Alpha 2, Alpha 3, Alpha 4, and Alpha 6 were all still swimming. Alpha 6's tracking system stopped functioning only a few days into its Lake Erie journey, but Z felt sure the fish was alive.

His plan was simple. He wanted to see at least one of his creations in real time, in real life, before winter set in and most likely killed them all. He had the Shooter arrange to charter a boat for the afternoon. The plan was to visit Susan at the museum and then spend the rest of the day chumming for sharks. He was certain that with his tracking devices he should be able to find at least one. If he got close, the chum would do the trick. First, he had unfinished business with Mary Susan Massimino.

Z was proud of this fact: no one knew about both operations, the execution of William Krupp for the crime of despoiling Lake Erie and threatening the lives of those yet to be born; and the introduction of sharks into Lake Erie to draw attention to global warming and its impact on the Great Lakes. Z liked to be in front of things. He wanted to be an aggressor, a player, like he imagined his grandfather, General Otto Schmeltzer had been. But he knew he had to play good defense and had told his pilots to be ready to leave very quickly if need be.

This would be a surprise visit.

It was only a 15–20-minute drive from the Port Clinton Airport to downtown Sandusky. He left the Shooter in the car outside the Museum of Lake Erie and walked in the front door. He even bought a ticket. He asked the woman at the entrance if the director was in. He handed her a business card and followed up by asking her if it would be possible for him to pop in and say hello. He smiled as he said it. The woman just waived him in and enjoyed smiling back at him. It never got old, he thought, the smiles, as he started down the hall toward the offices.

The receptionist chair was empty, possibly she was at lunch. He saw Susan sitting in her chair looking out the window toward Sandusky Bay holding her phone to her ear.

He knocked on the glass partition that functioned as a wall. She immediately swiveled her chair and looked in his direction. For an instant, her face had the look of someone who had seen a demon, but she recovered very well.

"Paul Gutten," she said, "here for your tour?"

He walked into her office and advanced as far as the two chairs in front of her desk.

"Tell me about the flowers," he said. "I want to know why you deserted me on the boardwalk in front of the Cedar Point hotel. All I did was mention some of the beautiful flowers I saw in the amusement park that night."

Susan wanted to itch her nose, but instead she said:

"You know why."

'No, I do not."

"You recited to me the names of eight flowers you had seen at Cedar Point, the same eight flowers that were used to decorate the corpse of William Krupp in a horse stall at the Erie County fairgrounds. That would be wild blue indigo, butterfly weed, cardinal flower, corn flower, delphinium, cone flower, coreopsis, day lily. No one had that list but me —just me and Chief Cleary. That list is kryptonite for you. It tells me you are the originator of that list. You either killed Krupp, or you arranged to have him killed."

"Actually, it was both," he laughed. I killed him from my big chair in the media room in my castle. "But it was mostly business, not personal. I didn't choose William Krupp. Someone else did. But yes, I executed him."

"So why flowers?" she asked. "And why me?

She was not afraid. He admired her for that.

"I don't know what you mean?"

"Why did you even rattle off the names of all those flowers? You took a chance with me."

Susan had activated the alarm system in her office as soon as she saw Paul Gutten at her door.

Z knew the look of horror on Susan's face when she first saw him. It was fleeting, but it was there, which meant that she believed that Paul Gutten had killed William Krupp. Well, he did. He certainly did.

"Show me Eric's museum," he said. "We can walk and talk."

She hesitated for a moment, but then stood up. "We can do that. Yes, you should see it." Susan had bear spray in her desk, but there was no way to get to it without Gutten seeing it. One of the undercover unit, a young woman, watched Susan enter the museum with the person she knew from pictures to be Paul Gutten. The woman sent the appropriate message to her supervisor and started to work at getting closer to Susan. A moment later she got a text telling her to observe but back off until support arrived.

Eric was going to stop at the museum "sometime after lunch." He was leaving Sandusky early the next day to return to New York. The museum had a decent crowd for a fall weekday, perhaps 50 people scattered around the building and grounds. The museum never looked better. Susan walked Z from exhibit to exhibit, giving its history and what they hoped to accomplish with it. Thanks to Eric Vankirk, the museum did not live hand to mouth like so many other museums. It all seemed so strange. She felt like she was walking and talking in a soft cloud.

"Did you know Krupp very well?" Susan was leading them into the section of the museum devoted to the agricultural history of the region dragging out the time to give time to whoever was monitoring the system.

"Not well," she said. "Different generations. And he was a farmer."

Z nodded his head as if to say he understood.

"Why did he die the way he did? Why kill him like that? He wasn't a very likable man, but in his manner of death he was elevated to sainthood in some quarters."

If she had to ask the question, then she didn't understand.

"Susan, he died because of what he conspired to do to future generations; there is no more heinous crime." Z let it sink in. "Susan, there is irony, don't you think, in being poisoned by something which had been developed to poison flowers and plants? The natural world is fighting back. We are the natural world, too."

Susan was wearing her name tag. A guest suddenly approached and asked for directions to one of the local motels. Z looked away and began to visually canvass the room. He saw nothing that didn't look right to him. Susan took her time answering the guest's question. A second guest was now standing in line to talk to Susan.

The Shooter was not daydreaming, despite the warm sun. He had positioned the rental car in the lot with its nose pointed toward the exit. He felt he could be back at the airport in less than 20 minutes if the situation required it. He did not understand why they were here, but he had to give Z the benefit of the doubt. As he was watching the entrance, he saw a black Mercedes pull up and then park in a back area where there was a RESERVED sign. Then he saw a tall, good looking man get out and walk toward the main entrance. There was no doubt it was Eric Vankirk. They did not expect to see him here. Z's instincts told him to leave at once.

The part-time receptionist working the entrance to the admin offices told Vankirk that Susan was out on the floor with an "international visitor." Vankirk held back from immediately going out onto the floor, his first inclination, and instead called Chief Cleary to let him know he thought Paul Gutten was with Susan at the museum.

"Not my jurisdiction," Chief Clearly said, "but I will alert the Sandusky PD and start listening to the playback. I'm going to call the FBI, too. We have to keep him here—we can't let him get on that plane, assuming he's got his jet over at Port Clinton."

"I just heard from your security people. I'm out on the lake. I'm in the middle of a fishing charter. I have called the Sandusky PD. This is their jurisdiction. But I am calling

O'Brien at the FBI. I called Quick. He's headed to the museum, too. We need to keep that son of a bitch here. We can't let him get on the damn plane."

"Wow, what a surprise," said Eric, walking up to Susan and Z in the Agriculture gallery.

"I'm very impressed, Eric," Z said, with a sweep of his arm.

"It's all Susan."

"I'm sure it is."

Z felt Susan to be the most attractive woman he had every known, starting the day he first saw her at the press conference following Krupp's execution. He had been with many women in his life, but none had inspired him as she did. He did not know why.

In the end, Z had decided to abdicate, to *get out of Dodge*, as the Americans would say. He was going to disappear, like his grandfather did. When he returned to Europe, he would activate a plan he had developed over several years. He would create a new identity and then live in it for a while and see if it suited him. It would be much harder for him than it had been for his grandfather, who didn't live in a digital and connected world, but Z knew that with discipline, financial resources, and a bit of luck it could be done. He would clear as many financial assets as he could to his new world, but he knew he would have to give some up as well. Going underground had always been a contingency. He was a rational man and knew nothing was forever. He wanted to share this new life with Susan for at least for some portion of it. He knew she was attracted to him. The embrace on the stage in the Ballroom at Cedar Point was real.

He trusted the Shooter, at least as much as anyone could trust anyone, especially in their line of work, to cover for him. The Shooter was that rarity, a true believer and good at what he believed in. Father Nature need not die. The Shooter could carry it on, at least for a while. The Shooter did not know about the cave. Z was the only person alive who did. It was a comfortable feeling, not a scary one.

The sharks. No one had tied Paul Gutten to the sharks. There were so many people involved, however, that Z was sure someone would figure it out eventually, or someone would get a tip to follow up. The good thing was that no one had been given the whole picture, just slices, just pieces of the pie. Going forward he would not have two lives, just one, and in many ways, it would be preferable. But he did not want to be alone. He had a fourth home in Canada, well protected and well hidden, where he would go.

Vankirk knew his job was to keep Gutten in the museum until the cavalry arrived.

Chief Cleary got Agent in Charge O'Brien on the phone. He was in Cleveland. He ran through the plan. They would attempt to arrest Z while he was in the museum and charge him with conspiracy to commit capital murder. O'Brien thought the recording would be the key. What he said about killing Krupp was a clear confession.

It was beginning to get a little weird, Z thought. It was a bad feeling. He put his hand on his back to feel the Glock. Yes, it was time to go.

As Z walked down the front steps, two Sandusky police officers approached him and asked him to stop. Z did not hesitate. He pulled out his Glock and fired twice, missing both times, but he managed to get in the car before the officers could respond. There were too many people around, too much risk of collateral damage, to return fire.

"I will see you again soon," he said to Vankirk and Susan. He did not wait for a response, but instead turned and walked as quickly as he could to the main entrance.

Z jumped into the front seat of the rental car, a Chevrolet Blazer, and told the Shooter to get to the airport as quickly as possible. He then called the pilot and said they had to be ready to go in 10 minutes. The pilot knew Z well enough not to object. He gave a one-word answer, and then signaled the co-pilot and started toward the plane, already running through the checklist in his head.

Susan called Chief Cleary. It was his day off and he had a fishing charter. He answered just as one his clients was landing a lunker walleye, a seven pounder.

The Chief called Agent O'Brien. He was on the east side of Cleveland. "We've got to get him," Agent O'Brien said. We won't have an opportunity like this again. I'm calling DHS. They are just across the street from the airport. They have staff and they have firepower."

"I am calling the Sheriff's Office and Port Clinton PD. They have got to have a unit close by," Chief Cleary said.

Z checked his weapon. "This may be a contested take-off," he said to the Shooter. They will have assets deployed in a manner of minutes. We've got to GO!" The Shooter was an excellent driver. He hit 100 mph on the Edison Bridge. A few minutes later they were on the off ramp.

"Just drive to the plane."

"Will do."

The plane was waiting for them at the start of the runway. The Shooter drove right up to the plane. So far, no opposition. Z and the Shooter jumped out of the Blazer and up the steps and into the plane. The pilot started to power up for takeoff. At the same time two vehicles from DHS pulled out from the building across the road and headed toward the runway, breaking through some chain link fencing. Three officers got out, two holding long rifles with scopes. On the radio, the CO gave them the order to shoot. "Take out the pilots," a voice calmly said.

The DHS crew had been smart enough to drive to the end of the runway. The plane would have to pass in front of them. The front window was small, and it was a moving target. But they were expert marksman and they had trained for this contingency. Using the hood of the SUV for support, they began shooting.

One of the first shots hit the pilot in the head and killed him instantly. Blood and brains spattered all over the cockpit. The co-pilot took over and held the throttle and the nose of the plane started to lift. Then he was hit in the shoulder, as the cockpit glass started to shatter. The pane continued to lift until it was 300 feet in the air, then the co-pilot started to feel woozy and started to lose his vision. The plane was over the lake now. Then the nose started to dip as the co-pilot lost consciousness. Z tried to get up and see what was going on in the cockpit, but the plane was going down too fast. The plane hit the water about between Catawba and South Bass island, about five miles offshore.

The Shooter was unconscious but still alive. Z left him in the plane. He had flown enough that he knew the basics of getting the door open. It was his only chance. The water was 35 feet deep where the plane crashed. He was cut in several spots and bleeding steadily. He managed to grab a life jacket and float outside the plane. It was settling very slowly.

Sharks are curious animals. Large sonic disturbances register as worthy of investigation. Alpha 1 and Alpha 4 were not far away. They both headed for the sound.

Z held on to the life jacket but was hurt too badly to put it on properly. He was floating back and forth into full consciousness. The closest rescue craft was two miles away. One was skippered by Officer Neubacher. Another was skippered by Chief Cleary. He and his fishermen had watched the plane go down.

Z 's face and eyes kept filling with blood from wounds on his scalp. He blinked constantly. He had trouble focusing. Suddenly his field of vision revealed a large dorsal fin moving in his direction.

His toes started to tingle.

CHAPTER 35

Frankie and Sheila are on Frankie's boat. She is driving, as Frankie points the way. They are returning from a long day trip to the southern tip of Pelee Point in Canada. It is the end of the boating season on Lake Erie. Summer is gone, the lake has slid into fall and winter is approaching at full gallop. They are both feeling the power of the lake. She can feel it in her feet and legs and then her hips and back as the bow cuts the surface of the water at 30 mph. She can feel it in the soles of her feet as the boat flies through the nearly calm water. The first big fall gale is forecast in two days. It could be a big one, an *Edmund Fitzgerald* kind of storm. By then the boat will be safe in her winter home.

The early November light is weak and filtered and incredibly beautiful. Neither makes this observation because they are seeing it together and know the other knows it. North Bass is on the horizon, a little dusty in fall color, and Middle Island, the southernmost bit of dry land in all of Canada. There are perch and walleye in the ice bucket. They are costly fish, especially considering the fuel the boat will burn today. It will be a race to the dock to beat the darkness, which is already creeping in from the edges of the horizon.

Across the transom of Frankie's boat, in shiny black lettering, is the name **PRISCILLA**.

There are few boats, none to the east. There are some faraway specks to the south and west.

Ten minutes into the run, she feels the sensation in her upper arm, and then across her chest and down her legs. She smiles, greeting her old friend.

"Hey, Babe!" she yells, over the purr of the engine, "it's a mystical moment. Come along with me. Can you feel it?"

He cannot, but he says that he can, if just a little. This is enough for Sheila.

"We are guardians," Sheila says. Frankie puts his arm around her shoulder and squeezes. "We are guardians."

The shark's fin cut the surface several miles to the south, between Kelleys and South Bass. It was feeling more cold than hungry. The surface water was to her liking, but when she went to the bottom it was cooler than what she would have preferred. She did not know it, but she was a dead shark swimming.

Maybe.

Maybe not.

Two weeks after the plane crash Mary Susan Massimino received a call from a lawyer in Switzerland informing her she had been named the sole beneficiary of the estate of Mr. Paul Gutten. In addition, there was a letter addressed to her by Mr. Gutten that was only to be opened by her and in the presence of legal counsel.

Monroe, Michigan is six miles west of the mouth of the Detroit River, the connector between the lower lakes, Erie and Ontario, and the upper lakes, Michigan, Huron, and Superior. The load/unload facilities structure is four miles inland and there is not enough open water for a large freighter, such as the

John Byrne, to turn around and head downriver to the open lake. Instead, she is required to reverse engines and back up the length of the river. It is a tricky operation and requires two mates on deck carefully watching the clearance between the boat hull and the channel buoys. The ship is moving only four mph. Everyone is on their game.

Captain John Mullen stayed on the main deck to watch the process, only 20 feet above the water. The stern was now clear of the river entrance and slowly but steadily she continued to move backward with the wind helping to push the huge boat to the west. There were gulls everywhere, as is often the case where water mixes and small fish ride the currents. The big bow started to swing out toward the lake, to the east. The gulls were on a rampage, squawking like badly tuned pianos. Captain Mullen was just about to head up to the bridge when he saw something flicker on the surface, something that did not seem right. Then he saw it, a huge head lifting a bird out of the water, feathers flying. He could see enough to know what he was seeing; a large herring gull being ripped to pieces by a bull shark. The animal was only 30 yards away from him.

————————∧————————

Those who live on the water are a superstitious group, going back to when humans first saw big bodies of water, salt or fresh, and felt the awe and the mystery and the power of the creatures who lived there.

ACKNOWLEDGEMENTS

Years from now, when my grandchildren and others ask me what I did during the pandemic, I will hold up a copy of this book.

That said, the genesis of *Sharks in Lake Erie* goes back more than 20 years to a series of conversations my wife, Marie, and I had about the Master Gardener program at Ohio State University. It was her idea to cast an Erie County Master Gardener as a character in a thriller or murder mystery set in our area. A voracious reader, she has a natural eye for the poorly chosen word, and I thank her for pointing out many words in the story that needed to be replaced by better words.

Although a work of fiction, *Sharks in Lake Erie* contains a great many facts about a great many things, and I have endeavored to respect what is and what isn't factual.

I want to thank a number of people who answered my questions about everything from the walleye population in Lake Erie to the history of the Great Black Swamp to native wildflowers. Jeff Reutter, PhD, former director of the Ohio Sea Grant program and Stone Laboratory, now retired, and a longtime friend and colleague, critiqued numerous aspects of the book and did his best to keep me on the straight and narrow in dealing with the natural world. Richard R. Keller, MD, also a longtime friend (and fishing buddy) reviewed the manuscript from a medical perspective. Chief Ron Gilson of the Cedar Point Police Department provided insight into law enforcement protocols. Thanks to Dave Jessup for many hours of conversation over the years about law enforcement issues. Lee Alexakos, longtime Cedar Point colleague who knows boats as well as anyone I know and who loves Lake Erie, read the manuscript, and offered numerous suggestions. Lou Schultz, fellow member of the Erie County Historical Society and an expert on the War of 1812 in northwest Ohio, reviewed the manuscript for historical accuracy (and for all things German). Jude Brown, naval architect and lifelong sailor, and Paul Berger, captain of the *Mesabi Miner*, introduced me to the fascinating world of the lake freighter. Old friends and voracious readers Michaela and Tim McCarthy read the manuscript and offered several good suggestions.

Jennifer Wright designed *Sharks in Lake Erie*, including the cover, and created a unique map of the western basin of Lake Erie. Her contributions to the project are significant and much appreciated.

I would also like to thank Charlene Margetiak, a Master Gardner from Huron County, for valuable service as a proofreader.

My brother Greg, an art teacher, photographer, and naturalist reviewed the manuscript and made numerous suggestions which benefited the book. He also gets credit for the images of the author.

My editor, Tim O'Brien, did a great job, as he did with my first book, *Always Cedar Point*. He is an advocate for the reader, and in that role challenged me on several issues. Those challenges resulted in a better *Sharks in Lake Erie*. Thanks, Tim.

BULL SHARK

Carcharhinus leucas

- Worldwide distribution in warm temperate latitudes.
- Habitat: coastal seas and slow-moving freshwater rivers.
- Bull sharks can move back and forth from saltwater to freshwater. Bull sharks have been found as far north as Illinois.
- Can reach lengths of 11 feet and weight up to 700 lbs.
- Aggressive predator, varied diet includes bony fishes, small sharks, some mammals (including dolphins), seabirds and sea turtles.
- In freshwater, diet expands to dogs, rats, cows, small antelopes, birds, sloths, even horses and hippos, and their own kind.
- Large adult bull sharks have no natural enemies.
- Usually hunt solo.
- Poor eyesight but strong sense of smell. Often hunt in murky or turbid water.
- Favorite hunting technique is "bump and bite," where the shark head butts the victim to determine if it's prey, then backs off to make a determination. If it determines the victim is prey, it returns and bites for keeps.
- Responsible for more human attacks and fatalities than any other shark species, in part because of shared environment in freshwater rivers and lakes.

LAKE ERIE WALLEYE

Sander vitreus

- Common name, "walleye," comes from the fact their eyes push outward as if looking at the walls. This adaptation allows the fish to see well in turbid waters and at dusk/dawn.
- Generally, olive and gold in color. Color shades to white on the belly.
- Mouth is large (vs. overall body size) and armed with many sharp teeth.
- Range: southern Canada, northern United States
- State fish of Minnesota, Vermont, and South Dakota
- Walleyes grow to about 31 inches in length and weigh up to about 20 lb. Typical length is 12-20 inches
- Females are larger than males
- After 40-60 days, juvenile walleye begin eating fish; adults eat fish almost exclusively, frequently yellow perch, minnows, crayfish, and leeches.
- Walleye population in Lake Erie is estimated 150 million.
- All commercial walleye fishing is done on the Canadian side of Lake Erie. The U.S. side of the lake is managed for sportfishing.

REFERENCES + RECOMMENDATIONS

Lake Erie Foundation
236 Walnut Avenue, Lakeside, Ohio 43440
419.301.3943
info@lakeeriecoundation.org
www.lakeeriefoundation.org

Lake Erie Waterkeepers
3900 North Summit Street, Toledo, Ohio 43611
419.367.1691
info@lakeeriewaterkeeper.org
www.lakeeriewaterkeeper.org

Ohio Department of Natural Resources
www.ohiodnr.gov
614.265.6860

Ohio Nature Conservancy
6375 Riverside Drive Suite 100, Dublin, Ohio 43017
614.717.2770
ohio@tnc.org

Franz Theodore Stone Laboratory
Ohio State University
878 Bayview Avenue PO Box 119, Put-in-Bay, Ohio 43456
614.292.8949
www.ohioseagrant.osu.edu

Encyclopedia of Water: Science, Technology and Society
"Lake Erie: Past, Present, and Future"

Human Dimensions

Water, Society and Law

Jeffrey M. Reutter

www.doi.org/10.1002/9781119300762.wsts0085

ABOUT THE AUTHOR

A native of Cleveland's West Park neighborhood, John Hildebrandt spent 40 years working at Cedar Point. He started as a staff writer in the PR Department in 1974. He retired in 2014 after nine years as General Manager of the park.

H. JOHN HILDEBRANDT
Author Photo: Greg Hildebrandt

Hildebrandt is a graduate of the University of Notre Dame, where he majored in English; he has an MFA in Creative Writing from the University of North Carolina at Greensboro.

He is the co-author, with his wife, Marie, of *Lake Erie's Shores and Islands*, a history of the tourism industry in the Lake Erie West region, published in 2015.

In 2018, Hildebrandt published a memoir of his time at Cedar Point: *Always Cedar Point, a Memoir of the Midway.*

In 2000, Hildebrandt received the Paul Sherlock Award from the Ohio Travel Association in recognition of his contributions to Ohio's tourism industry. Hildebrandt served as OTA president 1996.

Hildebrandt is a past president of the Erie County Historical Society. He currently serves as a director of the Sandusky Library and the Sandusky Library Foundation and Follett House Museum, and the Sandusky Area Maritime Association.

He and Marie live in Sandusky. They have two adult children and four grandchildren (who love to visit in the summertime).

CPSIA information can be obtained
at www.ICGtesting.com
Printed in the USA
LVHW052347010721
691623LV00005B/31

9 781736 899908